Cold my Heart

Also by Sarah Woodbury:

The Last Pendragon

The Pendragon's Quest

The Good Knight: A Medieval Mystery

Daughter of Time: A Time Travel Romance

Footsteps in Time

Prince of Time

www.sarahwoodbury.com

COLD MY HEART

A NOVEL OF KING ARTHUR

by

SARAH WOODBURY

Cold my Heart: A Novel of King Arthur
Copyright © 2011 by Sarah Woodbury

This is a work of fiction.

Cover image by Christine DeMaio-Rice at Flip City books

http://flipcitybooks.com/

For my boys

A Brief Guide to Welsh Pronunciation

c	a hard 'c' sound (Cadfael)
ch	a non-English sound as in Scottish "ch" in "loch" (Fychan)
dd	a buzzy 'th' sound, as in "there" (Ddu; Gwynedd)
f	as in "of" (Cadfael)
ff	as in "off" (Gruffydd)
g	a hard 'g' sound, as in "gas" (Goronwy)
l	as in "lamp" (Llywelyn)
ll	a breathy "th" sound that does not occur in English (Llywelyn)
rh	a breathy mix between 'r' and 'rh' that does not occur in English (Rhys)
th	a softer sound than for 'dd,' as in "thick" (Arthur)
u	a short 'ih' sound (Gruffydd), or a long 'ee' sound (Cymru—pronounced "kumree")
w	as a consonant, it's an English 'w' (Llywelyn); as a vowel, an 'oo' sound (Bwlch)
y	the only letter in which Welsh is not phonetic. It can be an 'ih' sound, as in "Gwyn," is often an "uh" sound (Cymru), and at the end of the word is an "ee" sound (thus, both Cymru—the modern word for Wales—and Cymry—the word for Wales in the Dark Ages—are pronounced "kumree")

Cast of Characters

<u>The Welsh</u>

King Arthur ap Uther (b. 480 AD)
Ambrosius—King of Wales (d. 501 AD), Arthur's uncle
Geraint—Knight
Gawain—Knight, Gareth's brother
Gareth—Knight, Gawain's brother
Bedwyr—Knight, Arthur's seneschal
Cai—Arthur's half-brother
Myrddin—Knight (born 501 AD)
Nell—Myrddin's friend (born 507 AD)
Dafydd—Archbishop of Wales

<u>The Saxons</u>

Modred—Arthur's nephew (b. 497 AD)
Cedric—Lord of Brecon
Edgar—Arthur's nephew, Lord of Wigmore
Agravaine—Lord of Oswestry
Wulfere—Modred's captain

(Translated from the Latin)

To Archbishop Dafydd:

    We must speak of the evils wrought upon us by my nephew Modred and his Saxon allies, how the peace formerly made has been violated in all the clauses of the treaty, how churches have been fired and devastated, and ecclesiastical persons, priests, monks and nuns slaughtered, women slain with children at their breast, hospitals and other houses of religion burned, the Welsh murdered in their homes, in churches, yes at the very altar, with other sacrilegious offences horrible to hear . . ..

    We fight because we are forced to fight and are left without any remedy . . . I do not ask for your blessing in these last endeavors. Only your understanding.

Arthur ap Uther,
King of Wales and Lord of Eryri
November, 537 A.D.

1

11 December 537 AD

"**G**et over here, Myrddin!"

I urged my horse across the clearing, through the ankle-deep snow and towards Gawain, the captain of my lord's guard. He resembled a greyhound, whip-thin but muscled, his grey-streaked hair held away from his face by a leather tie at the nape of his neck.

"Sir," I said.

Gawain pointed to a stand of pine trees some hundred yards away on the other side of the Cam River. "What do you see?"

At thirty-six, after a lifetime of soldiering, my eyes weren't what they used to be. I stared anyway, trying to glimpse what Gawain had noticed. *Christ! It can't be!* Cold settled into my belly. "The branches are moving." I glanced at Gawain. "Didn't our scouts check those trees?"

"Yes." The word hissed through Gawain's teeth. "They did. I saw to it myself."

"The company must move now," I said. "It isn't safe here." I forced myself to remain calm instead of shouting the words at Gawain as I wanted to.

"No, it isn't," Gawain said. "I said as much to the King before we began this journey."

"Maybe he'll listen now."

"I'll speak to him," he said. "For your part, take four men—Ifan, Dai, two others. Clear out those trees. I don't care how you do it." He clapped a hand on my shoulder, punctuating the command.

"Yes, sir."

I directed my horse towards the north, riding past the church, St. Cannen's, that squatted in the middle of the clearing. An up-and-coming half-Saxon lord, Edgar, son of King Arthur's youngest sister, had sent a letter asking to discuss the transfer of his allegiance from Modred to Arthur. That his overture was genuine had always seemed unlikely, yet Modred's war had gone on so long that Arthur felt he had to grab any chance that came his way, on the hope that he could shift the balance of power in his favor. Recent victories had given us real hope that we might prevail, but if those trees held Saxon soldiers, then the King was going to die, along with all of his men. Including me. He'd walked into a trap from which none of us would escape.

"Ifan!" I waved my friend closer.

He spurred his horse to intersect mine. "What is it?"

"Mercians," I said. "Possibly."

Ifan, as pale as I was dark such that a man could mistake him for a Saxon, had campaigned beside King Arthur even longer than I. He didn't ask for details. Once I'd collected several more men, we circled behind the church, heading for the ford of the River Cam on the northwestern edge of the church property. The trees along the river shielded us from the field beyond. Once across the Cam, however, we left their cover.

"Shields up," I said—and just in time. An arrow slammed into Ifan's shield and a second into mine.

"Back, back!" Ifan shouted, wheeling his horse to retreat down the riverbank. "We'll have to go around!"

But before we'd ridden halfway across the river, a company of Saxon cavalry burst from the woods to the west of the church. A quick glance revealed their considerable numbers—more than the eighteen men the King had brought to the rendezvous. Along with half a dozen of our compatriots who reacted at the same instant, we raced to intercept them, splashing through the water and back into the clearing. Our numbers wouldn't be enough to turn them aside, but as I met the first Saxon sword with my own, I put our chances from my mind.

I slashed my sword—once, twice, three times—before my horse stumbled, a tendon severed by a man on the ground. I pulled my feet from the stirrups, leaping free in time to meet the advancing sword of yet another Saxon. He glared through his visored helmet, a thick, red beard the only part of his face I could see.

"Retreat!"

3

The call came from behind me. I almost laughed. *Retreat where?* The church had little advantage in defense over the clearing. Admittedly, I'd last seen Arthur standing alongside the priest in the nave near the altar. In the back of my mind, I'd held onto the hope that if he made his last stand inside, even a heathen Saxon would be loathe to kill my King before the cross.

I ducked under the Saxon's guard and then burst upwards, one hand on the hilt of my sword and my gauntleted left hand on the blade. I thrust my weapon at his mid-section, forcing it through his mail armor. I pulled the sword from his body and he fell. Then I turned and ran full out for the front of the church, hurtling past the small knots of men battling between me and the front door.

But the King had already left the safety of the nave. A pace from the church steps, Arthur faced two men at the same time. The King had twenty years on me yet fought like a much younger man. He slashed his sword at one Saxon soldier and snapped an elbow into the face of the other attacker a second later. Blood cascaded from the man's nose.

I launched myself at the Saxon soldier, driving my shoulder into his ribs and sending both of us sprawling. Hardly pausing for breath, I pushed up on one knee and shoved the tip of my sword beneath his chin. Helmet askew and blood coating my surcoat, I stood, spinning on one heel, determined to defend my king to my last breath.

Except King Arthur had already fallen, overcome by a third knight coming late to the fight.

Aghast, I drove my sword into the man's back, just as he raised his arms for a final strike at the King. As the Saxon died, I knocked him aside and turned to stand astride the body of my lord. Even if it meant my death, I would gainsay anyone who dared come against me. But as my sword met that of the next Saxon warrior, the back of my head exploded in sudden pain from a blow I hadn't seen coming. Barely conscious, I fell across the failing body of King Arthur.

2

2 November 537 AD

Nell surged upwards from her pallet, disturbed far more by the shouts echoing through the stone corridors of the convent than by the abrupt ending to the dream. It felt real every time she dreamt it, but once awake, she acknowledged it for what it was: a dream, a *seeing*, if such a thing were possible, and a weight around her neck since she was a girl. Arthur ap Uther was going to die a little more than a month from now at the hands of the Saxons. A man she knew only as Myrddin—a man she'd *lived* for more nights than she could count—would die with him. And Nell had no way to stop it.

The shouts came clearer now. Thrusting her heavy braid over her shoulder, Nell pulled on her habit to cover her night shift, adjusted the thick wool around her waist more comfortably, and slipped into her boots. She slid through the cloth doorway that separated her room from the hall. As the infirmarer and a senior member of the convent, she had her own cell, separate from the dormitory where the novices and younger nuns slept.

"What is it?" Nell reached out a hand to stop Bronwen, a blond-haired, blue-eyed initiate who was far too beautiful to have chosen this life at such a young age. Unfortunately for her, she was heiress to extensive estates and her uncle had seen to her speedy incarceration in the convent after her father died. The old abbess wouldn't have allowed it, but all discipline had broken down since the Saxon invasion of Anglesey, which had followed hard on the heels of the abbess' death.

"Soldiers!" Bronwen said. "They came to the door and the watchman let them in. The Saxons are coming!"

Dear God. They'd been foolish to think their lone convent could escape the Mercian barbarism that had become so common in recent months. Lord Modred's soldiers had pushed King Arthur's forces out of every haven but his last stronghold in Eryri, or Snowdonia as the Saxons called it. They would overrun all Wales if Arthur died as her dream promised. Once upon a time, that moment had resided in the impossibly distant future. Not anymore.

Bronwen made to run but Nell still held her arm. "Not that way. Did you see Sister Mari?"

"Yes. In the dormitory."

Nell nodded. "Good. Tell her I said to gather as many of the girls as she can. If we can get to the chapel, we can bar the doors from the inside. Bring them quick as you can.

SARAH WOODBURY

Remember—the chapel, not the church. From the shouts outside, the Saxon soldiers are already there."

"Yes, Sister," the girl said, Nell's evident calm easing her fears.

Nell released her and Bronwen ran back the way she'd come. The Saxons hadn't penetrated the convent this far as yet. Sister Mari was not only a good friend, but reliable. She would come. Meanwhile, Nell needed to discover what had happened to the abbess, who had left her room. Nell hiked up her skirts and trotted down the stairs towards the common areas of the convent. As Nell arrived in the dining hall from a back entrance, having already searched the warming room and the scriptorium, two sisters spoke to one another, alone and in quiet voices, near the main door a dozen yards away. Her abbess' posture was as if nothing untoward was happening in the courtyard beyond.

"What are you doing here?" Nell hurtled up to them, heedless of decorum or her dignity. "We must flee!"

"Lord Wulfere told me to wait here for him and he would explain everything." Abbess Annis' eyes were wide and guileless.

"And you believed him?"

"Of course," she said. "He told me that his soldiers merely needed to commission a quantity of our foodstuffs."

"Commissio—" Nell broke off the word as a man flung open the door to the dining hall. Tall and dark, with a bushy black beard that obscured his face, Wulfere, the commander of the Saxon forces on Anglesey, strode towards them. He towered over Nell who was slightly less than middle height for a woman. His

8

heavy boots left a muddy track across the floor, evidence of the unrelenting rain that had fallen over the island during the last week.

Wulfere had set up his camp to the southwest of the convent, in preparation for the moment Modred allowed him to cross the Menai Straits and attack King Arthur's seat at Garth Celyn. The *Traeth Lafan*, the Lavan Sands, had served as a crossing point of the Menai Straits for millennia, but the waters in the Straits were unpredictable and treacherous, even to those long accustomed to their moods. To counter that unpredictability, the Saxons had built a bridge of boats, a hundred of them lashed together and anchored at both ends. Wulfere was waiting for Modred's signal to cross. Meanwhile, he amused himself the best he could. *Apparently, now, with us.*

"Madame Abbess," Wulfere said, in butchered Welsh and Saxon, giving Annis a slight tip of his head. "Thank you for your hospitality."

Annis simpered back, the loose flesh around her mouth giving way to a vacant smile. "It is our honor to serve Lord Modred, our rightful king, in whatever way we can."

Nell bit her lip. King Arthur had no heir and whispers had begun already that when Arthur died, stability under Modred and his Saxon allies was preferable to the chaos that would inevitably ensue as Welsh stakeholders fought among themselves for Arthur's crown.

"Are you mad?" Nell kept her voice low and even so Wulfere wouldn't react to the tone, if not the words themselves.

"It's not just foodstuffs they want!" Sister Ilar chimed in, for once supporting Nell's position. "They've turned Queen Gwenhwyfar's coffin into a horse trough!"

"It is our duty to bring peace to Anglesey," Annis said.

"Do you object, sister, to assisting those in need?" Wulfere asked Nell. "Are not my soldiers as much God's children as any other men?" He gazed at the three women, amusement in his face, and although Nell wanted to stare him down, she didn't dare defy him. Annis might be blind to what was happening in her convent but Nell was not. It was time to leave. Annis wouldn't act, so it was up to Nell to stand in her stead.

"Excuse me." Nell curtseyed to both Wulfere and Annis. She backed away. Just as she turned towards the side door that led to the cloisters, a half a dozen Saxon soldiers came through the door behind Wulfere. Nell didn't wait to see what they wanted.

I can't believe she just opened the convent to them! How could she betray us so? But Nell knew how it was possible. In an effort to quell what the Church viewed as a convent of too-independent women, Archbishop Dafydd had appointed an un-ambitious innocent to lead them. For all that Annis was approaching her fiftieth year, she knew nothing of men, the world, or anything in it. Nell was not so naïve.

Nell closed the door to the dining hall. It had no lock but it was futile to try to stop the men from reaching the cloister, since it could be accessed by four other entrances. They hadn't found it yet, but perhaps that was because the cathedral church and food stores were keeping them occupied. They would ransack them and then turn their attention to the women. The Welsh were hardly more than animals to the Saxons and they treated them as such.

Nell was relieved to see Bronwen and Mari, a cluster of sisters in their wake, hustling towards the chapel from the dormitory entrance. Nell intercepted them at the chapel door. "Thank the Lord you've come!" She grasped Mari's hand and squeezed it, trying to convey her relief and reassurance.

Mari leaned forward and spoke low, so as not to alarm the other women. "What's happening, Nell?"

Nell let the rest of her sisters file inside the chapel before replying. "The worst," she said. "I must see to those in the infirmary. Some might be well enough to travel with us. Perhaps I can hide the rest."

"I'll come with you," Mari said.

Nell shook her head. Mari's eyes were too wide and her hair had come loose around her shoulders, a match in color to Nell's, although Mari's red-tinged strands were shot with grey. "No," Nell said. "Stay inside the chapel. Without you, the younger sisters will fall to pieces. Bar the door until I get back. If I don't return within a count of one hundred, you must go with our sisters into the tunnel beneath the crypt."

"I can't leave you!"

"You can and you will." Nell's heart pounded in her ears but she fought the rushing sound and the panic, determined to hide her feelings so as not to upset Mari further. Mari was soft-hearted, which is why she mothered the younger novices, but not one to take charge. There was no one else to lead if Nell didn't. "But I hope you won't need to."

Without waiting to see if Mari obeyed her, Nell dashed towards the entrance to the infirmary, situated at the very rear of the complex and isolated from the rest of the living quarters by a narrow passage, in case a quarantine was ever necessary. The sisters could access the room from the herb garden beyond, and Nell had a secondary thought that her sisters could flee that way, if the tunnel proved impassable.

Nell pushed at the thick oak door to the infirmary and froze on the threshold. Hell on earth stared her in the face. Blood ran from the beds to the floor, soaking the undyed wool blankets a deep red. The half dozen sisters who'd lain under her care, along with the elderly sister who watched over them at night, had been murdered as they slept. The far door that led to the outside world bumped against the inner wall, moving in the gusting wind. Beyond, darkness showed. She couldn't risk escaping with her sisters that way, not with the men who'd done this so close. Nell stared at the carnage, then spun on her heel and fled back to the chapel.

Mari had disobeyed. She'd stayed in the doorway, hovering on the threshold to wait for Nell's return. "What is it?" Mari asked when Nell reached her.

"They're dead." Nell pushed Mari into the chapel, looking over her shoulder at the first Saxon soldiers spilling into the cloister, torches blazing in their hands.

"You there!" A soldier said, in Saxon.

"Hurry!" Mari's voice went high.

Nell slammed the door shut and dropped the bar across it. As more shouts filled the cloister, she faced the other women. Mari stood three paces away, taking in huge gulps of air, her hand to her heart. Nell's lungs refused to properly fill with air either.

A young voice piped up from the rear of the group. "What about the rest of our sisters?"

Someone thudded a fist on the door. "Open up!"

Nell set her jaw. She grabbed a candle from a shrine to St. Tomos and pushed through the small group of women and girls. "We can't help them." She led the way down the steps into the crypt, trotting past the ancient tombs, the voices of the soldiers fading behind them the deeper they went.

King Arthur had commissioned Llanfaes Abbey upon the death of his beloved wife, Gwenhwyfar. Her grave lay in the cathedral church, which the Saxons were sacking even now. The chapel was older, far smaller, and had served the people of Anglesey since Christianity came to the island, back when the Romans ruled it. Rather than pull it down, King Arthur had constructed his abbey around it—and refurbished the Roman tunnel that ran beneath it which matched the one underneath Garth Celyn.

Some might have said that the King was overly cautious to have expended so much effort on the chance that a hidden escape route might one day be needed. As far as Nell knew, none ever had, either here or at Garth Celyn—until today. Given the actions of the Saxons over the last month, King Arthur was proving not only cautious, but prescient.

Maybe he *saw* too.

The convent itself sat a hundred yards from the edge of the Menai Straits so that King Arthur could look across the water to the spot where he'd buried his wife. A current of air bringing the smell of damp and mold wafted over Nell as she approached the entrance to the tunnel. The near constant autumn rain on Anglesey, coupled with having built so close to the sea, meant they couldn't stop the water from seeping between the stones.

"Here it is." Nell came to a halt in front of a blank wall.

"Here what is?" Mari peered over Nell's shoulder at the unadorned stones.

"The entrance," Nell said. "I need more light."

Someone raised a torch so it shone at the wall. Nell handed her candle to Mari and then pressed both hands on a rounded stone at waist height. With a scraping sound, the door swung open on its central pin, revealing darkness beyond. The tunnel that led from the crypt stretched north, under the protective wall of the convent and beyond.

"We have to go inside?" Bronwen said. "What if there's no way out! We'll die in there!"

"The dark can't hurt you," Nell said. "Saxon soldiers most definitely can."

"But how do we know—"

Nell grabbed Bronwen's arm. She'd never thought of Bronwen as one of the more outspoken novices, but that was proving the case tonight. "Because all the sisters in the infirmary are dead, slaughtered as they slept. I don't want that to happen to you!"

"But Lord Modred wouldn't—"

Nell cut her off again. "It's time to grow up, Bronwen. All of you." Nell cast her gaze over the faces of each girl in turn. "It doesn't matter if you support Lord Modred's claim to the throne, or King Arthur's resistance. Both sides have committed atrocities in this war. Do you want me to list all the religious houses the men out there—and others like them—have sacked? The villages they've destroyed? The women they've raped?"

Bronwen shook her head uncertainly.

"If you don't want to be one of them," Mari broke in, "I suggest you do as Sister Nell asks."

"Yes, Sister." Bronwen said, her eyes downcast.

Nell turned away; she didn't think it her imagination that her sisters gave her more space now than before. It wasn't their fault they didn't know what went on beyond the walls. Many of them had lived at the convent their whole lives. At fifteen and newly married, she'd been as ignorant and innocent as Bronwen. But Nell had come to Llanfaes as an adult, ten years ago at the death of her husband and her two little boys, four year old Llelo and infant Ieuan. She'd seen—and she'd *seen*—what men could do.

Once inside the narrow passage, Nell let the others file past her, Mari in the lead still carrying the candle. She then pulled at the door and allowed it to close with a gentle *click*. Her shoulders sagged in relief that they were safe, at least for now. At worst, she was wrong about Wulfere's men and Annis could administer to Nell whatever penance she chose for leading her sisters astray and into the wild in the middle of the night. As unpleasant as that might be, Nell wished for it.

But she wasn't wrong. Now, the scent of smoke, from a source not as far off as she might like, drifted from the chapel through a crack underneath the door, pulled into the tunnel by the open air at the far end. Without further hesitation, Nell hefted her skirts and trotted after Mari.

"Are we almost there?" Mari asked when Nell reached the front of the line of women.

"It's not much further," Nell said. "Before her death, Abbess Alis entrusted me with the secret of the tunnel. As soon as the Saxons landed on Anglesey, I came here to make sure the tunnel hadn't collapsed. That was some months ago, of course."

Mari nodded, and then asked, her voice so low Nell could barely make out the words, "do I smell smoke?"

"I fear they are firing the chapel," Nell said.

"Why would they do that?" Mari said, and then answered her own question before Nell could, her voice flat and accepting. "Because they couldn't open the door. They think we're still inside."

Nell canted her head, agreeing, but not wanting to give more emphasis to Mari's guess than that.

But Mari wasn't finished. "Without this tunnel, our choice would have been to die, or to surrender to the soldiers."

"Llanfaes is an abbey patronized by King Arthur," Nell said. "Wulfere sees nothing wrong with leaving no one alive to remember it."

A hundred steps later, they turned a corner and the tunnel began to slope upwards. Mari's torch reflected off the wooden beams that supported the roof and then finally the trap door that led to one of the Abbey's outlying barns.

"This is it?" Mari said.

"Yes," Nell said. The height of the tunnel had shrunk to just above Nell's head. With the flat of her hand, she pushed up on the square of wood, three feet on a side, which loosened and then popped free with a snap. Nell froze, but after a count of ten, couldn't see or hear anything amiss. She shoved the cover to one side and grasped the edges of the opening. With a boost from Mari and another sister, she pulled herself out of the tunnel and into a sitting position on the floor of the barn.

Hay lay scattered about in the stall in which she found herself. While the hay loft above her head was full, the horse stalls were empty. They only used this barn at harvest time and when the overflow from the Abbey with visitors was such that there was no more room for equine guests in the Abbey stables. Nell got to her feet and walked to the far wall. Hidden in plain sight among the tools and farming implements was a short ladder. She removed it and brought it back to the hole.

"It may be we'll be safe here for the rest of the night." Nell looked down on Mari's upturned face. "Let's get them into the loft."

* * * * *

It wasn't quite light when Nell slipped through the barn door. It creaked and the wind banged it back against the jam, stilling Nell at the noise. Then she reminded herself that the entire barn was a half century old and patched here and there with scraps of wood or wattle and daub, when using wood seemed a waste of resources. A little creaking and banging was a given.

She'd left Mari in charge of their sleeping sisters, every one exhausted from the events of the night. As the sky lightened, Nell had noted smoke rising from the convent half a mile away and had felt obliged to discover what had passed there in their absence: to see if the soldiers had left, and if any of her sisters had survived. Mari had begged her to stay, fearing for her life if she went out, but Nell thought that daylight might bring some measure of security—that the soldiers wouldn't risk attacking a woman on the open road. To be safer, she'd removed her habit and traded it for a patched-together dress and cloak from one of the younger nuns-to-be who hadn't yet committed to her vocation.

Nell hadn't wanted to sleep anyway, although she hadn't told Mari why. She was afraid that the dream of King Arthur's death would come again and she couldn't cope with seeing it—not with what had happened to her sisters—not with the power of the Saxons so evident. Admittedly, it took far less strength to overpower a convent than to kill a king, but to live through one horror only to dream another immediately after was more than

18

Nell could bear just now. At least with her sisters, she'd taken action. That she could find a way to help King Arthur seemed as out of reach now as it ever had.

A bird chirped to Nell's left, a cheery counterpoint to the staccato of her heart. She gazed across the brown fields, harvested this autumn to the advantage of the Saxons instead of the Welsh, since the soldiers had captured the island in early September, intending to deprive the mainland of food. The convent continued to smoke, wisps spiraling skyward in the murky dawn. Nell braced herself for the effort—more emotional than physical—and set out towards what had been her home.

Twenty minutes later, she circled around to the east of the convent and crouched in the grass, screened from the entrance by a fence and blackberry bramble. The front gate of the convent sat wide open, revealing churned earth and grey stone beyond. From the looks, the Saxons hadn't fired the Church itself, just the inner chapel which Nell couldn't see from her present position.

What she could see were several bodies sprawled in the dirt, two inside the gatehouse and a third ten paces from Nell's hiding place. The body lay face down in the mud. Nell assumed this sister was dead along with the others until the woman moved a hand. Nell sprang to her feet. She sprinted the distance between them, fell to her knees beside the woman, and turned her over, revealing Ilar's battered face.

"Nell." Ilar opened her eyes. She raised her hand to touch Nell's chin and then dropped it.

"What—?" Nell stopped. It was pointless to ask what had happened. Any fool could see it.

"Annis is dead. All the others," Ilar said. "I thought you died in the chapel."

"We used the tunnel. Mari and some of the novices are safe in the barn this side of Coed Mawr."

"Coed Mawr?" Ilar lifted her head as if she wanted to stand and come with Nell; as if she hadn't bled out through the long gash along her right side. "No—" Ilar fell back and moaned, rocking her head from side to side.

"What's wrong? 'No'—what?" Nell grabbed Ilar's shoulders, wanting to shake her, but her hands came away bloody. She stared at her fingers, and then at Ilar's face. Ilar had closed her eyes again.

"They know of it." Ilar just managed to get out the words. "Annis told Wulfere about the tunnel . . ." Her head sagged to one side, spent.

Nell put a hand to Ilar's neck. Her pulse faltered and then stopped. Nell sat back on her heels, straightened Ilar's dress, and wiped her hands on the damp cloth of the skirt. Her stomach rebelled to know that even though no trace remained, she could still feel the blood on her fingers. Swallowing hard, she pushed the thought away. She had no time for a more proper remembrance and rose to her feet, searching the landscape for any sign of Wulfere's soldiers. *Why did I leave the barn? They'll have no chance without me!*

No movement caught her eye, either at the convent or in the distance, but then—*There! Along the road!* A company of Wulfere's men rode northeast, away from their camp and towards the spot where Nell had hidden her companions.

"No!"

Nell screamed the word. Knowing it was useless, that she'd never reach the barn in time, but unable to stop the cry or her tears from tumbling down her cheeks, Nell ran back the way she'd come. She stumbled and sobbed through the muddy fields and stands of trees, only staying on her feet over the rough terrain because she couldn't bear not to—until reason reasserted itself. She pulled up, having run two-thirds of the distance back to the barn. Breathing hard, as much from horror as from the exertion, she rested her cheek against the smooth bark of a willow tree, cool against her flushed face. She tightened her arms around the slender trunk, holding on for dear life, and gazed across the last two hundred yards to the entrance to the barn.

She had led her sisters to safety, only to abandon them to their fate. The completeness of her failure overwhelmed her as Wulfere's soldiers hauled the helpless girls and women out of the barn, arms wrenched behind their backs. When Wulfere's men had pillaged and burned the convent the night before, the majority of the women they'd encountered had been older or weakened like those in the infirmary. These were more to their liking.

Her sisters' screams echoed across the fields and into her ears; Nell sank to her knees in the bramble, her arms around her waist and her head bowed. She couldn't help them nor watch any longer. She leaned forward and sobbed.

3

4 November 537 AD

"Get over here, Myrddin!"

I urged my horse across the clearing, through the ankle-deep snow and towards Gawain, the captain of my lord's guard. He resembled a greyhound, whip-thin but muscled . . .

"**I** fear the weather will turn worse this evening." Lord Aelric tucked his fine, grey cloak closer around himself. "You'll have a cold ride home."

Myrddin blinked at the man, his breath choking him, trying to recover from the sudden shift in perspective. He gritted his teeth, stunned by the dramatic transition from dream state to consciousness. The vision of his defeat at the church had come so clearly to him, passing in front of his eyes with such intensity that he'd forgotten where he was. That had never happened to him before.

"Rain in the lowlands; snow in the hills," Myrddin said, in Saxon, thankful that Aelric hadn't noticed his inattention. The battle had occurred only in his mind—in a flash of understanding—and hardly ten heartbeats had passed in the real world in the time it took for him to fight and die inside his head. Myrddin took in a deep breath to ease his pounding heart. The vision had been clearer and more *real* than any he'd experienced before. Myrddin knew, even if he was loathe to admit it, that his dreams pressed on him more every day. They were getting worse—not to mention more demanding in their urgency that he *do* something. Yet as little more than a journeyman knight in the King's company, he didn't know what that something could be.

He maintained his seat on his horse, Cadfarch, and rode between the two grey standing stones that marked the pass of Bwlch y Ddeufaen, the highest point in the road that led from Garth Celyn, King Arthur's seat on the northern coast of Eryri, east to Caerhun and then across the Conwy River into the part of Gwynedd controlled by Modred. They'd reached the high moor, long since denuded of trees, but the windswept countryside provided a magnificent contrast to the mountains behind them and the sea in the distance. Rain was normal for Wales this time of year, and every time of year for that matter, but it had abated today.

Myrddin's answer satisfied Lord Aelric, who continued to saunter down the road with Myrddin, their horses at a steady walk. Three other knights followed. Myrddin hadn't spoken to them since he'd led them out of Garth Celyn, and they'd been content for him to entertain their master.

"I've never liked passing among the pagan stones," Lord Aelric said, once they lay behind them and the company had headed down the hill towards the Conwy River valley, still green in places despite the imminent winter weather. "I'll suggest that Lord Modred pull them down in due course, once your king has bowed to the inevitable."

He shot a glance at Myrddin, a sneer on his lips. Lord Aelric was baiting Myrddin and waited to see if Myrddin would respond to his arrogance. Aelric had no qualms about speaking his mind and keeping any Welshman in his place, one far below his. Myrddin kept his face expressionless.

As he'd just reminded himself, Lord Aelric was counselor to Modred and Myrddin was a middle-aged warrior, worn around the edges from a lifetime of warfare and rough living. From an impoverished, if noble, beginning, he'd risen among the ranks of Arthur's company. Thanks to his reckless courage as a young man, King Arthur had knighted him after a battle in his twenty-fourth year. At the time, it had served to increase Myrddin's devotion to him. Since then, that devotion had been tempered by a certain, frank realism. Twenty years of war—and dreams of death—did that to a man.

"The populace will object, my lord," Myrddin said, his voice mild.

Aelric sniffed, indicating what he thought of the populace. Myrddin smoothed the mustache that grew along each cheek, less flamboyantly than many a Welshman's but still of considerable size. Then it struck him that in his dream, he no longer wore it. *Had that always been the case?* Myrddin had dreamt the fight so many times he'd memorized it. Or thought he had.

Twenty miles later and after hours of stilted conversation—such that Myrddin feared he'd bitten right through his tongue in his attempts to contain what was in his mind—the road connected to another one running north/south which would take Aelric the remaining miles to Denbigh. By the time they reached the crossroads, the sun had nearly set. Although Aelric urged Myrddin to continue on to Denbigh Castle, he declined. His King had given him his orders and they didn't include dinner in Modred's hall—in a castle that a few weeks ago had belonged to Arthur's brother, Cai. That Cai had been more treasonous than not over the years was beside the point, since he again fought at King Arthur's side. Myrddin didn't think he could have stomached it anyway.

The troop of men flowed around Myrddin without a second look. As they disappeared around a bend, he gazed after them, unseeing. The first time he'd had the dream of the King's death—and his own—he'd been no more than twelve. At the time, he'd come awake shocked and alert, with his heart racing, although part of him had thrilled at the vision of the future, of battle, and that he'd fought for Arthur. He'd had the dream perhaps a dozen times between twelve and twenty. Fifteen years ago, however, the dreams had begun to change, becoming darker in intent, richer in color, and yet more stark, the white snow standing out against the blackness of the forest. They'd also grown more detailed, more urgent, and unfortunately, more common.

Lost in thought, Myrddin drifted to the edge of the road and into the trees that lined it. Cadfarch willingly cropped the grass that crept between the stones, unconcerned when Myrddin dismounted to leave the reins trailing. At first, Myrddin sat on the edge the road, his knees drawn up. Then, as darkness descended, nearly complete since clouds covered the sky from horizon to horizon, he lay on his back and stared upwards into the nothingness.

Over the years, Myrddin had learned to push the dream away, denying it, even as it dogged his steps. Yet, because it had come so much more frequently in this last year, every week certainly, sometimes every day, he could no longer ignore it or take it as casually as he wished. Just two days ago, Myrddin had downed enough wine and mead to blind a giant in hopes of heading off the vision, only to awaken halfway through the night in a cold sweat. Even as he pushed the events of December 11th aside, going about his business as if that day wasn't approaching fast—as if the dream was just a dream—he'd finally begun to admit the truth.

It wasn't just a dream.

Myrddin focused on the leaves above his head. Who was he to *see* like this? He was a nobody. His mother, the orphaned daughter of a landless knight, had lived as a lady-in-waiting in the household of a minor Welsh lordling. She'd birthed him out of wedlock. The Welsh ignored illegitimacy provided a father acknowledged his offspring but Myrddin's mother had died at his birth before she revealed his father's identity. Consequently, he grew up an orphan in the lord's house, living off the scraps of the high table and grateful to have received even that.

At the same time, Myrddin was Welsh. It was in his blood to *see*. Didn't the priests speak often of the native saints, whose visions had led them on despite the death and despair that surrounded them? Myrddin snorted under his breath at that thought. He might be many things, but a saint wasn't one of them.

Myrddin might have lain beside the road the whole night, his limbs growing stiff from the cold ground despite the warmth of his wool cloak, if a woman's scream hadn't split the air and forced him back to life. The depth of fear in her cry carried her panic through the trees to where he lay. Myrddin was on his feet in an instant. He threw himself onto Cadfarch's back, turned him in the direction from which the sound had come, and urged him forward.

Myrddin couldn't see a damned thing in the dark, but Cadfarch's eyes were more capable than his at night. The horse rode unerringly along the road at a gallop, his head pushed forward and his tail streaming behind him while Myrddin pressed his cheek against the horse's neck.

Ahead, off the road in a cleared, grassy patch, a torch flickered, revealing the shapes of three people hovering over the prone figure of a fourth. The woman hadn't screamed again, but she writhed on the ground before them and managed to lash out with her foot at one of the men, who cursed aloud. "St. Dewy's arse! I'll teach y—"

But he didn't finish his sentence. As Cadfarch's hooves pounded on the stones of the road, the three men rose to their feet and turned to look at Myrddin, although only one reached for his sword. The other two men had removed theirs, strapping them to their saddlebags in preparation for molesting the woman. Now that they'd trained their attention on Myrddin, she rolled into a hollow at the edge of the clearing while Myrddin raised his sword and swung it at the armed man. He stupidly chose to stand his ground.

He caught Myrddin's sword against his but the force of the blow threw him backwards. Seeing that he'd gone down, Myrddin flung himself off Cadfarch, landing hard in the grass beside the man. Myrddin thrust his sword through the knight's midsection, under his ribs, before he could recover. The blade slid in easily. The man may have worn a sword, indicating his high status, but he'd neglected his armor this evening, perhaps thinking he'd have little need of it and it would only hinder him in his carousing.

Myrddin pulled the sword from the man's belly and looked around for more men to fight, but the other two were already away. Well-horsed themselves, and in train with the third, now masterless, they raced north along the road to Rhuddlan, preferring an ignominious departure to facing an armed and angry knight. The woman crouched in a ditch where she'd come to rest, her hands in front of her mouth and her eyes wide and staring. The dress she wore might once have been fine but the men had ripped the fabric from neck to waist, revealing her shift. At least no blood marred the front. Her eyes were shadowed but Myrddin didn't know if the cause of that was the torchlight or men's fists.

"It's all right," he said, in Welsh, guessing at her nationality. "You're safe."

"I never thought—" she began in the same language, and then stopped, swallowing hard. "I didn't think anyone would come."

"I heard you scream," he said.

Myrddin took a step nearer and though the woman shrank from him, she didn't run away. Moving slowly, more as if she were a wild animal rather than human, Myrddin put a hand under her elbow and urged her to stand. The top of her head didn't even reach his chin. Then he stepped back, thinking to keep his distance so as not to frighten her.

"Let me take you home." Myrddin checked the road. No sign remained of the men who'd run but that didn't mean they weren't close by, waiting for a second chance. It made sense to hurry.

The woman didn't speak so he grasped her left arm and urged her towards Cadfarch. Her feet, thankfully still shod in well worn-boots, stuck to the earth at first, but he got her moving, glad that she wasn't in such shock that she ran away screaming. Myrddin had lived a long and varied life, but even for him that would have been a first.

Myrddin wiped the blade of his sword on the tail of the dead man's cloak and sheathed it. The torch the men had carried had almost burned out but he still needed it. He picked it up to hold it close enough to illumine both the woman's face and his. He wanted her to see that he wouldn't hurt her and he needed her to talk. "Tell me your name." He lifted the torch high. "And where you're from."

The woman shivered. She pulled the ends of her torn dress together and crossed her arms across her chest. Myrddin loosened the ties that held his cloak closed at the neck, removed it, and swung it around her shoulders so that the fabric enveloped her. She clutched at it while Myrddin lifted the hood to hide her hair which had come loose from the chignon at the back of her head. He didn't bother trying to find her linen coif.

Myrddin gazed at her and then swept his eyes up and down to take in her appearance from head to foot. The woman raised her eyes from the ground. They were a deep green that complemented her hair and Myrddin acknowledged that he was correct in his initial assessment: she was beautiful. Myrddin guessed that she was close in age to him, although she could have been younger. The events of the night had hollowed her cheeks and eyes but time and warmth could reveal her youth. Her diction, given the few words she'd spoken, was that of an educated woman.

"My name is Nell ferch Morgan. And I have no home."

"But you must have once," he said. "Did the Saxons turn you out of it?"

That garnered a response. To Myrddin's relief, it wasn't tears she expressed but anger. "I come from the convent at

31

Llanfaes, on the Island of Anglesey," she said. "The Saxons burned the Abbey to the ground and defiled the grave of Queen Gwenhwyfar." She spit out the words, her biting tone compressing all her hatred of the Saxons into one sentence.

"You've come far." Myrddin didn't even blink at the Saxon sacrilege. Their barbarity was well-practiced and well known among his people. "Where is your father? Your family?"

"Dead," she said.

"And the rest of your sisters?"

"I don't even want to say." She looked away from Myrddin now, her sadness conquering her anger. "They're dead too. I knew of what the Saxons were capable, but we were too vulnerable—too unprepared for when they came. I managed to hide a few of my sisters at first, but . . . ."

"But what?"

Nell gazed down at her shoes and a tear dropped onto the rough, brown leather covering her left foot. "I left them. I thought they would be safe in a nearby barn so I went to see what had become of the convent after we escaped. To find other survivors. In my absence . . . the Saxons found them . . . and . . . and . . . ." Nell stuttered, swallowed hard, and finished, even if Myrddin already knew what she was going say, "took them."

Myrddin studied Nell's down-turned head, going over her tale in his mind. The garrison at Garth Celyn had smelled smoke blowing across the Straits, but the fog and rain had been so unrelenting, they'd not known what was happening. Perhaps the

King had received word of this today, in Myrddin's absence, but . . . "You must come to Garth Celyn."

Although she'd expressed no fear of him up until then, now Nell paled. She took a step back. "I don't think so." She shook her head.

"I saved you," Myrddin said, nonplussed at this sudden reversal. He took a step towards her. "I won't harm you." Finding Nell here might be fate—might be one more nail in his coffin—but as the wind whipped the dead leaves from the trees, bringing the strong scent of the sea and the smell of winter, Myrddin felt a change in the air. By lying on the road for longer than he should have, he'd been given the chance to save one life out of all those that might be lost between now and December 11th. Whether by her choice or his, Nell was riding home with him, even if he had to tie her up and throw her across Cadfarch's withers.

Nell must have heard his thoughts. Without warning, she turned on her heel and ran for the trees that lined the road. She'd dropped his cloak within two steps and hiked her skirts above her knees, to run flat out along a trail only she could see. Cursing, Myrddin started after her. Where she thought she was going to go in the middle of the night, in Saxon territory, with a torn dress, was beyond him.

"Stop!" Myrddin said. *Goddamn it!*

In the end, it was an unseen root that undid her. She tripped and fell, falling forward onto her hands. Myrddin was a few paces behind, unhindered by skirts and with longer legs. He came down on her back and pressed her to the earth, grasping each of her wrists and holding her arms out to either side, trying to contain her struggles.

"Get . . . off . . . me!" Nell rocked her hips back and forth.

At half again as large as she and with twenty years of fighting under his belt, she hadn't a chance. "I won't hurt you." Myrddin repeated the words again and again until her movements calmed and she breathed heavily into the musty leaves. "My name is Myrddin. I serve Arthur ap Uther."

Silence. Nell put her forehead into the dirt, arching her neck. Myrddin could practically hear her thinking, although he couldn't discern her thoughts.

"If you were at Llanfaes Abbey, the King must hear of its burning," he added. "He would have my head for setting you loose east of the Conwy River."

"Then don't tell him."

Now it was Myrddin who had no answer. Finally, he said, "That I cannot do."

Nell mumbled something into the muddy leaves, something Myrddin didn't catch, other than the word 'men', which she spit into the earth. He eased off of her and then stood, taking a step to leave her free. She twisted onto her back and gazed up at Myrddin for a long twenty seconds. He held out his hand. After another pause, she grasped his fingers and he pulled her upright.

"Will you come with me or do I have to tie you up?" He released her hand before she threw it from her.

It was dark under the trees so Myrddin couldn't read her expression, but the words came grudgingly, subdued at last—at least on the surface. "I'll come."

They walked back to Cadfarch, who was waiting where Myrddin had left him. Myrddin swathed Nell in his cloak once again, swung into the saddle, and pulled her up after him. Nell had to rest on the saddlebags. It wasn't the most comfortable seat but would provide her a better cushion than the horn at the front of the saddle. Her hem rode up her legs, revealing the undyed leggings she wore underneath her dress. She tugged the skirt down before spreading his cloak wide for modesty. Myrddin waited for her to wrap her arms around his waist, which she eventually did, resting her small hands on his belt.

Cadfarch, of course, had no dreams of the future, good or ill, or any thought but when he might rest or next find his feed bag full. Uncomplaining, he pointed his nose west, in the direction of home.

4

5 November 537 AD

Past midnight—in November—in the rain—was not the best time for riding, even on a road as well made as the one that ran from St. Asaph to Garth Celyn. Nell was grateful for Myrddin's cloak which protected her from the deluge that fell from the sky. The cloak she'd borrowed from that poor almost-nun had gotten trampled in the mud and muck beside the road and Myrddin had left it where it lay. In his generosity, however, Myrddin had left himself open to the elements.

Although Nell wasn't happy to be heading back towards Eryri, she was content for the moment to ride behind Myrddin. He'd driven her attackers away and knew enough not to touch her unless he had to. It was she who was touching him, her arms cinched around his waist, keeping both of them warm and her fears at bay. *How can this be anything other than my fate? Perhaps God isn't done with me yet.*

She'd run from Myrddin before she knew who he was. Because of the dark and that enormous mustache masking his face, it wasn't until she lay under him in the dirt and he'd said his name that she'd recognized him. Once she knew him, the dream of King Arthur's death had come into vivid relief. It felt for a moment as if going with Myrddin would tie her to a future she didn't want to be true. But the truth remained inescapable. He was here, and real, and had saved her. It occurred to her that few girls ever got to meet the man of their dreams.

Myrddin had decided that they shouldn't seek shelter before they reached the garrison at Caerhun, an old Roman fort that Arthur had resurrected to watch the Conwy River. Even then, Nell wasn't sure how she felt about sleeping in a fort among a dozen unfamiliar soldiers. Fear—of men, of the future—had hounded her all the way from Anglesey to St. Asaph. If anything, her terror had grown as she replayed the events at the convent in her head mile after mile—as if she were living them and dreaming them both at the same time. But despite what she knew of men, she'd been unprepared for the attack on the road. Without Myrddin, those Saxons would have taken her and killed her. Nell knew it and her heart caught in her throat every time she allowed her mind to focus on it.

"Tell me who you are again," she said, after they'd ridden five miles, retracing both her steps and his. It had taken her that many miles to steady herself and to be able to speak without a hitch in her voice.

"My name is Myrddin. I serve King Arthur. I escorted the Lord Aelric to St. Asaph yesterday afternoon, and was preparing to return when I came upon you."

That sounded reasonable to Nell. Despite her fears about this journey and the notion of having anything to do with any man, she gave in to relief. At last, some of the horror of the attack drained away and she rested her forehead between Myrddin's shoulder blades. "Thank you," she said. "I haven't thanked you yet."

"Are you . . . much hurt?"

"I was terrified of the men, panicked beyond all measure, but they didn't rape me if that's what you're asking."

The word *rape* twisted on her lips and she shuddered into Myrddin's back, but she was glad she'd used it. They didn't need to dance around the question now.

"Praise God," Myrddin said. "Why were you traveling that road? Alone?"

"I had a family, once," Nell said, "and sons, although they're all dead now. I've not spent my life behind stone walls. I have no one who depends on me, no husband, and no desire ever to have one again. With nothing to tie me to Anglesey, I saw no reason why I shouldn't travel where I wished."

"In the middle of a war," Myrddin said.

Nell's hackles rose at the distrust in his voice. "What do you mean?"

"What could have possessed you to travel so far on your own, unless it was for some nefarious purpose?" he said. "I saved you from genuine peril, but even spies can find themselves in over their heads when they meet men more devious than they."

"What? You can't mean that." Nell found laughter mingling with a mixture of incredulity and hysteria. Then again, she too could imagine a scenario in which a woman such as she imparted information about King Arthur's movements to the men who attacked her, only to have them decide she'd outlived her usefulness.

"Convince me otherwise," Myrddin said.

Nell thought for a moment, sure she couldn't tell him the whole truth—not about the dreams or that she knew him from them—but she could tell him something. "Our abbess died during the summer, just before the Saxons came. The new one the Archbishop appointed was . . ." she paused, searching for a word that would convey the truth but wasn't as stark as 'an idiot' . . . "ineffective."

"What was your role?" Myrddin said. "Were you the prioress?"

"I was the infirmarer," Nell said.

"So you left," he said. "All by yourself."

"I did," she said. "And nearly paid for my stupidity with my life."

"But why were you at St. Asaph?" Myrddin said. "After dark?"

"That close to so many fortified towns, I thought I'd be safe."

"You were safe—from masterless men—but not from Modred's men."

"I intended to seek shelter at the convent at Rhuddlan," Nell said. "I had another hour to walk, no more."

"An hour that proved your undoing," Myrddin said. "You should have sheltered instead at the convent at Conwy, south of Caerhun."

"I couldn't—" Nell paused, trying to explain what she'd come to understand, though she'd never articulated it to herself. "You misunderstand. I wasn't going to stay at the convent at Rhuddlan. I can't go back to that life."

"What do you mean?"

"I took vows, I know, but I chose the convent when I was so angry at God I couldn't bear to live with myself anywhere else."

Myrddin barked a laugh. "That doesn't make sense."

"It did to me; it does to me." She paused again. "It wasn't God who burned Llanfaes and killed my sisters."

"Some would say God allowed it to happ—"

Nell cut him off. "Don't be a child. With Llanfaes burned, my sisters dead or worse, not just the Abbey, but my life lies in ashes around my feet. I've come to realize that I will not rebuild it again as a nun."

"The entire world has turned upside down these last months," Myrddin said, nodding. "A clear path is hard for anyone to see."

Nell could only agree with that. She lowered her voice, less because she was afraid it would carry than because of the force of the emotion behind it. "I hate the Saxons, so much so I fear I'll be consumed by it. Yet I'm afraid of them also, and of the future they represent."

Myrddin's hand found hers at his waist and squeezed. "It burns through me too."

The pair rode through the night, the downpour turning into a gentle rain in the early hours of the morning. Still, the rain had soaked them through and Nell was glad when Myrddin turned into the entrance of the fort in the murky light that preceded sunrise. She checked the sky, thinking that if they left Caerhun shortly after noon, they could travel the ten miles to Garth Celyn before darkness fell. Desperation rose within her at the thought of journeying all the way back to a point just shy of the one from which she'd started. Then she had a moment of stark clarity: she would never leave Gwynedd now. She would have to ride this war out in Eryri, in the very castle from which King Arthur governed.

Myrddin brought Cadfarch to a halt. "There'll be provisions and dry cloaks to borrow here."

Nell accepted Myrddin's help dismounting but once on the ground, hesitated. She looked toward the central hall, some thirty paces away, and then back at Myrddin.

"You can wait for me inside." Myrddin started to lead Cadfarch away.

"No." Nell moved to walk beside him. "No, I can't."

Myrddin stopped and Nell strode past him, heading towards the stables. "Nell—"

She ignored him. Once inside, Myrddin, still shaking his head at her, unbuckled the saddle bags and Cadfarch's saddle. Nell picked up a brush and began to work at the horse's mane. The motion felt good after the long ride. Her muscles were stiffened and sore. As she worked, she sensed Myrddin watching her out of the corner of his eye. She could tell he wasn't sure what to say to her, or if he should say anything at all. Nell decided that since she already knew everything a woman needed to know about what kind of man he was—even without the clarity of her dreams—he knew nothing of her and she would save him from his perplexity.

"My mother died at my birth." She moved the brush to Cadfarch's legs. The horse closed his eyes, absorbing the treatment Nell was giving him. "My father didn't marry again nor have other children." She glanced up at Myrddin, a half-smile on her lips. "He saw no reason why I shouldn't become familiar with horses."

"Where was this?" Myrddin rested his forearm along Cadfarch's back and leaned on it, watching her face.

"In Powys," she said. "My father had a small holding along the Irfon River. We were never wealthy, but lived well for all that."

"And your husband? You said you had one."

"I married at fifteen," she said. "My two sons were born and died before I was twenty; then, my husband was killed in a minor skirmish ten years ago."

"So you went into a convent," Myrddin said.

"I did."

"A common enough decision," Myrddin said, "but why so far from Powys?"

"My father had died; the Saxons had confiscated his lands. I'd lived among them for most of my life, but my father supported King Arthur and had taught me to support him too."

Myrddin tipped his head, acknowledging her admission of allegiance even if he didn't necessarily believe it, especially since she'd now confessed that she'd grown up among the Saxons. They finished grooming Cadfarch, still not in accord, and crossed the courtyard, entering the main building through a side door. It led to a hall, forty feet on a side, with long tables for dining or congregating. The smell of cooking wafted through a far doorway, indicating an adjacent cookhouse.

"Myrddin! You look well!" A stocky man dressed in mail armor much like Myrddin's appeared from the kitchens and strolled towards them. Also like Myrddin, his broad shoulders told her he'd worn that armor for his entire, adult life.

"I disbelieve you, Rhodri, since I haven't slept in far too long," Myrddin replied, by way of a greeting.

Rhodri laughed.

Myrddin placed a hand at the small of Nell's back, pushing her forward with him as he walked towards Rhodri. "We need food and rest and a place to dry our cloaks, if we may. We must return to Garth Celyn before the sun sets."

"Done." Rhodri grinned. "As long as you tell me one piece of news."

"That I can do," Myrddin said.

43

Rhodri seated himself at the end of one of the long tables. Nell pushed back the hood of Myrddin's cloak and went to stand by the fire, her back to the heat. She met Myrddin's eyes across the distance that separated them and realized he'd been observing her, his lips pursed.

"And we need dry clothes," Myrddin said.

"We'll start there." Rhodri looked Myrddin up and down. Myrddin's surcoat was still damp, the water glistening on the links of his mail. Rhodri jerked his head in the direction of a side doorway. "Help yourself."

Myrddin tipped his head to Nell and she followed him to a supply room, reached by a narrow hallway. Once inside, she stopped, uncertain, but Myrddin had everything in hand. "I've been here before." He lifted up the lid of a trunk which held a variety of garments. "And been in need before."

"I wouldn't mind hearing that story some day," Nell said.

Myrddin shot her a grin and then turned back to the trunk. "This will have to do." He tossed her an ugly, grey dress.

Nell caught it, gazing first at it and then at him. He turned to face away from her to give her a measure of privacy and tears pricked at her eyes at his understanding. Hastily, she wiped them away before stripping off his cloak and the torn dress she'd worn continually since she'd borrowed it from the young novice whose fate Nell couldn't bear to think on.

When she'd finished, Myrddin swung around to look at her. He grunted. "I don't like it. The color doesn't suit you and it's too big. We'll find you better at Garth Celyn."

44

Nell had regained control over herself by then and tipped her head in what she hoped was calm acceptance. "At least it's in one piece."

Then, not entirely sure of herself, Nell moved forward to help him remove his armor. Myrddin accepted her touch with equanimity, even as he studied her with his calm, hazel eyes that revealed nothing of the thoughts behind them. When Nell traced with one finger the long scar that ran the length of his bottom left rib, Myrddin shrugged. "An errant knife. A small matter, considering what it could have been."

Up close and without his armor, Myrddin proved to be less squat and taller than her first impression, with long rangy limbs, albeit thick shoulders and neck from years of swordplay. For lack of a satchel, Nell wrapped Myrddin's armor in his wet surcoat. A squire at Garth Celyn would polish the links so they wouldn't rust. Then, while Myrddin dressed, Nell busied herself in returning the contents of the chest that Myrddin had upended to their place so that she needn't look at him.

"Ready?" Myrddin straightened and adjusted his sword at his waist.

Nell looked up and nodded. Myrddin took his armor from her, tucking it under one arm, and led the way back to the dining hall.

In their absence, the daughter of the garrison captain, a girl just entering womanhood, had put together a meal. Once they were seated, she laid a trencher in front of Nell and Myrddin and set a cup beside it. She assumed that they'd share, which was not out of the ordinary, but the action revealed to Nell that both the girl and Rhodri believed that Nell belonged to Myrddin. Nell gave Myrddin a quick glance, wondering if he knew it too. He was focused on Rhodri so didn't see her look, and then Nell decided that an explanation to the contrary was not in order. They could think what they liked. She could stand to ride pillion a little longer.

"I brought Lord Aelric as far as St. Asaph last night," Myrddin said, oblivious to Nell and her concerns. "The discussions between Modred and King Arthur continue."

"So we have a few days' breathing space." Rhodri nodded. To Nell, he added, "Modred, when he attacks Eryri, will come through here."

Nell had known that. Modred's intent was to open two fronts in Eryri, splitting King Arthur's forces and attention. Wulfere would attack from Anglesey and Modred himself from the east, along the very road on which Nell and Myrddin had traveled. But while the army on Anglesey had been in position for months, Modred had faced resistance all along the border between Mercia and Gwynedd which had delayed the combined assault.

Then, when all was in readiness to advance across the Conwy River, Archbishop Dafydd had stepped in. He'd been working on a peace settlement between King Arthur and Modred since the middle of October, loathe to have uncle and nephew fighting each other and despoiling Wales between them. Lord Aelric had merely delivered the latest missive.

46

"Indeed," Myrddin said. "Archbishop Dafydd has not given up, but I've no news beyond that. We met no Saxons on the road, once we headed west from St. Asaph."

"I'll tell the captain," Rhodri said, standing.

Rhodri departed, leaving Nell and Myrddin alone with their simple meal of bread, cheese, boiled onions, and sweet mead. Myrddin ate the fresh food with gusto. Nell, in contrast, picked at hers.

"You all right?" Myrddin asked between mouthfuls.

Nell pushed the trencher more towards him, having eaten only three or four bites. Over the last two days, it seemed the nervous pit in her stomach had become permanent. It wasn't going to go away just because she was behind stone walls and ostensibly safe. "I'm more tired than hungry."

Myrddin nodded and hurried through the rest of the meal. Rhodri hadn't returned by the time he finished, so, once again, Nell followed Myrddin out of the hall. This time, he led her up a staircase to the sleeping rooms set aside for guests. On the floor of one room lay six pallets, blankets folded at the end of each.

"You may sleep here," Myrddin said.

Nell took a few hesitant steps into the room and then looked to where Myrddin lounged in the doorway, one shoulder braced against the frame. "What about you?"

"I'll bunk in the barracks across the courtyard." He tipped his head to indicate their general direction.

"No!" The word burst from Nell, but once said, she didn't want to take it back.

Myrddin blinked and straightened, dropping his hands to his sides. "What?"

"I can't stay here without you," Nell said, surprising herself with how important this had become to her. "Please don't leave me alone."

Myrddin gaped at her. "You ask the impossible, Nell. I can't sleep in the same room as you!"

"Please, Myrddin," she said. "I can't—" She choked on the words. Once again, the terrors of the last three days which she'd been holding at bay threatened to overwhelm her and she buried her face in her hands.

"All right; all right," Myrddin said, one hand out to her. "I don't mind. I can sleep anywhere, but you must be certain. Last week you were a nun, and today . . ." He stopped.

Nell let the silence stretch between them while she took several deep breaths to calm herself. "Today I'm not." She walked to one of the pallets which was set against a far wall and sat down on it. She pointed to a second pallet near where Myrddin stood. "Could you shut the door and move the pallet to block it? If you sleep across it . . ." Her voice trailed off.

After a final, long look, Myrddin nodded. "I can sleep here," he said, although his expression told her otherwise. It was as if he was concerned, curious, and amused all at the same time.

Comforted that he would stay, regardless of what he really thought, Nell lay down, turned her back on Myrddin, and pulled the blanket to her chin.

* * * * *

Myrddin breathed in the high moorland air, pungent with the smell of dried grass, juniper, and agrimony, patches of which grew all along the road. They'd reached a point where they were still well above the farmlands of the Aber river valley, but could see all the way to the Irish Sea. The water showed grey-blue and reflected the clouds that had begun to blow in from the west.

"It's so peaceful up here," Nell said. "Not like down below." She removed a hand from Myrddin's waist and gestured towards the island of Anglesey, which squatted in the distance. Myrddin squinted, but couldn't see anything more than a grey smudge on the horizon. "The Saxons plan to conquer Eryri next and we can't let them. They will move soon."

Myrddin turned in the saddle, trying to see her face. "Do you know that for a fact?"

"The ferryman at Bangor took me across the Menai Straits on the evening of November 2nd, not long after Wulfere's men—" Nell swallowed and then continued as if the words weren't poisoning her heart, "found my sisters. But he only helped me because he was ferrying himself across. He felt an ill wind blowing and didn't want to be caught in the middle of it. He didn't intend to return to the island until it was over."

"You speak of Wulfere. Does he still head the Saxon forces?" Myrddin asked.

"Yes," Nell said. "The people of Anglesey call him 'the pig'."

As before when Nell had spoken of the atrocities at the convent, Myrddin sensed that if she were less well-bred, she would have spit on the ground rather than speak his name.

"If anyone deserves it, Wulfere does," Myrddin said. "He once chopped off a man's hand for failing to give him his carafe of wine as quickly as he liked."

"May he burn in hell for what he did to my sisters," Nell said.

"I will see to it if I can," Myrddin said. "Before I left yesterday morning, King Arthur's scouts were reporting unusual activity on and near the bridge of boats. When they come, we'll be ready."

In fact, one of Arthur's many spies had told him that Wulfere had become frustrated by the delay, openly commenting that Modred lacked sufficient courage to fight King Arthur when it came to it, and sought a way to force Modred's hand. Arthur believed that soon Wulfere would order his men across the Straits, hoping for a surprise attack and a swift victory. Instead, he would find himself facing an army of Welshmen. Myrddin could already hear the screams of dying men, blood coating them and him, taste salt and sand on his lips as the wind spit surf into his face, and feel again the slick thrust of his sword through an enemy's flesh.

Nell and Myrddin made their way out of the mountains and into the forests and fields that surrounded Garth Celyn, following the Roman road. An hour later, they approached the gates to the castle. Arthur's banner—the red dragon of Wales on a white background—flew from the flagpole. A shiver went through

Myrddin at the knowledge that if he couldn't stop Arthur from going to the church by the Cam River, that flag might never fly in Wales again. While Myrddin never had any intention of allowing that to happen, it was dawning on him only now—so late he was embarrassed to admit it—that it was *he* who would have to see to it.

The certainty of Myrddin's new knowledge grew in him—along with his fear. All his life, he'd lived as other men had directed and been content with that. His lord pointed and he went; how was he going to change course so late in life? How was he to face the oncoming storm when he couldn't tell anyone his thoughts, his fears, his *dreams*? How was he to stand his ground against this fate?

A head popped over the battlements. It was Ifan, Myrddin's old compatriot. Myrddin waved a hand.

"You've returned." Ifan rested his forearms on the wooden rail at the top of the wall so he could see Myrddin better. He raised his eyebrows at the sight of Nell but didn't comment, for which Myrddin was grateful. Through the arrow slits, the shadows of other men paced along the wall-walk.

"You expected something different?" Myrddin said.

Ifan laughed. "When one rides among the Saxons, one can never be too sure of one's safety." He lifted his chin. "The garrison at Caerhun is secure?"

"It is," Myrddin said. "And the mead excellent."

Ifan snorted laughter and waved them in as the guards below pushed open the gate.

Two torches in sconces lit the front of the gatehouse. Garth Celyn was much more a fort or manor house than a castle, for all that a high palisade surrounded it. It perched on a slight hill overlooking the farmland and sea to the north and had a line of sight in all directions so the defenders could see the Saxons coming before they reached the castle—in order to give them time to flee.

Which they would need to do since Garth Celyn wasn't defensible. It lacked both the height of most of King Arthur's bastions and the elaborate ditch and rampart construction that were mandatory for flatland castles. It did contain many buildings, including a great hall and kitchen, behind which sat a two story house with many rooms for guests. A barracks lay near the gatehouse, along with the armory, chapel, and craft halls.

At Nell's convent, the tunnel which King Arthur had repaired had been intended as an escape route for early Christians who'd worshipped under an edict of death when the Romans ruled Wales. Garth Celyn, in turn, had two tunnels. One headed north, leading to the sea, and the other emptied into a meadow near Aber Falls. A grown man could walk easily along the underground passages.

Myrddin's stomach clenched at the thought of Nell navigating the tunnel underneath Llanfaes Abbey, leading her sisters to what she hoped was safety, only to find that her Abbess had compromised her safe haven. Such courage was rare, even in a soldier. He'd not have expected to find it in a nun. *Or rather, former nun.* That she'd asked to share a room with him at

52

Caerhun still stunned him. They'd slept apart, but nobody else knew that. He still couldn't believe she'd wanted it.

Nell's arms clenched Myrddin's waist. "What is it?" he asked, hoping his thoughts hadn't influenced hers. When she didn't answer, he added, "There's nothing to fear."

"I—" Nell stopped. "I am not at home here."

"You worry needlessly," he said. "The King will not hold the news of the Saxon depredations against you."

Once inside the walls, Myrddin dismounted onto packed earth, dryer than at Caerhun from today's limited sunshine. Looking around, Myrddin was pleased to be a part of the bustle and activity of the castle. Nell caught him smiling.

"I see soldiers." She pulled her cloak close around her and put up the hood. "I see war. Death. You must see something different."

Myrddin surveyed the courtyard. Three men-at-arms slouched near the smithy, waiting for their horses to be reshod. A handful of men watched two others wrestle by the stables and a host of peasants, servants in the kitchen and the hall, moved in and out of the huts that sat hard against the palisade. A boy holding a stick urged a pig towards its stall while another ran towards Myrddin and reached for Cadfarch's reins.

"My lord!" he said. "All is well?"

"It is, Adda." Myrddin tousled his hair. "I'll be in to see Cadfarch later."

"Yes, sir."

Nell watched the exchange through narrowed eyes. "You are a knight," she said, as if there had been some doubt on that score.

"I am." Myrddin turned to look at her, surprised she hadn't known it.

She wrinkled her nose at him. "I should have guessed it since you were charged with the welfare of Lord Aelric. But you traveled alone . . ." Her words tapered off.

"And my cloth is poor, for all that I wear mail armor," Myrddin said. "I know. I have the look of a man-at-arms but, in truth," he spread his arms wide like a bard preparing to sing a paean to Arthur, "I'm an impoverished knight." Myrddin laughed and tossed a small coin to Adda. "We do what we can with what we are given."

Nell didn't respond, still embarrassed perhaps, so Myrddin grasped her elbow and steered her towards the great hall. Despite her fears, she would have to speak to the King about the events at Llanfaes and the desecration of his wife's grave, as well as confirm that the populace on Anglesey believed the Saxons would move across the Straits soon in hopes of striking here, at Garth Celyn.

The guards who watched the entrance to the great hall pulled at the eight-foot doors at the top of the steps to allow Myrddin and Nell to enter. A wave of warmth enveloped them, along with that familiar musky smell of damp wool, herbs, and humanity. Nell relaxed beside him. Often in winter, it was cold enough to see one's breath in the hall, but darkness had fallen and it was dinner time, so men—eating, drinking, and talking—filled the room. The fire in the hearth blazed.

King Arthur sat at the high table at the far end of the hall, as was his custom, and it was so warm next to the fire that he'd shed his cloak. Two senior advisors flanked him: Geraint, one of his foremost commanders, and Bedwyr, his seneschal. Bedwyr was a grizzled, thick-set man of Arthur's generation who had supported Arthur since the early days of his reign. It was Bedwyr who kept order in Eryri when Arthur was away. More often than not, the two of them could communicate without speaking.

Myrddin stared at the King, feeling the familiar punch to the gut that seeing him alive after having dreamed of his death always gave him. Myrddin was sick of the dreams, terrified of the waking vision he'd had the day before, but there was no denying that King Arthur had acted as the beacon of Myrddin's existence in a world gone mad for his entire adult life. Myrddin may have long denied the future that stared him in the face; he might not know what it was going to take to change that future; he didn't know how he was going to become other than he was. But he knew, somehow, that he had to find a way. *By God, there has to be an answer here.*

As Myrddin urged Nell forward, pushing through her hesitation, Arthur noted their appearance and beckoned them to him.

"You'll do fine," Myrddin said. "Come."

And then before his eyes, Nell transformed herself from an insecure girl to the confident nun who'd taken charge of her sisters when nobody else would. She straightened her shoulders and raised her chin, as aware as Myrddin that if everyone in the room hadn't noticed them at first, they watched them now. They threaded their way between the closer tables, many of which had been added because of the increased number of men in the garrison, and then walked up the aisle to King Arthur's seat. They stopped before him. Myrddin bowed while Nell curtseyed.

"Myrddin," Arthur said, with that particular, dry tone he often used when addressing him.

"My lord."

"Lord Aelric reached home safely?" King Arthur said, his eyes tracking from Myrddin to Nell.

"He did," Myrddin said. "Neither he nor Lord Modred can have any cause for complaint."

"And yet, you come back in one piece." A smile twitched at the corner of King Arthur's mouth.

"As you say, my lord," Myrddin said. "For all Modred's perfidy, the Archbishop would countenance nothing less."

"Good." The King turned to Nell. "Welcome to Garth Celyn, madam. I remember your attention to the details of my wife's funeral." Somehow it didn't surprise Myrddin that Arthur recognized her. She was certainly memorable, and he was the King of Wales. It was his job to remember faces. "I confess I'm concerned to see you here, however, dressed as you are."

"The convent is dissolved, my lord," Nell said.

Arthur's face darkened. When he became angry, he rarely shouted or overtly lost his temper. Instead, he grew still and his voice became lower and colder. At Nell's words, the temperature in the room dropped ten degrees.

"Tell me," he said.

Nell enumerated the Saxon crimes while Arthur sat, still and silent, his jaw clenched and bulging. Once she finished, Myrddin took the liberty of stepping into the conversation before King Arthur's heart gave out.

"My lord," Myrddin said. "Nell has heard that the Saxons intend to cross the Straits soon."

"So my scouts at Penryhn tell me," Arthur said. "Modred attacks me despite the peace."

"Or rather, Wulfere does," Myrddin said, and then swallowed hard at his impertinence in correcting his king. Still, he didn't take it back. The man he needed to be wasn't going to come without taking risks.

"Certainly." Arthur looked amused rather than angry at Myrddin's interjection. "But we aren't supposed to know that, are we?"

"Modred isn't interested in peace, regardless of what Archbishop Dafydd hopes," Geraint added, from Arthur's left.

Nell shifted from one foot to another beside Myrddin and he glanced at her. Her clear skin had gone paler than its usual white. Concerned, he slipped an arm around her waist to support her. Also noting her distress, Arthur waved a hand to one of the ladies of the court who came forward. He looked into Nell's eyes. "You have a home here as long as you want it. If there is anything you need, ask Myrddin, here, or Bedwyr."

"Yes, my lord," Nell said. "Thank you."

To the girl, the King said, "See to our guest's comfort."

Meanwhile, Myrddin murmured under his breath, "Will you be all right?"

"I'm fine." Nell looked up at him, placed a hand on his chest, and patted once. Myrddin released her. Nell followed the girl without wavering on her feet. When she reached the door to the stairs, she looked back at Myrddin, her face expressionless. Myrddin liked that even less than her show of weakness. He nodded his encouragement and she disappeared.

Myrddin focused again on King Arthur.

"I hope you weren't planning to sleep tonight," the King said.

"No, sir," he said. "I slept at Caerhun."

All the way down the road from the standing stones, Myrddin had been thinking of the battle that was to come. He'd drawn his sword yesterday in defense of Nell, his muscles moving in their remembered patterns, but it wasn't the same as a real battle. Myrddin hadn't fought in formation since the brutal defeats of the previous year after which King Arthur was forced to surrender far too much to Modred and confine himself to his lands in Eryri. Myrddin wasn't glad to have killed a man yesterday, but it gave him confidence that he still knew how to fight, even at thirty-six. He needed to get his head in the right place if he was going to be the knight upon whom his companions depended. Myrddin touched his sword at his waist, reassured at its comforting weight.

The King had turned to speak to Bedwyr. Because King Arthur had not yet dismissed him, Myrddin remained standing on the opposite side of the table from his seat, trying not to shift from one foot to another in awkwardness and impatience. Geraint, who'd remained on Arthur's left throughout the conversation, winked at Myrddin in a rare moment of camaraderie, his eyes alight with amusement. Myrddin bowed gravely back.

Arthur spoke another few words, so low Myrddin didn't catch them due to the hubbub in the room, and then turned back to him. The King sat, slouched a bit in his chair, an elbow on the armrest and a finger to his lips, and studied Myrddin. "There is something different about you today, Myrddin."

Myrddin straightened his shoulders. "Is there?"

"How many years have you served me?"

"Since I became a man," Myrddin said. In Wales, legally, that was at the age of fourteen, although Myrddin was sixteen when he'd come to Garth Celyn and marked his transition from boy to man by that event.

"Perhaps it's time you found yourself a wife," he said. "Or I did."

Myrddin blinked. Nothing could have been further from his mind than that. Wives brought complications that were of no interest to him, both because of the commitment involved and the logistics.

"A wife, my lord?" Myrddin said. "I have no means to support a wife."

"You should," Arthur said. "In the new year, I will see to it that you are rewarded for your long service."

Myrddin's mouth fell open and he managed not to choke on his astonishment. "Thank you, my lord," Myrddin stuttered, bowing.

Arthur smiled and waved his hand, dismissing him. With King Arthur's attention again elsewhere, Geraint grinned at Myrddin and raised his cup in a salute. Myrddin shook his head, simultaneously bemused and appalled. Ever since the dreams had started to come more often, he'd felt himself haunted. He'd kept himself aloof and behind walls no woman could penetrate. He'd long since tallied the cost of letting anyone get inside them and found it too high.

But now here he stood, among friends he would trust with his life, in the hall of a King for whom he'd willingly die—and had died in his dreams more times than he could count—surrounded by people he knew so well he could recite their conversations for them. Whether he liked it or not, the walls were down. He was going to save them all, or die in the attempt.

With nothing left to say, Myrddin turned away, heading towards a vacant spot at one of the long tables next to where Ifan sat. Ifan moved over to give Myrddin room and handed him a trencher for his food.

"What was that about?" Ifan said.

Myrddin poured a cup of wine, studied it, and slaked his thirst, while reminding himself not to drink too much. He wasn't interested in drinking himself into a stupor. Perhaps if he paid closer attention to his dreams, and dreamed more often, he could cull the necessary details that might give him an edge in saving Arthur. "The King plans to find me a wife," Myrddin said. "Or, rather, he told me that he would choose one for me if I don't do the deed myself."

Ifan had been taking a drink as Myrddin spoke, and now choked and laughed at the same time, spraying wine across the table. Coughing, he used the tail of his cloak to dab at his mustache. "A wife?"

"That's what he said."

Shaking his head, Ifan set to his food once more. "Myrddin with a wife," he said, between bites.

Myrddin shook his head too and laughed into his cup. Unless he could find a way for Arthur to live into the new year, the entire discussion was moot. It was comical to even think about. *A wife. Instead, how about a life that lasts beyond the next thirty-six days?*

5

6 November 537 AD

Nell stood on the rampart above the gatehouse to watch
Myrddin, Lord Geraint, and all but a handful of the men-at-arms
from the garrison ride away from Garth Celyn in the pre-dawn
hush. Myrddin rode among the leaders, just to the left of Geraint.
It was a promotion of a sort, apparently, which hadn't gone
unremarked among those left behind. Anything that distinguished
one man from another—anytime a man found favor in the sight of
King Arthur—invited comment. The soldiers rode without
torches, relying on the moon to guide them, which at present was
playing hide and seek with the clouds.

Damn all men for their love of battle! Even as Nell
thought the words, she knew they weren't fair. This war had been
forced on King Arthur by his brother, Cai, who'd attacked one of
Modred's strongholds without consulting Arthur. Modred had
used the ill-advised assault as an excuse to restart the war. The

son of one of Arthur's many sisters, Modred had set his sights on Wales from the moment he realized that he was the eldest nephew and that Arthur wouldn't produce a son of his own.

His Mercian allies, on the other hand, had never forgiven Arthur for defeating them at Mt. Badon on his way to controlling all but the most southern regions of Wales. For thirty-seven years, they'd carried that grudge. By now, even the most die-hard apologists didn't doubt that Arthur's choices were few: to fight, to die, or to give up his patrimony entirely.

Nell braved the wind until the hoof beats faded, and was the last silent watcher left by the end. The men had long since disappeared into the mist when she turned away. It was strange to be so alone, with no responsibilities, no young novice to reassure or put to work depending on the hour, no religious office to keep. Even odder was the preponderance of men around her. Few women lived in the castle with whom she might associate—and should she even try, with hardly more than a month to live?

At the entrance to the hall, King Arthur himself greeted her and gestured that she should sit with him while he ate his meal. He'd watched his men ride away and contrary to her expectations, didn't retire to his office rather than allow his people to observe him in such a stressful moment.

Arthur took a sip from his goblet and put it down. "Anxious?" he said, once she'd seated herself on his left.

"Yes," she said, opting for the truth. She felt confident that Myrddin himself would live through this battle if he was to fight for the King in a month's time. The King had few enough men, however, that the loss of even one was a tragedy.

"Myrddin is one of my best men," Arthur said. "There is less need to worry for him than for most. He was a stripling when he came to me and I took him on despite the reservations of some of my counselors. I've not regretted it."

"He's not as young as he once was," Nell said.

"Nor are any of us," King Arthur said, with a laugh. "But there will be little enough fighting today, by my reckoning."

"How's that, my lord?" Nell said.

"The Saxons don't know the Straits like we do," Arthur said. "We take its temperamental nature for granted, but Wulfere has only been here a few months. He's arrogant. His bridge won't hold."

"I admit it's an odd construction," Nell said. The Saxons had hammered boards over the top of their bridge of boats to make a makeshift road from Anglesey to the Eryri shore. Even at low tide, the bridge wouldn't provide an easy crossing.

"It's not so much the bridge, but the tides," King Arthur said. "Slack water occurs four times a day: an hour before high or low tide. Geraint's got a boy severing the ropes and pins that hold the bridge together. Either the Saxons will discover the damage and it will delay them past the optimum time to cross and they'll have to wait six hours for the next slack water, or they won't, and the bridge will break and dump them into the Straits."

"And you think that Wulfere plans to cross this morning?"

"Yes. That's what the girl said."

Nell had been shredding the remains of a biscuit that a servant had set in front of her and now glanced over at the King. "Girl?"

The King gazed at her over his goblet and then set it down. "Wulfere's new doxy wasted no time in finding a way to reach one of my men. The Saxon camp is full of followers and hangers on. I've at least a half a dozen men and boys among them who confirm her information."

Nell's heart was in her throat and she could barely speak around the lump. "Do you know her name?"

King Arthur's forehead wrinkled in thought, and then he turned in his seat. Bedwyr was just entering the hall from the corridor beyond and Arthur called to him. "Do you know the name of the new girl in Wulfere's bed?"

Nell clamped her teeth together, trying to keep them from chattering at the casual way he asked the question. The girl meant nothing to him but as a source of information.

"Bronwen, I think." Bedwyr didn't even break stride as he headed towards the front of the hall.

"That's it." Arthur snapped his fingers. "Bronwen."

Nell placed her palms together and her fingers to her lips, but instead of prayer, she was trying to force back the tears that threatened to spill from her eyes. All she could think of was the sweet-faced, sharp-tongued girl Bronwen had been in the convent. Now she was Wulfere's whore, but had enough courage behind that pretty face, despite everything she'd endured, to defy him and spy for Arthur. "That poor child."

65

"Bronwen is a common enough name," Arthur said. "You don't know that she was one of your sisters."

"Perhaps," Nell said, pretending for Arthur that she wasn't certain, although inside she knew the truth.

"And what about you?" Arthur said. "You're welcome to stay at Garth Celyn as long as you choose. Your knowledge of herbs and healing is a most welcome addition to the castle, but surely you would prefer a different haven? Perhaps the convent in Gwytherin?"

"No, my lord," Nell said. "Thank you, but I can't go back to that life."

"Can't," Arthur said. "Or won't?"

Nell tipped her head in acknowledgement of the King's distinction. "Won't."

"As you wish." Arthur kept his voice level, but she could tell he was curious as to her reasons. Fortunately, he was too polite to ask.

Just then, Bedwyr reentered the hall, leaving the front door wide. The sun had risen and the grey dawn filtered through the scattered clouds, revealing an unusually clear day that would give the watchers a fine view of the Menai Straits and Anglesey beyond.

"My King!" Bedwyr strode towards Arthur. "The Saxons are delayed, but there is no doubt they intend to come today!"

Arthur's eyes lit and he stood. Nell stood with him. "Excellent."

"Will you go to see it, my lord?" she said.

"No," Arthur said. "I will not undermine the authority of Geraint and Gareth. My faith in my men is not misplaced."

That showed remarkable patience. Nell, for her part, couldn't keep still. Instead of trying to tame her emotions, she curtseyed to Arthur and left the hall for the battlements. Nell told herself she was going outside again so she could see what had become of Llanfaes. It wasn't necessarily that she was going to spend the day watching for Myrddin.

The sun shone and the wind was calmer than in the pre-dawn hours so it was warmer than before. Nell paced along the wall-walk, stopping every few feet to look over the rail at the sea sparkling in the sunshine less than a half a mile away. Penrhyn Castle, Gareth's hereditary estate, lay between Garth Celyn and the bridge of boats, but she could see it in her mind's eye.

Sweet Mary, mother of God, keep him safe! She sent another prayer to Saint Jude, patron saint of fools and desperate causes. And then she laughed because she didn't know if she was praying for Myrddin, or for herself.

* * * * *

Wulfere's men did discover the break in the ropes that bound the bridge together. Repairing it delayed them past their intended, early starting time so it was exactly noon when Wulfere ordered his men to march. It was the perfect opportunity. The Straits were as calm as they ever got.

"Here they come." Ifan broke the expectant silence that had seeped among the men over the long hours of waiting.

"Nervous, are you?" Myrddin said to his friend as they watched the horsed Saxon knights navigate their engineering marvel.

"They'd better make it quick, is all I can say," Ifan said. "I'm tired of sitting doing nothing."

"And your back aches," Myrddin said.

"Worse this week than ever," Ifan said. "Must be this rotten weather."

Although from Myrddin's perspective, the weather wasn't that bad for November. It was just that Ifan was nearing forty and so many years of fighting had given him aches and pains no remedy could ease. Myrddin counted himself lucky that while his eyes were failing him, his body so far hadn't.

Twenty minutes later, the lead riders had cleared the mainland end of the bridge. They rode across the sand, with Wulfere as one of the foremost knights, recognizable by his black head plume and matching beard. Nell had shuddered at the mention of his name. Given his composure and presence, Myrddin couldn't blame her.

Myrddin's fellow knights and men-at-arms stayed in the trees on the edge of the beach, waiting for the fifty archers on the hill above them to loose their arrows. Geraint held their fire until the cavalry were almost to the woods and the entire company of Saxons foot soldiers marched on the bridge. Then he gave the signal.

"Fire at the horses!" Geraint shouted, his voice carrying all the way down to Myrddin's position.

The arrows flew from the bows in a hail of metal and wood, turning the beach into chaos in seconds. Six of the Saxon horses went down in the first volley. Saxon knights knew about archers, having encountered them in battle with the Welsh many a time (to their loss), even if they hadn't employed any of their own in this venture. Therefore, instead of retreating, they did the smart thing, which was to charge. Holding their shields high to protect their chests, they urged their horses to close the distance to the woods. Perhaps they thought they'd find safety there. If nothing else, their action ensured that the tops of the trees restricted the archers' angle of fire.

Gareth commanded the cavalry in this battle and took Geraint's words as a signal to move.

"Charge!"

The Welsh cavalry came out of the woods in a phalanx, fifty feet wide, Myrddin among them. His heart pounded in his ears, drowning all sound but the relentless beat and making him oblivious to anything but the Saxons soldiers in front of him. *Christ, I'd forgotten!* Directing Cadfarch with his knees because he needed his left arm to hold his shield and his right hand held his sword, Myrddin plowed through the front rank of the opposing force.

His momentum carried him past a knight sporting an ostentatious, red plume on his helmet. When the man swung around to face Myrddin, his horse's hooves sank into the soft sand, throwing him off balance. Myrddin slid the tip of his sword along the man's blade and with a flick of his wrist, disarmed him. Myrddin then shifted the other way. Using his left arm, he hit the Saxons soldier full in the face with the flat surface of his shield.

The man fell, no longer a threat, and the noise of battle broke over Myrddin like an unexpected wave, assaulting his senses. He froze for a heartbeat, adjusting to the cacophony. Above him, Geraint's archers rained their arrows down on the Saxon soldiers on the bridge. To the east, the Welsh foot soldiers who'd come out of the trees at the same time as the cavalry, roared, starting their run towards the Saxons lines, their axes and pikes raised high and their mouths open in the universal cry that gives men courage in the face of death. Fewer than half the Saxon foot soldiers had reached the beach. Thus, the Welshmen outnumbered the initial Saxon ranks and they went down under the onslaught.

Myrddin turned his attention back to the Saxon cavalry and found himself face to face with Wulfere himself. Myrddin clenched his teeth and almost bit off the end of his tongue. This was the one man he'd most wanted to meet—and the one of whom he was also the most afraid.

Wulfere's black beard covered his face from chin to eyes and was split by an unholy sneer. Blood coated Wulfere's sword and he met Myrddin's with enormous force—enough to make Myrddin fear he'd lose his grip. They struggled together, neither finding the upper hand but hacking away at each other, all elegance or restraint lost in the desperation of battle.

"Back! Back! Back!" The words came in both Saxon and Welsh as one of Wulfere's captains tried to reach everyone who fought with him. Wulfere might have been doing well, but that wasn't true of many of his companions.

"No!" Wulfere's refusal carried across the whole of the battlefield.

Myrddin took that instant of distraction to launch himself at the Saxon lord. Their brief sword play had shown Myrddin what he'd feared—that he would have trouble defeating this man in a straight fight. At one time in his life, he'd relished the fear and power of exchanging blows, but he was no longer interested in trying. Thirty-six wasn't twenty-four. Instead, Myrddin wrestled Wulfere from his horse.

The two men fell to the ground, Wulfere beneath Myrddin. The force of the fall knocked the breath from Myrddin's lungs, but the jolt dazed Wulfere long enough for Myrddin to rise and straddle him. He stared into Wulfere's eyes. They were fogged and unfocused. Wulfere moaned, undone by the fall and suddenly human. Myrddin swallowed hard—and with a mighty thrust, forced his sword through Wulfere's armor and into his heart. Wulfere would never rise again.

Myrddin, for his part, got unsteadily to his feet. The death left an acid taste in Myrddin's mouth, but he swallowed it down too. Of all the men he'd killed, this was one he wouldn't regret.

Overall, the battle had been short and brutal. By the time Myrddin looked up, a dozen dead Saxons lay on the sand. The rest had begun the retreat. The Saxon foot soldiers had the numbers to push back at the Welshmen but at the sight of their horsed superiors passing behind them to the bridge, they turned as one and ran back the way they'd come. By now it was almost one in the afternoon—high tide—and the most dangerous time to cross the Straits. The bridge of boats bucked and bent from the strain of so many men and horses.

It seemed the entire Saxon army had taken to its heels and was fighting each other to be the first to reach Anglesey. They appeared oblivious to the fact that the Welsh were less dangerous to them now than the water. Following Geraint's orders, the Welsh let them go. They didn't want to get stuck on the Saxon bridge and didn't have the manpower to fight them on Anglesey, or King Arthur would have tried it already.

Then with only an ominous creak as warning, the bridge snapped, just as King Arthur had predicted. The separation occurred so suddenly, few men were able to stay upright. The two ends of the break swung apart, moving away from each other at a speed of two and a half knots. Within a count of five, the Saxon army had fallen into the treacherous waters of the Straits, with just a few men hanging onto the wooden planks, face down and gripping the wood as if their lives depended on it. Which they did.

"By all that is holy, I've never seen the like." Geraint came to stand beside Myrddin.

"We could retake Anglesey," Gareth said, as he halted on Myrddin's other side. Blood stained his sword and he'd lost his helmet at some point in the battle, but he appeared otherwise undamaged. He was a twenty-five year old, bachelor knight and a child of a long and powerful lineage. It wouldn't have done for him to die just yet.

"We don't need the lands they hold until the spring planting." Geraint looked past Myrddin to Gareth, his gaze piercing. "And I say that, even with the knowledge that your lands languish in the hands of your cousin."

"He's down." Gareth's voice carried no emotion. One glance showed an iron set to his chin. It occurred to Myrddin that Gareth might have taken on his traitorous cousin himself. Both men were grandsons of a great warlord who'd been steward to Arthur's uncle, Ambrosius. That family had been torn in pieces by this war, half fighting for Modred and half for Arthur . . . and this cousin had come down on Modred's side. To his loss.

Geraint nodded. "I will give the order to kill any Saxons who wash ashore." He slapped his hand on Myrddin's shoulder. "Ride to King Arthur and tell him of the victory. You are his favorite messenger."

"Today is your reward for all those times you've brought bad news." A smile hovered around Gareth's lips despite the grimness of the carnage before them.

Geraint shot Myrddin a grin. "And once again, you've shown yourself in possession of the Devil's own luck. I saw you vanquish Wulfere. It was well done."

"Thank you, my lord," Myrddin said.

His legs stiff from the aftermath of the fight, Myrddin returned to Cadfarch. When he'd leapt from the horse's back to bring down Wulfere, Cadfarch had stayed close in case Myrddin needed him, unafraid of the smell of blood or the clash of weapons. The war horses in Wales were bred smaller and more versatile than their Saxon counterparts so as to more easily navigate the rocky and uneven ground on which the Welsh lived and fought.

Myrddin was glad to see Ifan on his feet not far away, his head resting against his horse's neck.

Ifan waved a hand half-heartedly in Myrddin's direction. "You off to see the King, then?"

"As I am bid," Myrddin said.

"Better you than me, friend," Ifan said. "I've a mind to lay down right here in the sand."

"You do that," Myrddin said, more glad than he could say that Ifan still lived.

He mounted Cadfarch and directed him towards the road from Bangor to Garth Celyn, skirting the manor house at Penrhyn to which they'd bring the wounded. They'd lost no more than two or three men-at-arms and a dozen foot soldiers, but many more had surface wounds that could suppurate if they weren't treated. Over the years, more out of chance than design, the doctoring of the company's wounds had fallen to Myrddin, who'd found himself more adept at it than he might have expected. Gareth and Geraint would need every healer of whatever skill today. Myrddin intended to aid the men as soon as Arthur gave him leave to return.

The north coast of Wales was endlessly green, even in the middle of winter. The beauty of it drew Myrddin forward, easing the tension of the battle and draining away the adrenaline that had allowed him to fight it. By Myrddin's calculation, at least a dozen Saxon knights and an equal number of squires had died, in addition to the hundreds of Saxon foot soldiers. It wasn't a staggering total, but would be devastating to Modred, if only because of the knights he'd lost. Many were of his own household, his and Arthur's close kin.

From some distance away, Myrddin spied the towers of Garth Celyn and noted the great number of people atop the battlements. They were watching for him. He raised a hand, knowing they would understand what it meant. If they'd lost, he would have been moving faster—if he'd been able to come at all. As it was, the gates were open while Myrddin was still fifty yards away. He rode inside and was instantly besieged by questions. Myrddin glanced up from his inquisitors to see King Arthur standing on the top step to the hall, Nell beside him.

Myrddin dismounted, trotted to where Arthur stood, and didn't make him wait for the news. "It is a great victory, my lord," he said. "The bridge is broken."

"What are our casualties?" Arthur said.

"Slight," Myrddin said. "Geraint has their names. I do know there were few, mostly among those who were unhorsed or came to the battle on foot."

"Well done," the King said. "That is good news, indeed."

Arthur gestured for Myrddin to enter the hall, but Myrddin hesitated to obey. "I must return to Penrhyn, my lord." Myrddin bowed to indicate his continued respect. "Nell and I thought we'd help the wounded."

The King studied Myrddin, eyebrows raised. In the silence that followed, Myrddin realized his error. The man he'd been before St. Asaph would have aided the wounded only when he'd had no choice. He certainly would have taken a drink in the hall and thought that the following morning was soon enough to return to a battlefield.

"Of course," the King said.

Nell broke in. "I surveyed your infirmary earlier, my lord, I made a satchel of herbs and linens in preparation for the aftermath of the fight and the number of wounded who'd need attention."

"Very well," Arthur said, his puzzlement turning to amusement that Myrddin and Nell had taken matters into their own hands. "You have leave to go. However, I will come as well."

A few minutes later, Myrddin pulled Nell behind him on Cadfarch again. She didn't resist, placing her hands around his waist as before.

"Are you well?" Without apology, Nell had already inspected Myrddin's armor, surcoat, and head for damage, and now she patted down his arms and sides, checking for wounds.

"I took a hard fall with Wulfere beneath me. Otherwise, I'm uninjured," Myrddin said. "Although, I find that I am too old for this."

For the first time since they'd met, she gave him a genuine laugh. Myrddin was glad. She'd had little reason for amusement these last two days and there wasn't going to be much smiling in the coming hours. Regardless of the victory, they had injured men, and dead ones, and loved ones to inform of the loss.

Arriving at Penrhyn, Arthur strode up the steps to the hall while his company—with the exception of Nell and Myrddin—stayed with their horses. Gareth met him at the entryway. Wounded men lay spread across the floor in the same chaos that followed every battle. Myrddin swallowed hard at the sight of so much blood. He never got used to it, and it was probably better that he didn't.

"I have something to show you," Gareth said to the King, minus his customary formal greeting.

Arthur didn't blink at the impertinence but gestured as if to say *lead on!* Gareth turned on his heel and led the way to the back of the hall and then through a doorway on the right. Myrddin followed, unsure if he should come too but as he wasn't stopped, came anyway.

They entered a hallway that had several small rooms leading off of it. Gareth turned into the first doorway on the left, striding straight through it. Arthur came to an abrupt halt on the threshold. Myrddin managed to stop before he ran into the King's back. After a ten-second contemplation, King Arthur continued forward while Myrddin hovered in the doorway. Gareth's cousin lay on a pallet on the floor. He wasn't dead, but didn't appear to have long to live.

King Arthur directed his attention at the wounded man who stared up at him. "I loved your father and grandfather," Arthur said.

"Sir." The man's voice was stronger than it should have been given the enormous hole in his midsection. Even if the King gave them the opportunity, neither Myrddin nor Nell would be able to do anything for him.

"I couldn't leave him on the beach," Gareth said. Myrddin sensed defensiveness rather than anger or sadness in his clipped words, but Arthur didn't remark on the reasons Gareth had brought his cousin to Penrhyn, despite the order to leave no survivors. Given the difficulties among the members of Arthur's own family over the years, he undoubtedly understood them.

"Why?" Arthur said, his patrician nose aimed at the man on the floor.

This man, Hywel, along with his two brothers, Rhys and Llywelyn, both churchman, had swung over to Modred's side five years before when Modred had consolidated his alliance with the Mercians—and again pressed his claim to the Welsh throne even though Arthur still lived. Once Modred had agreed to a treaty with King Arthur, the brothers had returned to Eryri as if they'd never betrayed Wales. Since then, as one could imagine, their interactions with the King had been stilted, taking place in formal situations where they all avoided speaking to each other.

Hywel attempted a shrug. "My father was the youngest son. Our inheritance wasn't enough for the three of us to share. My brothers and I agreed that if one of us joined Modred, we all would." That didn't explain everything, of course, as Gareth had many brothers too and he still stood beside the King.

"How noble of you." Gareth looked down his nose at Hywel, in imitation of the King.

"I can't say it was my first choice," Hywel said, "but Rhys and Llywelyn insisted on it."

"Rhys is a supercilious, avaricious snake and a disgrace to the Church and the cloth he wears," Gareth said, "and Llywelyn is no better. Were they also at Llanfaes?"

"Yes," Hywel said, selling out his brothers without compunction.

King Arthur's face grew even more rigid. Gareth pursed his lips. Gareth's family had gotten themselves into a mare's nest of shifting allegiances, but it looked as if at least one of them was about to be released from his burden.

"Modred bought you with the promise of land?" King Arthur said. "That was enough to sell out your country? To take up arms against your companions and loved ones? Against me?"

"I have a family," Hywel said. "I have to think of them. It is a choice any man would make."

Arthur snorted his disbelief. "Inform me when he's dead." He turned on his heel and strode out of the room before anyone else could speak.

Myrddin had ducked through the doorway and into the room before the King reached him and now stayed, leaning against the wall in case Gareth had need of him. Myrddin shared the King's loathing for Gareth's cousin. But he'd been a soldier long enough to turn physician, and it was the latter role that prevented him from leaving the room.

Hywel tipped up his chin to look at the exposed rafters that formed the frame of the ceiling. "I don't need your forgiveness," he told Gareth.

"Good," Gareth said. "Because you don't have it." Gareth had been gazing out the window into the courtyard of his manor, and now glanced over at Myrddin. "You can go."

Myrddin had noted Hywel's glazed eyes, so didn't yet obey Gareth, taking a step towards the wounded man. "I can fetch some wine," Myrddin said. "He doesn't have to suffer this much."

Gareth swung around to face Myrddin full on. In contrast to the anger in his voice, his eyes showed tears he'd so far refused to shed. "Doesn't he?"

It was strange to see Gareth in this light. He rarely revealed anything of himself; he'd brushed off the betrayal of his cousins like a man would flick a crumb from his shirt. Gareth appeared different to Myrddin today, more emotional and passionately Welsh. *Perhaps I'm not the only one among the King's men who's had an epiphany in the last few days.*

Myrddin countered Gareth's obstinate glare with a calm face and nodded his acceptance of his wishes. "As you say, my lord." Myrddin left the room, although once he passed through the doorway and was out of sight, he froze in mid-stride at a sudden sound emitting from the open door behind him. Myrddin made to return, and then thought better of it. It wasn't Hywel in his death throes that he'd heard, but Gareth, choking back a sob.

"Hold my hand." Gareth's boots scraped on the wooden floor as he crouched beside his cousin.

Myrddin turned away. He could do nothing for either of them.

6

7 November 537 AD

"**D**on't turn around, but we're no longer alone," Myrddin said.

Nell glanced up from the man she was tending, a smile twitching at the corner of her mouth. "You mean we were alone before? There's two dozen wounded men in front of you."

"Lord Cai is here."

"And you don't like him," she said.

"I grew up under the roof of one of his men. A man named Madoc. My foster brother, Deiniol, still serves him," Myrddin said.

"And from the venom in your voice, those are days you'd prefer to forget," Nell said.

Myrddin didn't answer, instead blanking his expression as Cai came to a halt at the head of the man they tended. Cai held his helmet under one arm. He appeared to have traveled through the night to reach Penrhyn at this early hour. Myrddin stood, more comfortable in this lord's presence on his feet, and moved to a spot that half-blocked Nell from view. He couldn't help it; he wanted to protect her, even if reason told him that for all Cai's perfidy—he'd conspired to murder Arthur once after all—the notion that he presented any kind of threat today was more than ridiculous.

"Will he die?" Cai said.

They all looked down at the man. Myrddin hadn't recognized the soldier as a member of Arthur's company. Cai's presence revealed that he might be part of his household, much as Myrddin's foster father had been and Deiniol still was. "I cannot say as yet, my lord." The title stuck in Myrddin's throat. "It's likely."

The door to the hall swung open and Arthur appeared, striding across the floor towards his brother. "Your man fought well, I understand," Arthur said as he approached the group, gesturing at the prone body on the floor.

"So Gareth said," said Cai. The brothers didn't clasp forearms as would have been customary and their eyes met for half a second before they flicked away. Disconcertingly, Myrddin found Arthur observing him. He hastily half-turned, so as to impose less on the brothers' conversation.

"Why are you here, Cai?" Arthur's voice remained mild, but the question was abrupt.

"I understand that Modred sits at Denbigh," Cai said.

"That is true," Arthur said.

"Those are *my* lands," Cai said. "My castle."

"I've said that we will get it back," Arthur said. "Our recent victory puts Modred in a difficult position, unable to force either the Straits or the Conwy River. When we are ready, we will push him and his Saxon allies out of Gwynedd."

"When?"

"Soon."

"You promised me this weeks ago."

"It was you who lost control of those lands," Arthur said. "From my castle at Dolwyddelan, you have the power to prevent Modred from advancing on us through the mountains. Our southern allies will see that the winds blow our way and together we will force Modred out of Wales, once and for all."

"You know the solution to our problems." Cai pushed closer to King Arthur, who stood his ground.

"We've discussed this before. Now is not the time."

"Modred must die."

Arthur made an impatient movement with his hand, which Cai ignored, pressing on undeterred. He put his face into Arthur's, so close their noses were a hand span apart. As Arthur was four inches taller, it had the effect of forcing Cai to look upwards, like a boy facing down a man. Myrddin couldn't help listening, although Nell had the modesty to look away so neither man would see her staring. Again, Arthur caught Myrddin's eye for a heartbeat, and then answered his brother.

"He is our nephew, Cai. I will countenance no further discussion of the matter."

"Then perhaps you don't have the balls to be the King of Wales," Cai said. "But then we knew that already, didn't we?"

Cai shot these last words at King Arthur in a loud hiss that had the unfortunate effect of carrying throughout the hall. His words sucked all the air from the room. Cai didn't appear to care—and remarkably, was still breathing himself since Arthur had the restraint to keep his sword sheathed and his brother in one piece. Cai shoved past Arthur, knocking into his shoulder as he strode towards the door of the hall.

The offensive—and unfair—comment referred to the fact that in his long life, Arthur had fathered one child, a daughter, and no sons. As a result, it was either Cai or Modred who remained Arthur's heir, both with two legitimate sons to follow them. Myrddin could understand Arthur's pain. He'd bedded many women, but never fathered a child either—or at least none whose mother had named him. In Wales, a bastard was accounted as legitimate if his father acknowledged him. Therefore, nothing could be gained from hiding his identity; no mother would choose it.

Well, except mine.

Arthur didn't turn to watch his brother go, standing as Cai had left him, hands clasped behind his back, legs spread, and staring at the far wall of the hall. An enormous boar's head hung above the fireplace; rumor had it that Gareth and his brother Gawain together had brought it down. Myrddin didn't doubt it.

"You two," Arthur said, pointing at Nell and Myrddin with his chin, "will return to Garth Celyn." Myrddin turned towards him, surprised, and King Arthur moved closer. "Have either of you slept?"

Myrddin glanced at Nell and shook his head. This was one of the reasons Arthur was a great King. He could brush off his brother's insults in favor of concern for his own people. It was one of the many contradictions about him. Depending on whom one talked to, Arthur was worth dying for because of *who* he was and the position he held, or he was an arrogant son-of-a bitch whose regard for his own power was paramount. He wore his status and dignity with kingly bearing, while at the same time was obnoxiously protective of them. He carried a vision of a united Wales, but had fought and schemed for nearly forty years to hold onto what was his. And yet, despite his faults, there was nobody more suited to ruling Wales than he—and his people knew it. Myrddin knew it.

"You're no use to me exhausted. I want your full report this time, Myrddin." Arthur turned away and began walking towards the front doors. "I understand you were the one who brought down Wulfere."

"Yes, my lord," Myrddin said.

Arthur waved a hand, gesturing to Gareth who'd just come into the hall from the rooms beyond it. "Myrddin is with me."

Gareth nodded.

Arthur marched toward the entry doors, expecting Nell and Myrddin to follow. Myrddin took a long step after him before he noticed that Nell hadn't moved.

Myrddin looked back at her. "He meant you as well."

86

His comment shook Nell out of her reverie and she hurried to walk beside him. "I know," she said. "But why?"

"I don't even know why he wants me to come," Myrddin said.

"You are a most trusted companion." Nell stated this as a truth.

"Three days ago, I wouldn't have said that was the case."

And that, when he examined the facts, was his own fault. He'd lived no differently from every other man in his position: he fought battles and drank himself to sleep afterwards; he caroused with the other warriors and made love to any woman who'd consent to share his bed. He'd been an oft-chosen messenger for the King, and perhaps Arthur's sudden confidence in him was a natural outgrowth of Myrddin's ability to perform his duties as he asked. Still, Myrddin found it odd that just at the point he was ready to step forward, to take on more of a leadership role than he ever had before, and had practically forced himself upon his betters, Arthur had decided to accept him.

It had been dark in the hall, the few windows letting in glimmers of light. He and Nell had doctored the men by torchlight, so it wasn't until they exited the hall for the courtyard of the manor house that Myrddin realized the sun had risen and moved well into the sky. Nell bent her head to inspect her blood-spattered skirt and made an unhappy face. Arthur had already mounted his horse, surrounded by escorts. Perhaps he'd been astride when Cai had arrived and taken the opportunity to speak to him when he had the chance.

"There will be clothes for you at Garth Celyn," Myrddin said to Nell, mounting when the boy brought Cadfarch to him and hauling her up behind. It was a short ride to the castle from Penrhyn, and as before, they would take the road along the coast, riding down from the heights into the valley and then back up again to the hill on which Garth Celyn perched.

Nell wrapped her arms around Myrddin's waist and pressed her face into the back of his cloak. "So much death," she said. "How do you live with it?"

"Do I?" Myrddin said. "Is it any wonder that most men drink themselves into a stupor every night, rather than see the faces of the men who've fallen by their hands, or the faces of their friends who died instead of them?"

"You killed Wulfere," she said.

"I did."

Nell sat silent for a heartbeat. "And that man at St. Asaph too. In defense of me."

"Yes," he said. "I've killed more men then I can count and will kill many more."

"How do you live with it?"

"It's changed over the years, Nell. That first man—him I killed with an arrow. We were screened from the Saxons by trees, trying to pick them off one-by-one. It's dangerous work because there's always the fear that the enemy will charge into the wood to find you. Late in the day, I hit a man right through the neck and he toppled off his horse. I was not alone in that. We killed a dozen more before we retreated."

"And what did you feel?"

"*Nothing,*" Myrddin said, "at least not at first, not for hours. It came as a shock to me that killing could be the easiest thing in the world. One second the man was alive, laughing among his fellows, and then he was on the ground, felled by my arrow. At the time, when it first happened, I was so surprised all I could think was, *I did it! That wasn't so hard!* It was the difference between taking a breath and letting it out."

Nell's arms were around his waist, holding on. "And then?" It warmed him that she knew him well enough already to know there had to be an 'and then'.

"And then I woke in the night and couldn't get the man out of my head: watching the arrow hit, watching him fall. One of the men allowed me to sob in his arms. It was only then I realized they all knew, even as they congratulated me, that this was coming."

"How old were you?"

Myrddin's chest rose and fell as he breathed in more of the cold air. "I'd just turned seventeen," he said.

Nell made a sympathetic noise which Myrddin brushed off.

"And after that?" she said.

"I've killed so many times, Nell, with bow and sword. At first, I wouldn't expect to actually kill anyone, even in the midst of a battle. After that . . ." Myrddin paused. "After that, I learned to expect it, to admit my regrets, and to understand that I would owe penance for every soul I took. It remains a dreadful necessity."

89

"That's how you come to terms with the killing?" Nell said. "By telling yourself it's necessary?"

"Yes," Myrddin said.

"You can ask for absolution . . ." Her voice trailed off, perhaps because she realized how ridiculous that sounded.

"Absolution is for those who regret their offense and swear they will refrain from committing it in the future. Much of the time, neither is possible for me."

"That's partly why I can't be a nun," Nell said. "I no longer have either the certainty or the grace."

Myrddin pondered that, unspeaking, for another half a mile, at which point, he could no longer tolerate his own uncertainty. If he'd brought a snake into Garth Celyn, he needed to know. "What were you really doing at St. Asaph?" He kept his voice low and deceptively gentle.

"I . . . I told you," Nell said.

"You told me you traveled on your own, but to what end? What haven did you ultimately hope to reach?"

"I—" She stopped. "You wouldn't understand."

"Try me."

"Scotland," Nell said. "I fear King Arthur is going to lose this war and I will not watch it happen. I will not live in a Gwynedd ruled by Modred."

Those were strong words, forcefully spoken. He'd never heard anyone give voice to his own fears as clearly as this. "And if I were to accuse you again of spying for the man himself?"

Nell took in a sharp breath. And then, unaccountably, she began to laugh. "You really believe that? You still doubt me enough to ask such a question?"

Myrddin didn't reply and she laughed all the harder, burying her face in Myrddin's back and clutching at his cloak with both fists to keep her seat on the saddle bags.

They'd garnered some curious glances as their conversation had progressed, but with Nell's laughter, the looks turned to open smirks. Myrddin slowed Cadfarch and smiled back at his friends, covering for Nell. In truth, they were both well beyond their prime. Whatever was going on between them—whatever it was—had little import, other than the oddity of Myrddin's interest in any woman beyond a single night. Myrddin's companions turned away, all except Ifan who gave him a knowing smirk before straightening in his seat. Myrddin made a mental note to cuff him upside the head later.

"It isn't funny," Myrddin said.

Nell sobered enough to speak. "Yes, it is."

"You've not answered my question."

Nell swallowed hard, the laughter gone. "I'm not a spy, Myrddin. Whatever else I may have been or might become, never think that."

Myrddin nodded, somewhat mollified and yet more curious than ever. When they reached Garth Celyn a few minutes later, men and horses filled the bailey and they jostled against one another as Myrddin dismounted from Cadfarch. Just as his feet hit the ground, Ifan bumped into his back, unbalancing both Nell and him such that he clutched her to his chest.

"Whoops." Ifan shot Myrddin a wicked grin. "Looks like you don't need the King's help finding yourself a wife."

Myrddin's face froze and Nell stiffened. Myrddin had his arm around her waist to hold her upright, but now she turned in the circle of it and poked him in the chest. Her laughter had turned into a more manageable anger. "Wife? What's he talking about?"

Her eyes snapped in her upturned face. Myrddin hastened to appease her. "It's nothing to do with you."

"Then just tell me what this *is* about," she said. "You're avoiding the question."

"When we arrived at Garth Celyn—could that only be two nights ago?—King Arthur told me that I appeared different to him. He has begun to trust me more since the war was renewed and I've earned some honor in his eyes. I'm penniless, as I told you, and he said that he will give me the land to support a wife in the new year."

"Myrddin!" Nell's anger melted. "That's quite an offer, especially when he's besieged on every side." Together they observed Arthur's retreating back as he entered the castle's great hall.

"But perhaps a hollow one, too," Myrddin said. "Many battles stand between this moment and that promise. As you yourself said, there is reason to fear for his life and for the future of Wales."

Nell's eyes narrowed, surveying the bailey and the activity around them. "I've lived shut away from the world too long," she said. "How could I have forgotten that I couldn't ride or dine or spend any time in your company—any man's company—without causing talk?"

Given the trauma of the last few days, as well as her wish (that she'd expressed) and Myrddin's (which he hadn't) never to marry, Myrddin opened his mouth to apologize. "Nell—"

She cut him off. "Leave it. It's not your fault. Besides, if everyone thinks I belong to you, so much the better. It will give me the freedom to come and go as I please, unremarked. I would prefer to avoid attention from any other man."

"Are you sur—?"

She cut him off again. "I'm long past having any interest in sitting in the solar amongst the other women, Myrddin." She turned to face him. "You helped me before. You protected me before. Will you help me again?"

Oh, yes, I think so. Myrddin nodded.

"Good," she said, "I'll find us a place to sleep." She set off for the great hall. Myrddin, leaving Cadfarch once again in Adda's care, followed, more bemused than surprised. Nell might not be a spy, but she was *something*, knew something, that was out of the ordinary. Myrddin had a mind to find out what that was.

7

8 November 537 AD

"Myrddin! Get over here!"

I obeyed, riding toward Gawain, my captain. At his grim look, I pulled up beside him, reaching for my sword—not to fight him, but because he already held his.

"The Saxons are here!" he said.

I squinted in the direction he pointed, but could see nothing beyond movement in the branches opposite. "I'll root them out, my lord."

Within minutes, I gathered my men together and we crossed the creek to the north of the church where King Arthur waited even now to meet with Lord Edgar. I knew it was a trap. It was always a trap. I struggled to turn aside but we rode relentlessly on, across the creek, up the bank, and through the trees. Once we left the protection *of the woods, the arrows flew and Ifan shouted that we must turn back.*

"Myrddin! No!" As I charged the Saxon line, a woman screamed. The screaming grew louder but I ignored it, instead spurring my horse forward, my heart racing. "Myrddin! . . ."

Nell sat up with a start, her breath coming in gasps. She could still see the dream, hanging before her eyes like a veil, even as Myrddin sprang from his pallet and came towards her through it.

"What is it?"

"Just a dream." Nell put a hand to her chest in hopes that it would ease her racing heart.

"Of . . . St. Asaph?" Myrddin crouched before her.

Nell took in a breath and let it out. "No," she said. She lifted a hand to him and he took it, warming it in his two larger ones. "Not that. It was one I often have. It's nothing."

"Is it?" Myrddin said.

Nell froze, hearing the change of tone in his voice, and looked into his face. She'd asked that he leave a candle burning in its dish and it still guttered, within minutes of going out but still giving off enough light to show his expression. "Yes. Why?"

"You called my name," he said. "Or rather, cried it."

"Oh."

"I'm curious that if it was a dream you've often had, that you would have dreamt of me before you met me."

Nell twitched her shoulders. For so many years she'd longed to tell someone of the dream, but now that it came to it, she couldn't. He would think her—no, know her—crazed. She gazed into Myrddin's face, warring with herself, unable to answer. "It—" She stopped. "I didn't—"

Myrddin sat back on his heels. "It's all right. You don't have to tell me right now if you don't want to."

Nell didn't know if that was really better or not. If not for the screaming, he'd probably have thought she was dreaming of him in a romantic way but was too embarrassed to admit it. It irked her how wrong that was but had no way to fix it. Under his gaze, she forced herself to relax and lie down. But she didn't turn her back to him as she had earlier. Instead, she studied him as he was studying her.

He'd made sure, once she'd found space for them in one of the small, closet-like sleeping rooms in the manor house, that this was truly what she wanted. The room had been empty as they'd entered. He'd closed the door to lean against it while she shifted one of the pallets so it no longer abutted any of the others.

"After this, there's no going back, Nell," he'd said.

Nell had laughed, the sound coming more harshly than she'd intended. "It's not very nun-like is it?" she said, and then arrested her movements to focus on him. "It's better this way, Myrddin. I slept that first night amongst the other women, ten of us strewn across the floor. My dreaming woke them three times. They don't want me there and I don't want to lie among them."

96

"I'm not saying it's uncommon," Myrddin said. "It's done all the time. Most of the men here haven't married their women, but none of those women spent the last ten years in a convent. This is going to ruin your reputation."

"Or yours?" She looked up at him, truly worried about the arrangement for the first time. "The King—"

"Couldn't care less," he said. "His concern, like mine, would be for you."

"This is my choice."

"If you say so." He gestured to a spot against the opposite wall from where she sat. "I gather my pallet is over there."

"You gather correctly." She shot him a grin. "If another woman catches your eye, just tell me and I'll make myself scarce."

"Damn it, Nell. " He'd turned on her, his hands on his hips. "This isn't funny."

"Isn't it?" she said. "I have to look at it this way. Otherwise, the only other choice is despair."

Now, Myrddin invoked that earlier conversation. "I know about despair, Nell." He eased backwards onto his pallet. "I didn't realize it at the time, but last night when you spoke to me of it, you weren't speaking just about what happened at St. Asaph, or even Llanfaes, were you?"

"No," Nell said. "Despair is a companion with whom I'm long acquainted."

Myrddin matched her, lying on his side with the blankets pulled to his chin. "I have dreams too, Nell."

Nell nodded, but still wasn't ready to reveal her true thoughts: *Not like mine, you don't.*

* * * * *

Myrddin slept past the dawn and awoke, his brain churning, thinking about Nell, knowing that she'd dreamt of him even if she wouldn't admit it. He hoped the dream was a good one but somehow doubted it.

Nell's auburn hair cascaded off the edge of the pallet, having come loose from her braid in the restless night. She turned her head, met his eyes, looked away, and then looked back. "Thank you for understanding."

Myrddin sat up. "I didn't say I understood," he said. "I just decided not to press you right away. At some point soon, I'm going to ask you to tell me what is going on behind that sweet smile."

"Oh, is that it?" she said, giving him the smile he wanted. "Well, not this moment anyway." She got to her feet. "While you wait, you can help me dress."

Myrddin took that for what it was—a chaste invitation. Well bred women wore elaborate skirts that scraped the ground, got in the way, and forced women to walk in a mincing fashion. At Arthur's insistence, Nell had given away both the homespun dress which the men had ripped at St. Asaph before Myrddin had rescued her and the coarse dress from Caerhun that blood-stains had irreparably damaged. In exchange, she now wore the fashionable gown of a lady, which was a bit harder to get into.

By the time they arrived in the great hall, it was full of people and rumors. A rider from Modred had arrived and the inhabitants of Garth Celyn were abuzz with what the letter he carried contained. Myrddin pulled Nell to a seat near Ifan, who (after a knowing look that encompassed them both and what he assumed had gone on between them in the night) shrugged when Myrddin queried him.

"Your guess is as good as mine," Ifan said. "Lord Aelric carried a letter from King Arthur to Modred; I assume this is Modred's response. It won't change anything."

"But with the battle at the Straits . . ." Nell said.

Myrddin shook his head. "Modred won't even mention it. He believes he has the better of King Arthur; such is his arrogance that he believes it is our king who is in rebellion and in danger of excommunication. By his lights, our only recourse is to beg for mercy."

"Bollocks to that," Ifan said.

Myrddin caught Nell's eye. "What do you think Archbishop Dafydd has told him?" Nell said.

"It's what Modred has promised the Church, more like," Ifan said, the same sour expression on his face.

Before they'd finished their breakfast, Gareth appeared at the table. He put his hands flat on the wood and leaned heavily on them, the weight of the world on his back. "The King wants you." He looked directly at Myrddin.

99

Nell, who wasn't invited, wrinkled her nose in annoyance. Myrddin shrugged back at her and got to his feet. He followed Gareth to the rear of the hall and down the corridor to Arthur's receiving room near one of the towers. In the room already were King Arthur, Lord Cai, his face a thundercloud, Geraint, and Bedwyr. The figure of Cai drew Myrddin's attention and his eyes narrowed.

Myrddin hated the man—all the more after the exchange from the day before. Nell, in her former life as a nun, would have told him that it was wrong to hate at all, but when speaking of Cai, anything less than hatred would have been doing him a disservice. The man begged for retribution, but to his regret, Myrddin would never be the one to give it.

Over the years, Cai had betrayed his brother in many ways and by diverse means, even to the point of conspiring with Modred to wage war against Arthur (twice), and an assassination attempt. Whenever Myrddin was in Cai's presence, he avoided looking at him at all and worked very hard not to show his disdain. Arthur's face didn't reveal what he thought of Cai either, but then, he'd spent a lifetime masking his feelings towards his brother. Most of the time, it was best not to think on it, especially since Cai stood beside Arthur once again.

Myrddin had arrived in the middle of a conversation between the Cai and Arthur and this time, they were in agreement, even if both were angry. Arthur stood, his back to the other men in the room, staring out at the heavily falling rain which was making muddy puddles in the courtyard.

Cai, for his part, snorted his derision, disgust in every line of his body. "At least he offers you land a plot of land in Mercia in exchange for Eryri. Modred's letter to me states that 'peace' means I must take the cross, travel to the holy land, and never return to Wales. I'll give him peace! He is a fool."

Arthur turned to his brother, his expression mild. "If we deny his requests, he will see to it that the Archbishop excommunicates us. He states his intention boldly."

"Archbishops have not always spoken for God to our kings," Cai said, spitting out his response. "If we are excommunicate for protecting our country and our people, then so be it."

The stance was a brave one and for the first time in his life, Myrddin found himself agreeing with Cai. He had more fire behind his words since he'd started this war. It almost made Myrddin think that he had concern for something or someone besides himself.

"And these messengers bother me," Arthur said. "They bear a white flag of truce, but they wear Agravaine's colors, not Modred's."

At the mention of Agravaine, every man in the room hissed under his breath. Everywhere Arthur had turned of late, there Agravaine had been. He was the key coordinator of military activity in Wales for Modred. He'd gained this position over the heads of all the other barons who supported him, including Lord Edgar of Powys and Lord Cedric of Brecon, Modred's cousins.

"These riders will do what they can to spy on us," Bedwyr said. "We don't want them running around Eryri unobserved."

"That's what I need you for, Myrddin," Arthur said, finally noting him in his corner. "Follow them as far as the Conwy River and then return to me this evening. Take Ifan. When I'm ready, you will carry my answer to Modred."

"Yes, my lord," Myrddin said.

"Take Deiniol with you as well," Cai said, halting Myrddin's progress towards the door. "He's your brother, I believe."

His stomach roiling, Myrddin inwardly corrected him: *foster brother*. "Yes, my lord," he said instead, and turned away.

Did he know how much Myrddin hated him? *He* being Cai, and *him* being Deiniol, who knew damn well that Myrddin despised him down to his ugly boots.

"What's wrong?" Nell caught Myrddin as he walked stiff-legged across the hall, heading towards the front doors, which opened as another soldier left the room, exposing the hall to the elements.

It was cold, even for November. A dozen men and horses were preparing to ride on similar missions—to other lords and barons whose estates were within a few days' ride of Garth Celyn. Modred had sent a letter to the Council of Wales, as well as one each to Cai and Arthur. The Council needed to see it, discuss it, and respond, just as Arthur and Cai did. Raindrops reflected off the links of the men's mail which were just visible beneath the thick wool of their cloaks. Myrddin didn't envy them even as he acknowledged that he would soon be one of them.

"I'm sent to follow the Saxon riders who brought the messages to the King," Myrddin said. "To make sure they return to their side of the Conwy."

"And that makes you angry?"

Myrddin halted and turned to her, forcing down the anger and the memories that had formed a film over his eyes.

The rain drips down my neck into the collar of my linen shirt. Ripped and torn after my struggles in the woods over the last hour, it provides little protection anyway. If I ever reach the safety of the castle, I will leave it in the rag pile on my way in.

I shiver. "Come on, Myrddin, you spineless bastard," I say. "Move!"

But I cannot. I bend aside a branch of the bush in which I'm cowering and peer though the murk, looking for my pursuer. I see nothing but the rain and the muddy track separating me from the gatehouse of the castle.

Bracing myself, I leave the safety of my bush. In ten quick steps, I'm through the gatehouse and cross the bailey at a run, heading for the stables. I reach it and then press my back against the wall beside the open doorway. I listen for movement, to calm myself and become one with my surrounding as I've been taught, but my beating heart and the pounding rain overwhelm my senses.

At last, I risk entry. I slip through the doorway and head for the shadow of the horse stalls. A horse whickers a gentle greeting and I touch his nose to quiet him. From the door at the far end of the stables, it's a dozen yards to a side door of the keep. Once there, I'll be safe. For now. I reach the last stall and quicken my pace, sensing freedom. Instead, the door swings open and I'm face to face with Deiniol. He grins.

I back away.

A single lantern lights the expansive space between the doorway and the horses. The light glints off a knife Deiniol holds. He shifts it from one hand to the other as I watch. Deiniol is a seasoned fighter, full grown and strong. Even though I'm already sixteen, I'm still a scrawny half-child, speaking in a voice that breaks instead of the low voice of a man.

Deiniol has always been bigger than I, possessing a cruel streak I'd discovered before I could talk. There are more ways to hurt than through physical pain and Deiniol has tried them all on me at one time or another. He's hounded me all afternoon and it's as if this moment is the culmination of a lifetime of animosity. I'll have one chance to escape him, if I've any chance at all.

Between one second and the next, Deiniol moves forward and I spring to my right, only to find myself caught between two large hands that grip my arms and twist them behind my back. A booted foot comes around my legs and pinions them. I twist and jerk my body, but cannot break free.

"Aeden," I spit out, recognizing this new foe as Deiniol's cousin on his mother's side. "Why do you help him?"

Aeden laughs. "Drop the weapon, Deiniol. I'll hold the rat while you hit him."

Deiniol's eyes glint alarmingly. They're almost more frightening than the knife he carries. Deiniol takes a step forward, knife outstretched; then tosses it aside into one of the stalls. I smirk. Instantly, I know I've made a mistake and try to tame my expression, but it's too late.

Deiniol's face twists in hatred. He rushes forward and drives his shoulder into me. Aeden has already backed away and Deiniol and I go down: me underneath and Deiniol straddling my abdomen. I rock my hips trying to throw him off. I scrabble my hands on either side for a fistful of hay to throw into his face, but the stable floor is unaccountably clean and smooth. I can feel the restlessness in the horses, as they, in turn, sense my distress. They cannot help me, however, and Deiniol ignores both them and my struggles. He grasps my wrists so tightly my hands go numb and pulls them above my head.

We glare at each other. There's blood on my lip where I bit it and my belly aches from Deiniol's pummels. Still, I don't look away, and at long last Deiniol sees something in me that gives him pause. His eyes narrow and we still.

105

I can't breathe. Suddenly, Deiniol tips his head back and screams his frustration to the sky. Only then does help come, in the form of Deiniol's mother.

"Boys!" she says, insulting all three of us without thought. "We leave for Mercia tomorrow and yet all you can think to do is scuffle in the dust!"

"So it's true," Aeden says. "Cai has defected to Modred."

"And we with him," my foster mother says.

Deiniol rolls off me. I get to my feet and meet his gaze. "I will remember this, mochyn,*" he says. It is the word for 'pig', but means bastard. "This is only the beginning."*

"Don't be ridiculous," his mother says, brushing straw from Deiniol's shoulders. "Myrddin, I expected better of you."

The unfairness of that leaves me speechless and unable to defend myself. Deiniol smirks at me from behind his mother's back. He tips his head to Aeden and prances after his mother, leaving me alone in the stables.

What Deiniol doesn't realize is that this time, the lesson I've learned is the opposite of the one he intended. When we meet next, four years later, Arthur is in the ascendancy and it is Deiniol, not me, whose stands downcast on the losing side.

"I find that I must travel to Caerhun in the company of my foster father's son. I spoke to you of him yesterday."

Nell's look was sympathetic. "I wish I could come with you instead," she said. "I'm useless here."

"That isn't true," Myrddin said. He reached out and smoothed the hair near her forehead. "Besides. It's impossible. You know that."

"This is all new to me," she said. "I'm at loose ends."

"There's an herb garden behind the kitchen," Myrddin said, "and a drying shed beyond. Perhaps you can be of some assistance there."

"Don't—" Nell broke off, swallowing the rest of the sentence. Myrddin watched her carefully as she looked away, took a deep breath, and turned back to him. "I've already found it," she said. "You're right. They have need of me here."

Unsure what her cut-short comment would have been but glad that Nell would make an attempt to be content, at least for today, Myrddin inspected the mustering men in the courtyard. The clouds hung low and the rain fell so hard it was like they were standing in a waterfall. He sighed and set out into it. It would be a hideously cold ride to Caerhun.

"You," Deiniol said, as his initial greeting.

They stood beneath the gatehouse archway while a stable boy used a cloth to dry Myrddin's saddle. Deiniol had already mounted and wore his hood pulled tight around his head to counter the rain. Regardless, even wearing wool cloaks, it wouldn't take long for the rain this heavy to soak everyone through.

"Deiniol," Myrddin said.

"I see you haven't changed," he said. "Still a sniveling child with a snotty nose and a craven look about you."

"Sweet Mary," Nell said, her words sincere, having pulled up her hood and come to see what kind of man Myrddin despised.

"Is that your woman?" Deiniol lifted his chin and pointed it at Nell. "I heard men speak of her in the hall."

Myrddin had an overwhelming urge to drive his fist into Deiniol's face. Nell, perhaps sensing this, moved closer.

"I hear she used to be a nun," Deiniol continued. "You'll have a cold bed to come home to, won't you?"

Now, Nell caught Myrddin's elbow and held on. "I'm a grown woman," she said. "I've heard worse, and experienced worse, as you well know. Don't get in trouble on my behalf."

Ifan muttered under his breath, turning towards Myrddin and pretending to inspect the length of his stirrups. "Does he rehearse these insults? A man could take lessons from him."

"It's been many years since I was forced into his company," Myrddin said.

"No doubt this was far too soon for a reunion," Ifan said.

"Twenty miles we've to go today," Myrddin said, "and each one will seem like an eternity."

"He hates you," Nell said.

Myrddin looked into her concerned face, her eyes flicking from Deiniol to him. Fortunately, Deiniol had turned his horse's head and urged him out from under the gatehouse, into the rain. Myrddin had a vision of the tower coming loose and crushing him as he rode beneath it.

"He does," Myrddin said. "I've never known why."

"Some men don't need a reason." Ifan straightened his saddle bags. "Did you say that he's your brother?"

"Foster brother. Don't remind me," Myrddin said.

"No wonder you rabbited about when you first came to the King, jumping at every shadow," Ifan said. Two years older than Myrddin, Ifan had been a squire in Lord Bedwyr's retinue when Myrddin had arrived at Garth Celyn. "I gather it was he who gave you those bruises that were just fading when you came to the King?"

"You never said anything about them," Myrddin said. "I'd hoped nobody noticed. It wouldn't do for a future knight to reveal so clearly how unable he was to defend himself."

Ifan shrugged, embarrassed perhaps to have brought them up. "You survived, didn't you?" he said. "Sometimes a man wears bruises because he's the last one standing."

That made Myrddin smile. It was odd to think that he'd spent nearly twenty years in Ifan's company and this was the first Ifan had mentioned the day he'd arrived. It had been a cold day in March, with snow in the mountains. Myrddin had come down the road to Garth Celyn all on his own, with little more than a broken down horse he'd taken from Madoc's stables and his sword, a not-insignificant inheritance from his mother.

The news of Cai's stunning defection had just hit and Garth Celyn had been in upheaval. Arthur had barely glanced at Myrddin, just informed his captain to find him a place to sleep in the barracks, a better horse, and decent armor if he was to be of any use to him at all. King Arthur had needed men and Myrddin had found being treated like a man to his liking.

"By the balls of St. Mari!" Deiniol swore as the rain turned to sleet, and then the first flakes of snow began to coat his shoulders.

Even Ifan blinked twice at that bit of blasphemy and reluctantly mounted his horse. "Would King Arthur be upset if I killed him? We could run him through and throw him into a chasm. No one would be the wiser."

"We'll do it on the way back if we're truly desperate."

"I'll watch his back, miss." Ifan nodded at Nell, and then turned his horse's head towards the sea to follow Deiniol.

Myrddin lifted Nell's hand from his coat. "I'm five years younger than Deiniol and the last time we spent more than ten minutes in company was the evening I ran away. He wanted to kill me. It was only the sudden arrival of his mother than stopped him."

"At least Ifan is with you," she said.

Myrddin laughed. "I would have said he would act as a barrier to me killing Deiniol today. But now I'm pretty sure I'll have to get in line."

Nell wrinkled her nose at him. If they hadn't had that conversation the day before about him sleeping across the room from her, Myrddin would have called it coquettish. "You be careful."

"Let's go, *mochyn!*" Deiniol had stopped some forty feet away for Ifan to catch up, and they both twisted in their seats to look for Myrddin. "The Saxons ride away."

Because it was urgent and he was right, Myrddin did as he was asked, telling himself that he was doing the King's will. Myrddin gave a final nod to Nell; then spurred Cadfarch forwards. The three men rode out of Garth Celyn, heading towards the southern pass.

8

11 November 537 AD

Nell perched on her stool, leaning over the narrow wooden table in front of her. Dried plants hung from the ceiling while herbs and spices crowded the shelves. In short order, she'd made the gardener's shed that lay across the herb garden from the kitchen a haven, installing a warming brazier and cushioned stool, taking Myrddin's advice and making the idea her own. The only light, other than from the brazier, shone from a pewter candelabra in front of her which held three glowing candles. A hole in the roof let out the smoke, but other than that, the room allowed no exterior light. Admittedly, a window would have done her little good, as it was four o'clock in the afternoon and already nearly dark.

"How are you doing?"

Nell looked up as Myrddin entered the hut. She'd been writing on a scrap of vellum, detailing the dream she'd had the previous night. If she closed her eyes, she could see it running in an endless loop behind her eyelids. It came so often now, night after night, that she sometimes felt she was more awake when she was dreaming than the other way around.

"Fine." She straightened, running through the last few minutes in her mind to see if she'd given anything away. She wasn't fine, of course. It was hard to see how she was ever going to be fine again. Myrddin, for his part, watched her warily, as if he knew she was lying to him. She hated feeling so vulnerable. She missed those high convent walls, keeping out the world. "How long have you been standing there?"

"Long enough to watch you fill the page," Myrddin said. "I heard a few phrases that could have been curses, too." He smiled. "You haven't been spending time among the garrison in my absence, have you? At least Deiniol isn't here to bother you."

She found that she couldn't smile back. It was no laughing matter that Deiniol had ridden with Myrddin and Ifan only as far as the pagan stones before taking a track south into the mountains. They'd let him go alone into the wilderness, rather than lose the Saxon messengers they'd been sent to follow.

Myrddin walked to her and peered over her shoulder, resting one hand on the table beside the inkpot. Nell hunched her shoulders, covering the page with one hand so he couldn't read her words. It was just like him to be able to read too: he pretended to be a bachelor, journeyman knight, but every now and then he would evidence some new, unexpected skill that belied his claim. He couldn't fool her anymore.

He stood at her shoulder, refusing to take the hint. After another count of ten, he sighed and eased away from her. But he didn't leave her alone as she wanted—or part of her wanted and the rest didn't.

"What is it, Nell? Tell me what's bothering you. You can trust me."

She glanced up at him. "It isn't that I don't trust you."

"Isn't it?" he said. "I would like to think that you're telling me the truth this time, but it's hard to tell. I share a room with you, and meals, but you never talk of anything more momentous than the weather. The world is falling in around us; we're in the middle of a war. Why won't you speak of it?"

Nell bowed her head. Endlessly patient as always, Myrddin leaned against the counter on which she prepared her herbs and ointments. Finally, she pushed away the paper and turned in her seat to face him. "I'm tired, Myrddin," she said. "I'm thirty years old and I feel a hundred."

"You don't look it." He tried to coax a smile. This time, she obliged, although it quickly faded.

"Why did you come to find me, Myrddin?"

"We've news from Powys," Myrddin said. "Lord Edgar has sent word that he might be persuaded to change sides, given the proper incentives."

Nell stared at him, her stomach sinking into her boots while a vision of the church by the Cam River rose unbidden before her eyes. "That couldn't possibly be true," she said. "His family has ever been faithful to the kings of Mercia—and now Modred. Does King Arthur believe it?"

"King Arthur has said nothing to me, but just this morning he sent a captain south to prepare to open a second front against the Saxons—on our terms this time, not Modred's. Geraint told me that given this new approach from Edgar, the King will want to lead his men himself."

Nell shook her head, an iciness taking over her limbs. Ten heartbeats ago she was alone with her dreams and her fears, and now the dream was a reality. "I don't think this is a good idea," she said. "Surely the King must see that?"

"The King needs to change the balance of power, and perhaps making Edgar an ally is the way to do it."

"What about—" Nell thought desperately for anything—any idea—that could divert this folly. Twenty years of dreaming and she'd never been this close to the King—or to complete failure. "You have the King's confidence. What if you suggested to the King that he look to someone else to turn aside from Edgar. Someone like Lord Cedric of Brecon. He hates Modred."

In 521, Cedric's father had fought against Modred and Icel, the King of Mercia at the time, in a war over the border territory between Mercia and Wessex. Cedric's family had allied with Arthur, who had some stake in the outcome, though not a large one. But Cedric's father had died of the wounds he received at Shrewsbury and Cedric himself, only sixteen at the time, had witnessed his father's wounding and subsequent death while in Modred's custody.

Myrddin laughed. "He's none too fond of Arthur either," he said. "And he's as mercenary as Cai."

"True," she said. "But he's more open about it. You never have to wonder at his motives. You just need to make sure your goals align with his. And from what I know of the man, he's always been up-front with his allegiances. If he walks away from an alliance with Modred, he'd probably tell him about it in advance, rather than stab him in the back."

"Yes," Myrddin agreed. "But it isn't he who has sent a message to King Arthur."

"But— " Nell stopped. A curious look had passed across Myrddin's face. *Could I have said something right?* "It was his family who sided with King Arthur sixteen years ago. They might do it again."

"Modred forgave Cedric's family their treason." Myrddin nodded as he thought it through. "But the death of a father due to the mercilessness of one's lord is not something any man can easily forget, or forgive, especially one arising from as ancient a lineage as Cedric."

"King Arthur wants to unite Wales as its King," Nell said. "Cedric wants his bit of land secure and to stop having to fight either Arthur or his own supposed allies for the right to it. He wants more land too, but it's unlikely that Modred is going to award him any more—not any time soon."

"The land would be at the expense of Agravaine, Aelric, or Edgar," Myrddin said, "staunch allies of Modred."

"Well, except possibly for Edgar," Nell said.

"And you say that . . . why?"

"Because Edgar's . . ." Nell paused and pursed her lips, uncertain as to whether or not she should say more.

"Edgar's . . . what?"

"Edgar does not prefer women," Nell said, as delicately as she could. "To my mind, this is why Modred has withheld Edgar's inheritance since his father died. None of the Mercian barons think Edgar is a fit heir, but it *is* his right."

"And how do you know all this?"

Nell stared at the floor, biting her bottom lip. She had so many things to tell him; so many things he might not forgive or understand.

Myrddin waited through the silence.

Finally, Nell waved a hand, apologetically, unable to avoid revealing to him this bit of the truth. "My husband served as a man-at-arms at Wigmore Castle."

Myrddin gaped at her. "He was part of the garrison? For Edgar's family?"

Nell couldn't mistake the anger and distrust that rose in his face—the same distrust he'd felt that first night on the road from St. Asaph. "Yes."

"Why didn't you tell me this before?"

"Because you're a staunch supporter of Arthur!" Nell's voice went high and tears pricked at her eyes in her anxiety. "You thought I was a spy! How could I tell you my husband served a Saxon lord?" A lone tear fell across her cheek and she angrily brushed it away with the back of her hand.

"I already suspected the worst," Myrddin said. "It would have confirmed my suspicions."

"And you still have them now." Her heart sank.

"No man can ever truly know what is in another's soul," Myrddin said, unrelenting. "Was your husband Saxon?"

"No." Nell crossed her arms and stared at the floor. "Many of the men-at-arms who serve the Saxons are Welsh."

"So who was he?"

Nell closed her eyes. "His name was Rhys," she said. "He was ten years older than I, the younger son of a landowner who held lands to the south of my father's." She'd been such a child when she married him. Not so much foolish, but innocent, in love with the handsome soldier she barely knew, even if she'd known him from infancy, but sure of her future with him. "Fifteen years ago there was peace between Wales and Mercia and my father didn't object to the marriage."

"But you didn't want to stay?" Myrddin said. "Once your husband and children died?"

"No," Nell said. "I didn't. I told you that before and it was nothing but the truth. It was Edgar, in fact, who helped me return to Wales."

"And you haven't been back since?" Myrddin said.

"No."

"And Edgar?" Myrddin said. "Have you a further thought, then, about his message to King Arthur?"

"I don't know about that," Nell said. "It's Agravaine who has the real power. Modred put him in charge of all his forces, including Edgar's, for a reason. I wouldn't be surprised if the letter to the King was Agravaine's idea, and Edgar was only going along with the deception because he wanted to prove to Modred his loyalty—to force him to acknowledge that he is his father's rightful heir."

"That is my thought too," Myrddin said. "If Arthur goes to meet Edgar, I fear he goes to his death."

Nell had been studying her toes, not looking at Myrddin as he interrogated her. Now she glanced up, surprised that he would say such a thing so openly and surely. "I feel that too," she said. "Can you think of a way to stop him? I will help you if I can!"

Myrddin studied her face and she let him, not looking away. His lips twisted. "We'll see." With a last nod, he spun on one heel and left the hut.

Nell stared after him. When his footsteps had faded, she leaned her head back against wall and closed her eyes. In twenty years of dreaming, nothing she'd tried had turned out right. This was obviously not working either. Perhaps she shouldn't have allowed Myrddin to bring her to Garth Celyn after all.

9

12 November 537 AD

As he stared up at the battlements of Rhuddlan Castle, Myrddin felt for the letter from King Arthur to Modred one last time, as reassurance. Arthur had selected him to bring it as he'd promised. Myrddin had come alone because in the end, the King had determined that it was better to lose one man to an early grave or Modred's dungeon than a company of them.

"I'm not too happy about this either, Nell," Myrddin had said, standing in Garth Celyn's courtyard that morning. Nell had held Cadfarch's bridle and fed him carrots while Myrddin adjusted his saddlebags. "Nor is the King."

"Take me with you," she said. "Nobody will know or care if I leave here, or what happens to me."

"I will care," Myrddin said, remembering her tears from yesterday and their effect on his heart. "The road I'm taking passes right through St. Asaph. You don't need to ride through there again."

"Maybe I do need to," Nell said.

"Nell—"

"I wouldn't be alone this time," Nell said. "I'd be with you, and I'd pretend to be your little brother. Nobody would give me a second look."

"In boy's clothes?" Myrddin said.

"Of course."

"No," he said, more firmly than before. "You're a nun."

"Not anymore," she said, "and I have no intention of ever being one again."

"The law—"

"*The woman shall not wear that which pertaineth unto a man, neither shall a man put on a woman's garment: for all that do so are abomination unto the Lord thy God,*" Nell quoted. "Give me credit for knowing at least that. But with Eryri about to fall to Modred, wearing a boy's discarded breeches is surely a small matter."

She gazed at him, disconcerting him because a vision of her lifeless and abused body had risen before his eyes. He blinked to clear them before she realized he'd seen it. That she'd experienced attempted rape and murder even once was unconscionable. She was crazed to think Myrddin would let her near the scene of the crime again.

"It wouldn't work." Regardless of his opinion, the request was ludicrous and she had to know it. But Myrddin understood it, too. She was vibrant and competent woman, adrift in the middle of a war; little wonder that she was struggling with it. But riding with him wasn't the answer.

"It isn't because you don't trust me, is it?" she said. "It's not because you still believe that I spy for Modred?"

"That's not it," Myrddin said, acknowledging at last, albeit grudgingly, that the idea had always been unlikely.

"Besides." Nell changed tack. "Masterless men didn't attack me. Those men were knights. I just happened to get in their way."

Myrddin snorted under his breath. "Don't you think I know that? Modred would never allow marauders so close to Rhuddlan. His men are disciplined and he would have taken care of any such men who'd dared roam his territory. But who's going to *be* at Rhuddlan? Those very same men! The thought of you left to your own devices at Rhuddlan Castle sends chills down my spine."

Nell studied his face and then sighed, backing down. "Yes, my lord."

Myrddin's eyes narrowed at her uncharacteristic use of his title.

Her shoulders fell for a second, but then she poked him in the chest. "But I'm holding it against you."

"I can accept that," Myrddin had said. He'd glanced back once as he left the castle to see Nell and Ifan standing on the battlements, watching him ride away. Nell had tucked herself into her cloak, with the hood up, but Ifan stood bareheaded, his crop of short, blonde hair unmistakable. Each had lifted a hand to wave him down the road. Myrddin had responded with a salute.

Now, at sunset, he followed the western side of the Clwyd River, past the drawbridge and its lesser gate, to the ford. Cadfarch splashed through the river, came up the bank, and stopped in front of the main defensive tower in the outer palisade. Myrddin waited, hoping that the archers who peered at him from the battlements would remain patient. He was Welsh but that didn't mean that he was an enemy. Sad, but true.

A guard called to him from the walkway above the gatehouse. "Give me your name and your purpose." The man, tall and helmetless, spoke in heavily accented Welsh.

"I come at the request of Arthur ap Uther, King of Wales," Myrddin said, answering him in Saxon, the language in which he was sure to be most comfortable. "I have a letter for Lord Modred."

The man studied Myrddin and then nodded. "You may enter," he said, now in flawless Saxon, confirming Myrddin's assessment, "provided you surrender your weapons."

Myrddin agreed with reluctance to what the soldier asked. Men wore weapons as a matter of course and for a man *not* to wear his sword was unusual—and insulting to the unarmed man, which is of course why the soldier intended to strip Myrddin of his. It wasn't that he feared Myrddin would use his sword against Modred, but because he sought to humiliate him, and by association, King Arthur.

Myrddin urged Cadfarch under the gatehouse and into the outer bailey. Once inside the curtain wall, a cobbled path led to the massive double towers of the second gatehouse which protected the great hall behind it. Modred's fort was impregnable. No one had ever taken it by force, although not for lack of trying. Cai had attacked it after taking down one of Modred's more eastern castles the previous spring, but other than causing some damage from fire, he'd gone away unsatisfied. It might be possible to starve the defenders out, but Myrddin wouldn't have been surprised to learn that Modred had built an escape tunnel under his castle, just like at Garth Celyn. Then again, he had less experience in losing wars and so perhaps hadn't thought he needed one.

Torches flared in sconces—dozens of them—lighting the bailey almost as if it were day. Like everything else about Rhuddlan, the expansive light was a display of wealth and power that the local populace would surely notice. Compared to any of King Arthur's castles, which tended to be coldly utilitarian, even if their castellans did everything they could to make them comfortable, Rhuddlan was a palace. Modred's image of himself had only grown more resplendent as his victories had increased in number.

Myrddin dismounted and instantly three men were upon him, two gripping his upper arms while a third disarmed him. He patted Myrddin down, finding one knife in his boot and a second tucked into the bracer on his forearm. Myrddin had hoped they'd miss that one and kicked himself for not having a maid sew a smaller knife into the lining of his cloak. A true spy, he wasn't. Perhaps it was time he learned.

Just as they finished, another man—of obvious rank, given his clothing and the artistry in the hilt of his sword—came out from under the secondary gatehouse. Even his walk was purposeful and distinctive. The men sitting outside the stables with doxies on their laps hastily put them aside to stand at his approach. The man didn't indicate that he noticed, although Myrddin guessed that if he was a captain worth his salt, he would confront them later. When the man reached Myrddin, he gave Myrddin a curt nod and said, "Lord Mordred will see you now."

Myrddin hadn't expected anything different in terms of courtesy, although it would have been nice to brush the dust from his clothes and polish himself up so as to represent Arthur better. With no help for it, he allowed a stable boy to lead Cadfarch away and then trailed after the man, followed by one of the men-at-arms carrying his weapons. Even Modred knew he couldn't have his men toss them in a corner—that Myrddin wouldn't countenance it. They were his livelihood and the value of the sword alone was that of an entire village.

Rhuddlan's walls and towers loomed even larger from the ground than on horseback. As Myrddin followed the knight through the second gatehouse, the second bailey, and into the great hall, he had to shake his head over the amount of time and treasure it had taken to build it. Modred's people must be suffering greatly to have given him so much in such a short time.

The hall was full of men at their evening meal. Myrddin and his escort by-passed them, however, and headed down a corridor to Modred's receiving room. The metal fittings of Myrddin's boots clacked loudly on the stones as he paced along the corridor, a match to the pounding of his heart which seemed to rise further into his throat with every step. Then he told himself that if he was to turn aside the fate set for Wales in the dream, if he was to become the man Arthur needed him to be, he'd have to do better.

When facing down an enemy, whether Deiniol as a boy or a hated upstart nobleman, confidence was everything. Much as Nell had done when she'd first spoken to King Arthur back at Garth Celyn, Myrddin replaced uncertainty with pride. Straightening his shoulders, Myrddin nodded at the man who'd brought him. The man's eyes crinkled at the corners, acknowledging the transition Myrddin had affected, and nodded back.

The man threw open the door to Modred's receiving room. It was the same size as the great hall at Garth Celyn, but as it was only a third as large as the hall Myrddin had just come through, Modred used it for his private meetings. Not that this was going to be private. Myrddin had walked into a room full of people and had their immediate attention. Deliberately ignoring everyone but the man in charge, Myrddin strode towards Modred. He no longer had a sword at his waist but he held a missive of defiance close to his heart, which was almost the same thing, and perhaps better.

His heart caught in his throat, however, at the sight of Archbishop Dafydd standing to Modred's right. Myrddin hadn't realized, even with all the discussion of peace lately, that the two men were so close—and that Modred had this level of support from the Church. For his part, the Archbishop observed Myrddin as he came to a halt five paces from Modred's throne, with its gilt frame, raised dais, and thick rug. Myrddin bowed, straightened, his hands at his sides, and looked straight at Modred.

"Come," Modred said. "Let's see what my beloved uncle has to say to me today."

Modred appeared exactly as he should, which was to say, like a king. He was forty years old, into middle-age, but didn't look it. He had a full head of dark hair, broad shoulders, and eyes that Myrddin would have avoided if he could. It was hard not to think they saw right through him. *Christ, I hate him.* Still upright, refusing to allow his thoughts to show, Myrddin advanced towards Modred's throne. He removed the letter from his breast pocket and with a second, short bow, held it out to Modred.

"My lord," Myrddin said. "King Arthur greets you and hopes that his royal nephew is well."

"How kind of him to inquire." Modred took the letter, watching Myrddin out of the corner of his eye as he did so, and broke the seal. He unrolled it and read for no more than a minute. Without re-rolling it, Modred handed the letter to the Archbishop, who took it. Myrddin kept his hands relaxed at his sides, wondering what would happen next. He didn't like the feeling he was getting from Modred or his lackeys, many of whom were watching him like he was a rare beast in a cage. Or a chicken intended for slaughter.

While the Archbishop read Arthur's letter, Modred sat still, his only movement the tapping of his finger on the arm of his chair as he waited. He didn't appear disturbed or angry by King Arthur's words, just impatient. The letter seemed no more or less than what he had expected.

"And Cai's response?" Modred said.

Myrddin had that letter too. He didn't know precisely what it said, but suspected it was far less polite than Arthur's. "Here, my lord." Myrddin pulled it from his pocket and handed it to Modred.

Modred took it, split the seal, and passed it off so quickly to the Archbishop he couldn't have read more than three words. Instead, he revealed that he had other things on his mind. "And what was your role in the battle at the Straits?"

Myrddin blinked, nonplussed. And then decided the question wasn't so surprising. Very few of Modred's men had survived the battle, and perhaps he hadn't yet had a good first-hand account. "I am one of the knights in my King's household guard," Myrddin said, deciding there was no harm in telling him this bit of truth. Eventually he'd hear it from someone else. "I was at the forefront of the initial charge."

"Tell me what happened," Modred said.

Myrddin took in a breath. Modred would hate what he had to say, but then, it was unlikely Myrddin's explanation could make it worse for him. "The Saxon forces crossed the Straits at noon on November 6th," he said. "Once the cavalry reached the beach and the foot soldiers were marching on the bridge, we unleashed our arrows."

Myrddin stopped.

"And then?" Modred watched Myrddin's face. The silence in the hall was complete.

"And then we charged," Myrddin said.

"Who killed Wulfere?" Modred said.

Myrddin hesitated. "I did."

A pause. Unaccountably, Modred smiled. Then he began to laugh. He continued, tears spilling out of his eyes and rolling down his cheeks. After a stunned ten seconds, the rest of the people in the room began to laugh too, even if they, as Myrddin, had no idea what their lord thought was so funny.

Myrddin remained standing in front of Modred. He shared a quick look with the Archbishop, who was the only other person not in hysterics. Then he glanced at the stars beginning to show through the glass in the window to his left. As in the courtyard, the wealth on display in the hall was palpable, from the glass in the windows, to the dual fireplaces, one on each side of the hall, to the tapestries that adorned the walls. Myrddin wished he was gone already but until the king dismissed him, he had to stay. Finally, Modred calmed enough to explain himself.

"Your King has quite a sense of humor," he said. "He sends his letter with the one man he knows I won't touch. He probably thinks I should thank you for doing to Wulfere what I would have done myself, except that you robbed me of my pleasure."

"My lord, my apologies if I displeased you, but Wulfere attacked me." Myrddin bowed again, for lack of anything better to do or say. Wulfere had disobeyed a direct order. If he hadn't lost his life at the Straits, if Modred was angry enough, he might have hung him from the tallest tower at Rhuddlan and afterwards stuck his head on a pike for display. On the whole, given Modred's cruel streak, Myrddin had done Wulfere a favor.

Modred barked another laugh. "No regrets, eh?" He fingered his lip. "To repay the loss of my prize, you can render me a small service while you're here, especially as you appear so adept at delivering messages."

"If I can, my lord," Myrddin said.

"Lord Cedric of Brecon awaits my pleasure," he said. "I think I've kept him waiting long enough. Bring him to me."

"Certainly, sir," Myrddin said.

He turned on his heel, his mind racing. *What a gift! The very man he'd wanted to meet!* Nell would have his head if he didn't take advantage of the opportunity—he almost wished he'd brought her with him to help him think of what to say. Myrddin marched towards the door, the space between his shoulder blades tingling with the force of the glare that he felt Modred directing at him. He would have run from the room if he could, but as it was, the instant Myrddin cleared the doorway, he heaved a sigh of relief.

Myrddin had no idea where Modred was keeping Cedric, whether in the dungeon, or the tower, or a private suite. It was a simple matter, however, to ask a servant, who gave him directions

and informed him, as a by-the-way, that Cedric had arrived by
boat just after dawn and had been cooling his heels in his rooms
ever since, waiting for Modred to send for him.

To give Modred credit, he *was* treating Cedric as an
honored guest. Given the disaster at the Straits, coupled with the
fact that the two men hated each other, that was somewhat
surprising. Still, Cedric had remained overtly loyal to Modred and
was a high ranking nobleman—and Modred's cousin—even if every
task he performed for Modred was accomplished with great
loathing.

As Myrddin approached Cedric's rooms, a disturbing
amount of mumbling and shouting began leaking through the
half-open door into the passage. He fought his instinct to run into
the room to quiet the man. Didn't Cedric realize he was in enemy
territory? Didn't he see the need to bury his emotions and keep
his thoughts more private?

"Fools!" Cedric said, the word echoing down the corridor.
"The indignity of being forced to wait in my rooms! To have my
honor called into question!"

Myrddin arrived in Cedric's doorway, knocked, and then
took a step back so as not to crowd the threshold. Booted feet
echoed on the floor and Cedric himself opened the door. Beyond,
the room was empty.

"Lord Cedric." Myrddin bowed and pretended he hadn't
overheard him. "Lord Modred requests your presence."

At the sight of Myrddin, Cedric's face transformed from
rage to a blank and expressionless façade—all except for his eyes,

which glinted, the sole indication of the fire behind them. He glared at Myrddin and then slid the sword he'd been brandishing at his unseen listeners into the sheath at his waist.

"Finally," he said. "Is the Archbishop beside him?"

"Yes, my lord," Myrddin said.

"And who are you?" He pointed his chin at Myrddin. "By your features, you are a Welshmen, yet your Saxon is perfect."

"Myrddin. A knight in the retinue of King Arthur ap Uther."

That got Cedric's attention. He examined Myrddin through narrowed eyes. Then he tipped his face to study the rafters above him and spoke in a low voice. "Why does Modred send you to me? What is it that I don't know?"

"I came to Rhuddlan because I bore a message from my King to Modred," Myrddin said, answering him even if the question had been rhetorical—and then decided that he would take advantage of the opportunity Modred had given him. Maybe there really was a way to prevent Arthur from meeting Lord Edgar at that damned church a month from now. "But it is well that Lord Modred sent me here, for I have a query for you on behalf of my King."

Cedric's head came down at that and he looked at Myrddin warily. He pushed past Myrddin to look both ways down the hall, and then gave Myrddin a curt nod. "Tell me quickly."

"You and King Arthur have been at odds," Myrddin said. "He would rather you were allies."

Cedric pursed his lips and looked away. He contemplated the hilt of his sword on which he rested his left hand and tapped a staccato with one finger at its end, in a similar thinking pose to Modred's. Then, moving quickly into the hall, Cedric caught a courtier off-guard who was hurrying down it. The man bowed low as he reached Cedric, and then continued on.

Unable to read Cedric and wondering how big a mistake he'd made, Myrddin turned to follow him. Myrddin assumed that Cedric expected him to walk behind him, given Myrddin's nationality and as befitting Cedric's rank which was so much higher than Myrddin's. Once the courtier had disappeared around a far corner, however, Cedric motioned impatiently for Myrddin to come abreast. Myrddin did as he asked and the two men walked together down the passage. Or rather, Myrddin walked, and Cedric stalked.

"What is his mood?" Cedric said, with no need to explain whose mood he meant. Apparently they were going to ignore Arthur's supposed message.

"I have no idea," Myrddin said. "The Archbishop stood beside him and said nothing either. I can't imagine Modred was happy with Archbishop Dafydd's attempts to mediate a peace settlement, but he would never reveal what he is thinking—to anyone perhaps, but certainly not to one of King Arthur's men."

Cedric grunted, but whether that meant agreement or disapproval, Myrddin didn't know. Then, as they approached Modred's receiving room, Cedric slowed. "You have served King Arthur for many years?"

"Yes."

"Does he strike you as a man with a temper?"

Myrddin glanced warily at him, not sure where this was leading. "No. He has one, of course, but when it rises he turns cold, not hot."

Cedric nodded. "Lord Modred is not one to cross. For me to do so would have ramifications for generations to come. You tell that to your lord."

Uncertain, Myrddin stood frozen to the floor for the half a second it took Cedric to push open the door leading to Modred's rooms. Then, galvanized by Cedric's retreating back, Myrddin hurried after him as Cedric crossed the twenty feet to where Modred sat, no longer on his throne but behind a desk that was set under one of the windows to the left of the central fireplace.

Modred had emptied the hall in Myrddin's absence. Now, Archbishop Dafydd was the only other man present. Both Archbishop and Lord Modred had been bent over a piece of paper, which the Archbishop now folded and slid into a hidden pocket beneath his robes. It was warmer in the room than before, despite the fewer bodies to heat it. The fires had been stoked and blazed brightly. Like Arthur, Modred had the best of everything. The remains of dinner lay on the corner of his table. The Archbishop held a goblet of wine and a hint of spice wafted from it.

Cedric reached Modred and bowed at the precisely correct angle that was required. In contrast, Myrddin's feet stuck to the floor just inside the doorway, near the bench where his untended weapons lay. For a heartbeat, Myrddin considered grabbing his sword and making a run for it. One glance at the guards by the open door who had shifted to more ready stances had him biding his time a while longer. The exit was a long way away, through the great hall and two well-guarded gatehouses. If Myrddin was going to reach it, it wasn't going to be at a flat-out run. Stealth would have to be the order the of day.

"You summoned me, sire?" Cedric said.

Modred leaned back in his chair and for twenty seconds sat unmoving, elbows resting on the arms, seemingly relaxed. Cedric's words hung in the air as Modred left his question unanswered. Cedric waited with what appeared to be patience for his lord's response.

"Tell me of the defeat at the Menai Straits," Modred said, finally, as if discussing the dreadful weather, and as if he hadn't just asked Myrddin the same question half an hour before.

"My lord—" Cedric began.

Modred cut him off, leaning forward to punctuate his next words with a pointing finger. "Explain to me why so many of my men are dead: Wulfere, Golm, Halfric, Dane, not to mention the equipment and horses that are now at the bottom of the sea! Do you understand the huge expenses I am incurring in this business? Of the criminal waste that this defeat has entailed?" By the end of his query, Modred's voice had risen to the point where the sound buffeted Cedric like waves.

"Wulfere refused to listen to me," Cedric said, lifting his chin and aiming to withstand the onslaught. "He, not I, was the commander in the field. He, not I, is to blame for the loss of so many of our men."

"And he, not you, paid for his error with his life." Modred sat back in his chair as if he'd never raised his voice. "By the sword of our friend, here." He gestured with one hand towards Myrddin. Cedric's eyes met Myrddin's. The corner of Cedric's mouth twitched before his face blanked and he turned back to his lord.

"As you say, my lord." Cedric bowed his head and then raised it to meet Modred's eyes. "I tried to convince Wulfere and the others that you would not countenance an attack on that day, not with the Archbishop in the middle of negotiations and hoping for a settlement between you and King Arthur. Wulfere thought he could ensure that a settlement was unnecessary. He supposed that a great victory could convince Arthur to submit to you, or at best, he could capture the King by driving down the coast to Garth Celyn, once he'd navigated the bridge. Regardless, he refused to listen to my cautions."

From what Myrddin knew of both Cedric and Wulfere, he believed Cedric's story. Myrddin had to wonder, however, how hard Cedric had tried to get Wulfere to change course. He must have despised Wulfere—everyone did. Even Modred couldn't have admired the man as a person. He had put Wulfere in charge of his troops because he could be trusted to get the job done.

That alone had to have been a huge sore point for Cedric, whom Modred had overlooked from the start of the war in favor of Agravaine in particular. To have put Wulfere in charge of the men on Anglesey added insult to injury. To Cedric's mind, if Wulfere had won the battle, Cedric could have gone along with it; if Wulfere made a fool of himself, Cedric wouldn't have been at fault. Nobody could have foreseen the total disaster the battle had become for the Saxons.

"On the day of the attack, a fault in the bridge of boats delayed us," Cedric said, continuing his story. "Wulfere had intended to cross at dawn but ended up crossing at noon. It was the optimal time, with the water high, but as we traversed the bridge, we failed to surprise the Welsh forces. They caught us on the beach, low ground, between the trees and the water. When we retreated, the swift waters of the Straits and the weight of the horses and equipment on the bridge ensured our near total defeat."

"And gave Arthur new reason to resist me." Modred surged to his feet. Myrddin would have said he was furious, but as always, his eyes remained cold, revealing nothing of the man inside. "He sits in his eyrie in Snowdonia, mocking me, as if I haven't the power to root him out! I will accept nothing less from that bastard King than complete submission!"

If the back of Myrddin's knees had not been resting on the edge of the bench, he would have taken a step back at the king's vehemence. Even Cedric, for all his confidence, thought better of any reply. Myrddin decided not to mention that Arthur, of all the Welsh lords, appeared to have been born legitimate.

For Modred's part, he wasn't done. "Arthur is arrogant! Impossible! Look at the letter he sends me!" Modred leaned over

the desk and shoved one of the pieces of parchment towards
Cedric who just managed to catch it before it fell from the table.
Unrolling the paper, he studied the words in silence, but Myrddin
knew well what they said:

> . . . *we are ready to come to the Archbishop's*
> *grace, if it is offered in a form safe and honourable for us.*
> *But the form contained in the articles which were sent to*
> *us, is in no particular either safe or honourable . . . indeed,*
> *so far from it that all who hear it are astonished, since it*
> *tends rather to the destruction and ruin of our people and*
> *our person than to our honour and safety . . . for never*
> *would our nobles and subjects consent in the inevitable*
> *destruction and dissipation that would surely derive from*
> *it . .*

Cedric handed the letter back to Modred who tossed it into
a wooden box on the floor behind him and sat heavily in his chair
once again.

"My spies inform me that Arthur has sent men south to
open a new front against me in Powys," Modred said.

Myrddin started at that, the pit forming in his stomach and
the chills running down his spine telling him that Modred's
attitude towards him had changed in the time he'd been gone.
Myrddin gritted his teeth, fighting back the cold certainty. Despite
what Modred had said earlier about not harming him because he'd
killed Wulfere, he must have decided Myrddin would never leave

Rhuddlan or he would not have spoken openly of this. Myrddin was a walking dead man.

"I've heard that Lord Gawain is marshalling a force to threaten Brecon," Cedric said.

"You wish to be relieved of your duties in the north, then?" Modred said. "To deal with this new threat?" Myrddin couldn't tell if he was mocking Cedric or asking a serious question. Cedric treated it as genuine.

"If it please you, my lord. A strong hand is needed at Brecon or my lands might fall to Arthur's army. That would serve neither me nor you."

Modred contemplated Cedric's face. Cedric, for his part, kept his back straight, looking forward, even if it might cost him Modred's favor. Modred tapped one finger to his lips, as was his habit, and spoke.

"I will not have a repeat of the Anglesey disaster. I had ordered Wulfere to delay his attack. It is fortunate for him that our friend, here, killed him before I could myself."

"I understand completely, my lord," Cedric said. "If I offended you in any way, it was not my intent."

"Is that so?" If anything, Modred grew more still. No doubt, he was thinking, as Myrddin was, of that long ago war. "It is I, and I alone, who will determine that."

"Yes, my lord." Cedric's jaw was set and he spoke through gritted teeth. "I have further news, sire, that might interest you. Lord Edgar has sent a letter to Arthur, inviting him south. If the

King wasn't already resolved to lead his men himself, this will confirm his intent."

Was there anything the Saxons didn't know?

Modred leaned forward, apparently truly interested for the first time. "The King has agreed to this meeting?"

"I know not, my lord."

Modred sat back. "Arthur will agree. I am sure of it." Modred sneered. "He is that desperate—and naïve. The notion that Edgar would side with a rebel such as he is laughable."

Cedric didn't respond to Modred's assertion any more than Myrddin did, even if Cedric's mind had to be revolving with the same calculations as Myrddin's. Did Modred know that Edgar's resentments were as great as Cedric's own, for all he was younger and less experienced? Did Modred know of Edgar's anger at being denied his inheritance?

"May I go, my lord?" Cedric asked instead, bowing yet again.

"Go." Modred waved his hand dismissively. "When we meet next, Arthur will be dead and I will have all Wales in the palm of my hand."

Cedric bowed one more time and turned for the door. He held Myrddin's gaze as he walked the thirty feet between them. Myrddin couldn't read his expression, but felt he was trying to tell him something. His eyes flicked to the door and then back to Myrddin.

Flee now?

If Arthur died, Wales would be left rudderless. Arthur had no sons to come after him and his death would solidify Edgar's station with Modred. The thought could not have been comforting to Cedric. He had to despise Modred's vision of the future of Wales. For Myrddin's part, he didn't like Modred's confident power. He didn't like it at all.

10

13 November 537 AD

The hours after midnight can be bleak. Certainly, the dungeon under the southwest tower of Rhuddlan Castle was not an enjoyable location in which to spend them. The castle was new, true, but the walls seeped water, which came from either the moat or the river—it hardly mattered which one, but given Myrddin's location, he suspected the river—and mold had formed in the corners of his cell. From his fixed position on the wall, he could smell it, although not see it, since darkness shrouded his cell. The sole light came from the torch in a sconce on the wall in the guardroom on the other side of the door.

The door had a hole cut in it, bifurcated by a single bar. Beyond it, the shadows and the occasional figures of Myrddin's guard passed. Representing almost a greater threat than the guards were the three rats that had found their way to a far corner. Those, Myrddin could see as well as hear and they ensured that any notion of dropping off to sleep in such an uncomfortable position was squashed before he took it seriously.

He was still cursing himself as to how in the hell he'd ended up here in the first place.

After Modred had dismissed Cedric, Myrddin had snatched up his weapons and followed Cedric out the door. With a confidence he didn't really feel, Myrddin had moved along the hallway, buckling on his sword and intending to make a quick getaway. Cedric heard his steps behind him, however, and pulled Myrddin aside.

"Modred won't let you leave," he said.

"I fear you are correct," Myrddin said. "But I must try."

"Wait a while," he said. "Dine with me. After the meal, I'll see what I can do for you."

Myrddin doubted he could trust him, but believed the guards would prevent him from walking out the front gate. So Myrddin went to the great hall with Cedric. Full darkness had descended shortly after he'd arrived at Rhuddlan, and by now they'd missed the bulk of the meal. But like Modred, Cedric got to eat whenever he wanted.

The hall was still full of men, all of whom would have been hostile to Myrddin if they'd known who he was. But since he entered as Cedric's new-found companion, if not friend, nobody approached them. Cedric was known for standing on ceremony and insisting on the comforts and accolades of his office—much like King Arthur.

A servant appeared with trenchers for their food and goblets for wine, which she laid before them. She wore the garb of a Saxon girl and was perhaps one of the villagers whom Modred had imported to Rhuddlan for this purpose. Although she was young and lovely, in a blonde, Saxon way, Cedric didn't spare her a glance. It supported the rumors Myrddin had heard that he was faithful to his wife—an unusual trait among noble men. And something else he didn't share with Modred, although Modred apparently did love his wife to distraction.

Myrddin shifted in his seat, peering around the room. "Is Agravaine here?" He'd never met the man and wanted to see what he looked like.

"No," Cedric said, without looking around. He ate with small, dainty bites, as if he wasn't quite sure as to the safety or spicing of the food. "He'd sleep in a barn rather than stay at Rhuddlan."

"Why is that?" Myrddin said.

"The man's a ghost; flitting in and out among Modred's possessions, never stopping anywhere for more than a day if the castle belongs to someone other than himself. Agravaine trusts no one. Modred puts up with it because he wins battles and does as he's told. Half the time it seems he can see the future before it happens."

Myrddin didn't like the sound of that and would have inquired further, but Cedric was done with the subject, taking a sip of wine and then gesturing to the servant for more turnips. Myrddin went back to surveying the hall. Plenty of Welshmen were scattered among the diners—both men who'd sided with Modred from the first and recent defectors. Beyond Cedric's left shoulder, two monks whom Myrddin thought he recognized sat at a far table.

A quick inspection of their undyed robes and cloaks confirmed his suspicions: they were the brothers Llywelyn and Rhys, cousins to Gareth, and brothers to the Hywel who'd died at Penrhyn after the battle at the Straits. Brother Llywelyn was the prior of the monastery at Bangor, and Rhys was the friar of St. Deiniol, the cathedral church, also in Bangor.

As Hywel had explained, it was Llywelyn who'd talked his brothers into betraying King Arthur. Myrddin's disgust for him and that loathsome act hadn't abated in the intervening years. Perhaps feeling the intensity of Myrddin's stare, Llywelyn glanced up, caught Myrddin's eye, and glowered. Once Rhys noted Llywelyn's attention, he turned to look at him as well. Myrddin didn't glance away, but returned their glares. It was childish of him but he refused to back down.

"What are you looking at?" Cedric said, noting Myrddin's odd behavior. He twisted in his seat to glance behind him.

"I know those two monks over there." Myrddin pointed at them with his chin.

Cedric pursed his lips, turning back to his food. "I don't like traitors. Not even ones on my side."

"I suppose it's a matter of perspective," Myrddin said. "One man's traitor is another man's loyal subject."

"Edgar won't betray Lord Modred." Cedric spoke as if they'd had a conversation about Edgar already which had been interrupted, even though they hadn't. "If Modred keeps Agravaine on a tight leash, Agravaine keeps an even tighter one on Edgar. He will do nothing of his own accord."

"Would that be true for you as well?" Myrddin said.

Cedric pointed his knife at Myrddin. "Don't let King Arthur come south."

Myrddin canted his head to the side. "And leave your lands alone?"

Cedric chuckled deep in his throat, but then cut it off. "I'd prefer it."

"What would Modred think of your warning?"

Cedric gave Myrddin a hard look. "He's the one who allowed you to hear of the danger that awaits your King in Powys. Weren't you paying attention earlier? I've not said anything that he hasn't already made clear."

Myrddin shook his head at the complexity of it all. His visions were incomplete and by now, nearly useless. He'd accepted that he had to take action, but while the dreams told him that Arthur shouldn't come south to meet with Edgar, they didn't tell him what would need to happen instead. To have Cedric informing him of what he already knew—even though it hadn't yet happened—was disconcerting.

Cedric pushed away his plate, the food on it half-eaten. He was gathering himself to get to his feet when Modred strode into the room, trailed by the Archbishop. He, in turn, was flanked by

146

two more churchmen whom Myrddin didn't recognize, and said as much to Cedric.

"Bishop Anian of St. Asaph." Cedric rose to his feet as they always did in the presence of Modred. "The other is the Archdeacon of Anglesey."

Myrddin's heart sank into his boots, for he knew what was coming, just as King Arthur had predicted to his brother. At Modred's raised hand, the room quieted. Modred lifted his voice so that it carried to the far corners of the hall.

"I present to you Archbishop Dafydd. Listen well and take heed of his words."

The Archbishop stepped forward, a piece of paper in his shaking hands. Maybe it was because he suffered from palsy, even though he couldn't have been much older than Myrddin, but Myrddin was willing to believe he understood the significance of what he was about to do and half-regretted it. Myrddin briefly felt sorry for him. Dafydd spoke in Latin, and then again in Saxon so everyone in the room would understand:

> *Arthur ap Uther, along with his brother, Cai,*
> *notwithstanding the formal canonical warning of 17 June*
> *last and the repeated appeals to desist from their*
> *intentions, have performed a schismatical act of*
> *disobedience and have therefore incurred the penalty of*
> *excommunication latae sententiae. The priests and*
> *faithful are warned not to support the schism of Arthur*

and Cai, otherwise they shall incur ipso facto a similar punishment.

There it was. Arthur was a devout believer, and would care—fearing for his soul—but this pronouncement would change nothing. The churches in Gwynedd—as opposed to those Archbishop Dafydd oversaw in the south of Wales—would continue to administer to the faithful: marrying, baptizing, and seeing to their spiritual needs, in defiance of the injustice of this act.

"This will make it easier for those who are so inclined to betray King Arthur." Cedric sat down again as Modred left the hall and the priests found seats at the high table.

Myrddin shrugged. "Or the opposite. The excommunication of their leader at the behest of a despised usurper might only confirm the rightness of their choice in their eyes."

"Did you say 'despised usurper'?" Cedric said. "You are too bold."

"A man must live by his conscience," Myrddin said. "When men say that they speak for God, in pursuit of their own power, it calls their words into doubt."

Cedric's hard look was back. Myrddin thought better of further conversation, but even if he'd wanted to speak, he wasn't given a chance. Two men-at-arms appeared, one on either side of Myrddin, grasped him under the arms, and lifted him bodily over his bench. Before Myrddin had a chance to do more than sputter, they had him up against the wall, his back braced and his legs spread.

"What's this?" Cedric gestured with his knife. "We were eating."

The man on Myrddin's right spoke. "Our apologies, my lord. Lord Modred has given orders."

In those first minutes of his captivity, his face already bruised from the guard's fists, Myrddin had hoped he could withstand their treatment and not submit. It was clear fairly quickly, however, that they didn't want any information from him. Perhaps they beat prisoners—and King Arthur's men—as a matter of course.

Five hours later, Myrddin's body was stiff from the cold, his wrists and ankles chained, and he had an almighty headache. The one positive note was that the blood along Myrddin's upper lip had dried and was no longer dripping onto his clothing and the floor. He didn't want to attract those rats to his toes, which absent his boots, were too easily accessible. Myrddin wiggled them, trying to increase their circulation.

A light flickered through the small window in the wooden door that blocked the entrance to Myrddin's cell. Myrddin shifted, awkward, the shackles digging into his wrists. A rime of blood seeped around the metal band every time he moved, the edge cutting further into his skin. Then the door opened to reveal Modred himself and two guards, one of whom carried an upright, wooden chair. He set it in the middle of the cell. Modred turned it around and sat facing Myrddin, his arms resting along the top rail.

"So," he said. "Now that we both are situated more comfortably, perhaps you'll answer some of my questions."

It was a jest, but Myrddin wasn't laughing. "I answered truthfully before. I would have answered whatever other questions you chose to put to me in your hall."

"Perhaps." Modred flicked a crumb off his sleeve with one finger towards the rats in the corner. The rats scurried to where the crumb had fallen and after a brief scuffle, the dominant one ate it. Myrddin watched, horrified, thinking of how easily one could take a bite out of him. "But not as quickly or completely."

Myrddin moved his eyes back to Modred's face. "Why would I be any more likely to do as you ask now, since you're going to kill me anyway?"

"Ah," Modred said. "But the manner of your death remains a mystery. It is something to be negotiated."

Myrddin had known all along that Modred was a murderous son-of-a-bitch. What Welshman didn't know that? But, naïvely, Myrddin hadn't expected him to direct this level of villainy at him. Then again, this was the man who hanged a couple of hundred his own people so he could confiscate their possessions—and pay for his war against Arthur. There was nothing that wasn't beyond this man. Worse, Modred knew that Myrddin knew it.

When Myrddin didn't reply, Modred nodded at one of the guards, who fisted his hand and shot it into Myrddin's midsection. If Myrddin's bonds hadn't held him tightly, he would have gone down and stayed down. As it was, he couldn't even bend forward to better absorb the blow.

"Now," Modred said. "I want the truth. What happened at the Menai Straits?"

"I told you already." Myrddin said. "Cedric did too. It was just as he said."

The guard backhanded Myrddin across the face and his head clunked against the stones behind him. Blood formed at the corner of his mouth and dripped down his chin. Myrddin turned his head and hunched his shoulders, trying to staunch it on his shirt. He couldn't reach, however, and fell back, moaning more from frustration at his helplessness than the pain.

"I want the rest." Modred said. "There's more. What haven't you told me?"

Myrddin was at a loss, both for something else to give and for what Arthur would think was acceptable for him to say. Myrddin took a stab at a new piece of information. "We sabotaged the boats."

"Better," Modred said. "Whose idea was that?"

"Mine," Myrddin said.

Another blow to the kidneys.

"I want the traitor's name," Modred said.

Myrddin must have looked as blank as he felt because he received another shot to the face. "Traitor?" Myrddin said. "You mean Lord Cai?"

Modred's face purpled, revealing a passion that was likely to give him heart failure. In his youth, Modred had been Cai's squire. They'd remained close companions for many years afterwards, even after Modred began to assert his own claim to the throne over Cai's. Whatever bond had survived the years had been severed with Cai's latest actions. Perhaps in Modred—as in Cai—love and hatred were two sides of the same coin.

Modred and Myrddin stared at each other and slowly Modred's color subsided. He barked a laugh. "I'll give you that. He betrays both sides as it pleases him. No, I want the traitor in my ranks. The one who informed you that Wulfere would cross the Straits that day. I want to know why you were ready for him."

Myrddin opted for a shrug. "We knew. I don't know all the people who told us, but there were many sources. Wulfere was too open about his plans, at least on the Anglesey side. Not all the people there support the Saxon cause."

Another slap, which Myrddin should have known was coming for being cheeky.

"Names," Modred said.

"I have none to give you," Myrddin said. Before he could elaborate on that lack of knowledge, he received another thrust to his abdomen. The pain was intense. His ears still rang from the previous blow and his eyes no longer saw straight. A black mist rose across his vision. Myrddin fought it, blinking and struggling to stay conscious, even though the blackness would have been a relief. "A doxy. A fisherman. A ferryman. A nun. They all told us."

Modred eased backwards. Myrddin had a brief hope that he'd leave, but Modred got to his feet and came around the chair to stand in front of Myrddin.

"You can do better than that," he said.

Myrddin tried to focus on his face, but there appeared to be several of him now. "You have two noses." He found the idea amusing, but the words came out slurred and his eyes blurred from tears he couldn't stop from falling. They hadn't even left him the dignity of wiping at them with the back of his hand.

Modred snorted his disgust. "He's done. For now." He turned away, followed by the guards who pulled the door closed behind them and left the cell in darkness.

11

14 November 537 AD

"**Y**ou are well and truly out of your mind!" Ifan followed
Nell down the hall towards Lord Cedric of Brecon's quarters, a
stack of logs in his arms for stoking the fire in Cedric's room.

Nell glanced back at him, careful not to tip her tray of food
and drink. "Am I?" she said. "And what was your plan for getting
Myrddin out of prison? A straight assault?"

They'd arrived at Rhuddlan in time to see Myrddin hauled
away from Cedric's table—and the protest, albeit slight, that
engendered from Cedric—and then spent the rest of that night and
the next day mingling among the lowlier members of the castle.
They both spoke Saxon, Nell better than Ifan, but only Welsh had
been required so far, which had caused a slow boil in Nell's chest
she was working hard to contain. Her people had done far more to
betray Arthur than the Saxons ever could. Well, except for his
looming death at the hands of Edgar of Wigmore.

"Better than all this sneaking around," Ifan mumbled, not so low that she couldn't hear him.

At the same time, he hadn't protested more than that, and so far had not objected to her taking charge of this aspect of the endeavor. Clearly, she'd spent far too many years in the company of women and her confidence was out of place in a castle run by men. "You got us safely to Rhuddlan," she said. "Trust me to manage this."

Ifan had caught her coming out of her room back at Garth Celyn, dressed as a boy. At first, Ifan hadn't recognized her, which was all to the good as far as she was concerned. Then he'd grabbed her arm, hissing. "What are you doing?"

"Going after Myrddin," she said.

"Alone? Are you mad?" he said. "Myrddin told me what happened at St. Asaph; what he'd arrived almost too late to stop. You'd risk that again?"

"Better than staying here and allowing him to go into danger alone," Nell had said. "To die at Modred's hands. I don't—I don't have a good feeling about this."

That had brought Ifan up short. He'd looked at her, suspicious. Nell gazed back. Unfortunately, it was no less than the truth, although as always, not all of it. Myrddin went off on his own all the time; the difference today was her dream last night. Frighteningly, instead of dreaming as Myrddin as she always had, she'd watched the battle from above, looking down on the King's death. Myrddin wasn't even there. Nell's breath caught in her throat at what that might mean.

Even admitting that, she had to acknowledge that her visions of Arthur's death took her only so far. Sometimes she simply had a *feeling* that she should do something, or that something wasn't right—like she could sense the currents and emotions of the people around her and they all added up to a conclusion that she couldn't explain. She'd felt that way in the first moments of Wulfere's attack on her convent. To her regret, she *hadn't* felt it when she'd left her sisters alone in the barn. But she'd learned not to ignore her sense of wrongness when it came.

Ifan nodded. "Neither do I. But this is not a task for a woman. I'll go."

"No!" Nell had said. "You're not going anywhere without me."

"I'll tell the King—"

Nell cut Ifan off with a finger to his lips. "Don't you dare. Besides, I'm a free woman, with no husband or obligations to anyone but myself."

"Except to Myrddin?" Ifan had said.

"That is my choice," Nell said.

Ifan had stared into her face for a long moment, and then nodded. "I'll talk to Geraint."

So here they were, thirty miles from Garth Celyn, in the very belly of the Saxon beast. Nell raised a hand to knock at Cedric's door.

"Come in."

Nell pushed the door open and entered the room, followed by Ifan. The room was less rich than some she'd seen in the castle.

She'd flitted in and out of many over the last hours, always accompanied by Ifan and his logs. Nobody had to know that those were the same three pieces of wood he'd carried all day. They'd simply moved from room to room, purposeful and diligent, determining the lay of the land. Nobody ever questioned them or wondered at their actions. Far more than at Garth Celyn, servants here were invisible—even to other servants, provided she and Ifan kept their heads down. Rhuddlan was so huge that it was impossible for any one person to keep track of all the comings and goings.

"My lord," Nell said in Saxon, curtseying, "I've brought you a meal."

Cedric glanced up. "I didn't ask for—" He cut off the sentence when Nell met his gaze with a sharp look she couldn't help. It had been far sharper than he'd probably received from anyone since he was in his nurse's care. "I see," he said, after a quick scan of her face and clothes. "Put it there."

"My name is Nell ferch Morgan," Nell said, abandoning the pretense that she was a boy. She gestured to Ifan, "and this is Ifan, from Garth Celyn."

"You're Myrddin's rescue party, are you?" Cedric said, his mind discerning the truth faster than Nell could have hoped. "Are there more of you?"

"No." Nell paused. "Unless you're willing to help us?"

"Now why would I want to do that?"

Nell gazed at him, her expression calm while she thought furiously for an answer.

But it was Ifan who spoke. "Because you've got bigger *ceilliau* than Modred."

Cedric smiled.

* * * * *

"We're getting you out of here," Nell said.

Myrddin swam upwards towards the faint light in his cell, coming to himself with his arms around Nell and his head on her shoulder.

"You," he said, feeling marvelous all of a sudden.

Ifan crouched at Myrddin's feet, working at the chains that bound his ankles. Myrddin imagined they too were blood-rimmed, but his lower extremities were so numb from the cold and being forced to stay in one position for so long, he couldn't feel them.

A voice growled from behind Nell. "*I'm* getting you out of here."

Myrddin lifted his head to squint towards the form in the doorway.

Cedric lounged against the frame, his arms folded across his chest. "Hurry up," he said. "We haven't much time."

"Not like his lordship couldn't help," Ifan muttered in Welsh, under his breath.

"I grew up in Wales," Cedric said, his voice mild. "I learned Welsh in my nurse's arms."

Nell lifted a hand to Myrddin's face. With shaking fingers, she touched his eyebrow. "It's the only part of you that isn't wounded," she said, trying to jest, although her voice wavered.

At last Ifan fitted the key into the final lock and opened it. "We need to move."

"I'm fine." Myrddin took a step. "Let's get out of here."

Just because the manacles were loose, however, didn't mean he could walk. If Nell hadn't still been holding him, he would have fallen. Seeing Myrddin's peril, Ifan came up on his other side, his arm around Myrddin's waist. Together, they hobbled towards the door, Myrddin's feet tingling as the blood rushed into them. Myrddin feared for guards, but Cedric kept a smirk on his face, unconcerned about the treasonous act in which he was openly participating. He turned at their approach, led the way across the stones of the foyer where Myrddin had seen guards earlier, and up the stairs.

They came out of the stairwell into a larger room containing three soldiers, all unconscious. One sprawled across the table at which he'd been sitting at dice, while his companion's head lolled against the right hand wall. The third guard had fallen off his bench onto the floor. He lay on his side, legs splayed in front of him. Like the others, his eyes were closed.

"Drunk." Cedric strode past the table at which they sat, not looking at them but at the same time not even attempting to be quiet.

"The poppy juice I brought helped," Nell said.

159

Myrddin swiveled his head, searching for his weapons, but Ifan had taken care of the problem. "Your sword's right here." He patted his waist. "We recovered it first, in case we had to leave in a hurry. I left mine outside the castle with the horses."

"Thanks," Myrddin said, the sound coming out more as a grunt than a word.

A moment later, they were through the far doorway and into the outer bailey. The dungeon—or at least Myrddin's dungeon—was situated in the basement of the southwest, square, guard tower that overlooked the Clwyd River. The guardroom door sat at the base of the tower wall, effectively in a ditch, looking up to the inner wall, over two hundred feet away. If Modred had held Myrddin in one of the six towers that defended the inner bailey, he'd never have escaped.

Myrddin had known where Modred had put him, of course, and now that he was being rescued, it seemed more suspicious than lucky to be so far from the central workings of the castle. Then again, maybe Modred didn't like to disturb the castle inhabitants, including his beloved wife, with screaming. Cedric led them along the curtain wall that fronted the river to the river gate. The drawbridge was up, as it had been when Myrddin had arrived, but the postern door was unguarded. As Cedric drew it open, a moan sounded from further along the wall in the shadow of the tower.

"He sent him a whore." Nell whispered to Myrddin as she and Ifan dragged Myrddin through the opening.

160

Cedric didn't come with them. "I leave you here." He halted in the doorway. "You may retrieve your horse at Brecon Castle, my home, should you care to do so."

Myrddin pulled his right arm over Nell's head and held it out to Cedric. "Thank you."

Cedric grasped Myrddin's forearm, nodded stiffly, and shut the door in Myrddin's face. He'd gone before Myrddin realized he'd never responded to Arthur's message.

But then, on second thought, perhaps he had.

Nell, Ifan, and Myrddin staggered down the sharp bank that descended from the postern gate to the river. They could have crossed at a low spot half a mile upstream, but it wouldn't do to walk under the walls and expose themselves on the castle side of the Clywd, even at this hour of the night. The sooner they left the vicinity of Rhuddlan the better.

"Can you swim?" Nell said.

"He's a fish when his arms work," Ifan said.

"I'm here," Myrddin said. "I can speak."

"In," Nell said.

Obediently, Myrddin plunged into the water and struck out for the opposite bank. At worst, if he couldn't have made it, he could have let the current carry him north to the ford that he'd ridden across on Cadfarch. Determined to succeed and not put Ifan or Nell into any further danger, Myrddin forced himself to stroke and kick long enough to reach the muddy bank. He crawled up it, bedraggled and soaking wet, although the cold water made his wounds feel a bit better. Myrddin could even sense his feet and for the first time was happy not to have worn boots. Nell and Ifan had kept theirs on and would have to stop once they were clear of the castle to empty them of water.

"How far?" Myrddin said, once they'd clawed their way out of the brush, onto the road, and then across it into the ditch on the other side.

"We left the horses close by." Nell grasped Myrddin's arm and lifted him out of the scrub. "You can make it."

"I'm not sure that I can do anything anymore without you." The words were out before he could censor them. Nell had her head up, watching the road, and didn't respond, for which Myrddin was grateful. Perhaps she hadn't heard him.

'Close by' wasn't quite as close as he'd hoped. Another twenty minutes passed, Myrddin hobbling on tender feet, before they reached the copse of beech trees in which Ifan had tied the horses. They'd only brought two, so once again, Nell and Myrddin would share. Ifan passed Myrddin his water flask but Myrddin's hands were so cold and he was so tired, he couldn't remove the stopper. Nell pulled it out, but even then, his hands shook so much that the water spilled out the top. In the end, Nell placed both of her hands on either side of his and helped Myrddin tip it up. Then she had to help him out of his wet clothes and into loose breeches and shirt.

"From Caerhun again?" he said as she fastened the cloak around his neck.

"Rhodri laughed when I asked for them," she said, "but gave way. It was better to be safe than sorry."

Finally, when they were all dressed, Myrddin had to face the notion of climbing on the horse. The saddle looked miles away.

"Come on, lad," Ifan said.

Myrddin rested a hand on Nell's shoulder while Ifan steadied him. With his foot in a stirrup, they shoved Myrddin hard upwards, shooting him towards the saddle. He sprawled across the horse's withers, exhausted. With some more pushing from Ifan, Myrddin managed to swing his leg over the horse's back and straighten. His forearm was one of the few limbs that didn't hurt, so Myrddin offered it to Nell. She grasped it, clambering into place behind him.

Every bone, muscle, and nerve in Myrddin's body screamed at him. The only reason he was even upright was because Nell held him on the horse. It had been a long time since he'd felt this terrible. If it wouldn't end up hurting him more, Myrddin would have rubbed his face to hide the tears—of pain and the frustration that he couldn't control—that threatened to spill from his eyes.

Myrddin swallowed hard. "Talk," he said, once they urged the horses out of the brush and had given them their heads.

"We followed you," Ifan said, giving Myrddin a chance to gather his wits. "I got permission from Lord Geraint—more or less—and we were gone within an hour of your own departure. As we knew where you were going, we hardly needed to trail you closely."

"Where'd you get the boys' clothes?" Myrddin asked Nell.

"From a stable boy," she said. "He'd outgrown them and his mother'd been saving them for his younger brother."

"And then?" Myrddin said, when neither wanted to continue.

"We followed you all the way here." Ifan shrugged.

"There was a chance you'd rest with the garrison at Caerhun," Nell said, "but Rhodri said they hadn't seen you."

"Or rather," Ifan added, "they'd seen you but you'd crossed the ford instead of turning in at the fort."

"Because we took time at Caerhun and had to hide the horses, we reached Rhuddlan a few hours behind you. It was full dark, but the villagers were still up and about."

"We entered the castle in the back of a hay wagon," Ifan said.

The tag-team story telling was giving Myrddin a headache, but they were in full spate and Myrddin chose not to stop them. "Go on."

"Hundreds of people work in that castle," Ifan said. "As I left my weapons and armor with the horses on the other side of the Clywd, it was a simple matter to pretend to be other than what we are."

"What I want to know, more than anything, is about Cedric," Myrddin said. "How did you convince him to free me?"

"That was my idea," Nell said. "We dined in the hall at the same time you did—after you'd met with Modred. To our eyes, Cedric didn't object to your company; although we didn't know how you'd met, it seemed fortuitous, given the discussion you and I had at Garth Celyn."

"So when the guards hauled you away," Ifan said, "and Cedric protested, albeit not loudly and not to Modred, we decided to take a chance on him."

"What did you do? Walk up to him and say, 'Greetings. We're with Myrddin. Will you help us free him from the dungeon?'"

Ifan laughed from deep in his chest. "Yes. If I'm ever in a tight place, I'd prefer to have Nell with me. She was as bold as Queen Gwenhwyfar herself."

"He deliberated only briefly before he agreed to help you escape," Nell said. "We watched for Modred to come to you again, but he didn't. He went to his bed and then we acted."

"Thank you for freeing me." Myrddin realized he hadn't yet said it. "It was quite a chance you took."

"I hope Cedric doesn't suffer for it," Nell said, "once Modred realizes you're gone."

The crisp air, along with their story, had perked Myrddin up considerably, even as his muscles stiffened from the cold. "He's Cedric ap Aelfric," Myrddin said. "He gave the guards wine and women, and if they remember what passed in the night, it will be a miracle. When Cedric tells Modred that he had nothing to do with my escape, if it even comes to that, it will be good enough for Modred."

"Cedric said he wouldn't leave Rhuddlan until the guards discovered your absence," Ifan said, "after which he and his men would travel south to Brecon." He paused, thinking. "I'm missing something, aren't I?"

"As in, the why of it?" Myrddin said. "Why did he risk his own neck to free me?" The sight of Cedric in the doorway was fresh in Myrddin's mind and he felt a weight lifting from his shoulders. "He is willing to consider an alliance with King Arthur."

"He said that?" Nell said.

"He showed it," Myrddin said.

12

15 November 537 AD

"Can you hear me, Myrddin?" Nell leaned over Myrddin's inert form.

Although Myrddin didn't reply, he did open his eyes to look into her face. The room was dark, except for a candle on the table at the foot of the pallet on which he lay. Nell smiled, even though it cost her. Myrddin didn't smile back, just stared, unseeing, and then let his eyes close. Nell stroked his cheek with one finger. And then she did smile, albeit mockingly, at what he'd think when he discovered that she'd shaved his mustache in order to tend to the gash above his lip.

It had been a long, grim ride from Rhuddlan Castle. Myrddin had been so much weaker than usual and the last few miles had almost been his undoing. It had been all she could do to hold him on the horse. Modred's men had wounded him inside and out, though she wouldn't know how bad the damage was inside him until the rest of him began to heal.

"Would you like to hear a story?" she said.

Again, Myrddin didn't answer. He'd squeezed the hand she was holding earlier, but now his grip softened. She gazed down at his closed eyes, thinking of what story to tell, and whether it was time to tell him a true one. "Once upon a time, there was a little girl . . .

She was just like any other little girl—shocking red hair, green eyes, pointed chin—doted upon by her father, especially as he'd lost his wife at her birth.

One day, as she was wandering in the trees along the river near her home, looking for any winter herbs that had survived the snow, she heard voices—men's voices—very close. They shouted at one another. Hooves pounded on the soft earth and then not ten feet from her, a company of five men wearing King Arthur's crest rode out of the woods, swords and shields raised high. They splashed through the water and up the bank on the other side.

The girl was frightened. She ran the opposite way, but instead of running into her father's field as she expected, she found herself in a clearing, next to a church. All around her men called and horses neighed. She ran for the entrance to the church, but just as she reached it, the door opened. A man appeared, older than her father,

*his dark hair shot with grey. She'd never seen him before,
but somehow she knew he was their king. He pulled his
sword from his sheath, shouted at the men behind him,
and retreated back inside.*

*Oddly, the man didn't see her. A moment later, the
men who'd ridden through the water returned, racing
their horses towards a line of Saxon soldiers that had
burst from the woods on the other side of the clearing. All
around her men fought and died.*

*Then, one man in particular caught her attention.
He'd lost his helmet and his black hair had come loose.
His shield was gone too and between forcing his sword
through a Saxon's belly and turning to race for the front
of the church, he thrust his hair out of his face with his free
hand.*

*In that space of time, she caught his eye. They
stared at each other. They couldn't have been more
different: her, small, scrawny, not yet blooming into
womanhood; and him, a tall, dark-haired soldier, older,
with lines around his eyes.*

*Then he broke away, racing to defend his King.
She watched him barrel into a Saxon soldier; she watched
him fall. She watched the Saxon soldiers celebrate their
victory. And it was she who pulled the man to the side, off
of the body of his King whose head the Saxons soldiers
had taken while they left the rest of him to rot. And it was
she who wept over his grave . . .*

169

* * * * *

"So now you've saved *me*," Myrddin said. From the way the light reflected from the hallway through the open door, it was late afternoon. He'd slept a long time.

"Does that make us even?" Nell said.

"Do you want it to?"

She smiled and didn't answer, looking down at her hands. She'd tucked her hair into her cloak, but the end of her thick braid peeked from underneath the hood. Then she looked up. "It hurts me to see you this way."

"It hurts me too," he said, trying to make light of it.

"I wish we could have gotten to you sooner."

"I'll heal," he said.

"Hidden away in my convent, I forgot the horror one man could do to another," she said. "I've been reminded almost daily since then."

"Believe me, Modred is capable of much worse."

Nell nodded. "I stitched the back of your head while you were asleep. I kept waiting for you to wake in the middle of it and argue with me about the proper method." She smiled, and then added, "I would have had Ifan cosh you to put you back to sleep."

Myrddin laughed and then tried to suppress it, moving his hand to his chest. "Don't!" He swallowed the mirth and the pain the laughter had caused. "Where's Ifan now?"

"He stayed up with you most of the night," she said. "Did you know *he's* in pain nearly all the time?"

"It's his back," Myrddin said. "He injured it ten years ago—doing less than nothing, mind you—and it's never been the same since. But a soldier who can't ride and fight isn't a soldier anymore."

"I told him I'd make a rubbing salve for him when we returned to Garth Celyn." She turned her head to look through the doorway. The scent of greenery and outside air wafted through it, indicating that the temperature had risen. "It's peaceful here, isn't it? I didn't notice the first time we came through."

"We're at Caerhun?" Myrddin said.

Nell nodded. "That was the longest twenty miles I've ever ridden."

Footsteps sounded along the corridor. "You're awake." Rhodri poked his head through the doorway.

"In a manner of speaking," Myrddin said. "Thank you for your hospitality, as before."

"I thought you'd like to know that the Saxons patrol the eastern bank of the river. Three separate companies have ridden to the ford, to turn around at the water's edge. I would not have said you were that valuable." A grin split Rhodri's face.

"Nor I," Myrddin said.

Rhodri shrugged. "Let me know if you need anything, miss," he said to Nell.

"Thank you."

Rhodri left.

Myrddin gazed up at the ceiling, thinking about the past and the future and all that lay between them. He didn't fear death. He hadn't for many years, not with living it every night in his dreams. But despair was as close a companion for him over the years as for Nell, and it had overwhelmed him after Modred had left the dungeon. To have come so close to making a difference in whether Arthur lived or died, only to die at Modred's hand, had left him bereft. Now that they'd fled the castle and were safe in Arthur's lands again, the emotions he'd been holding in check came flooding back.

"I should have guessed that you were up to something," Myrddin said. "When I turned to look back at the castle and saw you and Ifan on the battlements . . . I should have been suspicious. Had you already decided what you were going to do?"

"I'd already decided to come after you," she said. "But Ifan wouldn't let me come alone."

"I should hope not," Myrddin said. "Were you afraid?"

"Not during the journey; not even when we reached the crossroads at St. Asaph. Ifan is a strong swordsman or you wouldn't trust him. I was afraid for you; that Modred had already murdered you before we reached Rhuddlan."

"I was afraid of that too," Myrddin said.

"The only comfort," Nell said, "was the assumption that you knew what you were doing."

Myrddin started to laugh and then swallowed it, trying not to move. "I'm not so sure you should have relied on that notion."

Nell smiled. "Once Cedric said he'd assist us, however, things moved quickly and I hardly had time to think. He had it all in hand."

"Thank you," Myrddin said. "I don't know that Cedric would have freed me unless you encouraged him."

"I'm not so sure," Nell said. "It would depend on how much he thought he could gain from sticking his neck out."

"He stuck it pretty far," Myrddin said.

"He did," Nell said. "What did you say to him to make the two of you so friendly?"

"I told him that Arthur wanted to negotiate—to talk to him—even to work out an alliance."

Myrddin had closed his eyes again, as keeping them open was just too much work, but at Nell's silence, turned his head to look at her. A range of emotions crossed her face: shock, disbelief, puzzlement, and then understanding.

"Given that the King has never said any such thing, you took a risk," she said. "Suppose King Arthur doesn't want to talk to him?"

"Why wouldn't he?" Myrddin said. "The King is willing to talk to Edgar, and he's far less likely a turncoat than Cedric. Cedric, at least, has a history of rebellion. Edgar is the son of the only Saxon lord with interests in Wales never to waver in Modred's cause, for all Modred has angered him now."

"What are you going to tell King Arthur?" she said.

"The truth," Myrddin said. "Even your part of it—provided you do not object?" He studied her face. She had a smudge on her nose and a second along one cheek.

Nell lifted her hands and dropped them in an expression of resignation and helplessness. "Ifan and I made our choice. I don't regret it. Given that we rescued you, I'd hope King Arthur wouldn't either."

Myrddin nodded. "I'm glad you've told me everything now," he said. "I'm glad you know that you can trust me."

Nell sat silent for a long count of ten. "You weren't asleep."

"No."

Nell stayed frozen, her legs in front of her and her back against the wall.

"You have visions," Myrddin said, not as a question. "You've had them of me."

Nell swallowed hard. "Since I was a girl."

"Back at Garth Celyn you cried my name in the night. You've done so often in the nights that followed."

"You've haunted me all my life," she said. "The story I told you was a waking dream—my first and only. It's why I've always known that you were real, even when all I had were dreams."

Myrddin nodded.

"You're not upset by this," Nell said, now canting her head to one side and looking at him curiously. "Why aren't you afraid of me? Or at the very least, suspicious?"

"On December 11th, a month from now, if we do not stop it, King Arthur will die at the hands of a Saxon soldier, near a church by the Cam River," Myrddin said.

"That's what I see in my dreams," Nell said. "I just told you that story last night. That's what I dream nearly every night now. It's changed a bit in the last few days. But—"

Myrddin interrupted. "That's *my* dream, ever since I was twelve years old."

The relief he felt in admitting it to Nell—and that she would understand everything he felt—filled him. His was a true seeing and they'd been given this vision for a reason. It appeared to be *their* job—his and Nell's—by what means he didn't know and couldn't imagine from where he lay—to ensure that his King did not meet Edgar by the Cam. He met Nell's eyes as understanding entered them: *their* vision; *their* task; *their* destiny.

Nell stared at him. "It's not just me, then!"

Myrddin shook his head. "It's not just you."

13

16 November 537 AD

Myrddin slept again, woke in the early evening, and then slept in fits and starts throughout a second night at Caerhun. Every time he tried to roll over, he awoke in pain, but either Ifan or Nell was there to ease him into a more comfortable position. Ifan had a soldier's ability to watch or sleep in whatever situation he found himself, but the times Nell sat beside him, she talked. Some of what she said Myrddin remembered, but mostly he let the sound of her voice wash over him as she related a story from her girlhood, or another from the tales of the *Dôn*. She didn't speak of the dreams again, but then, Myrddin knew that story too well himself.

At dawn, Myrddin came to himself enough to realize that he couldn't delay any longer and neither Nell nor Ifan protested that they should stay. They knew as well as he that King Arthur awaited word of Myrddin's journey. Soon, the King would begin to fear that Myrddin would never return. Most importantly, Myrddin had information for him and Myrddin didn't want him doing anything rash because of lack of knowledge.

In the pouring rain, which was a match to the companions' low mood, they made their slow way out of Caerhun. By late afternoon, they had reached the last stretch, descending down the road from the standing stones to Garth Celyn; the men-at-arms on the battlements saw them coming and opened the gates, welcoming them home. In the muddy bailey, Nell slid off the horse. Myrddin climbed down with Ifan's help, his body stiff and a hand at his ribs. Even though they'd walked the horses the whole way, Myrddin could barely move from the effort the journey had cost him. Most of the day was gone, as slow as they'd taken it.

"Your face looks much worse." It came out as a matter-of-fact comment as Nell steered him towards the hall. "I have something inside to help with the bruising."

"It's my ribs that ache the most," Myrddin said. "I'm glad Modred's lackeys didn't puncture a lung."

"From my examination, all your bones are whole," she said. "Not to diminish the pain, but I felt you all over when you were unconscious and you're only bruised."

"*Only*," Myrddin said.

Nell tsked through her teeth. "Infant."

They'd taken one step up the stairs to the double doors that guarded the hall when one of the doors opened to reveal King Arthur. Nell and Myrddin froze, their heads tipped up, looking into his face. He pursed his lips; then took two steps down to where they stood. Without saying anything, either admonishment or praise, he placed Myrddin's arm over his shoulder. Taking most of the weight off Nell, he hobbled with Myrddin into the hall, across it, and down the corridor.

"I need to rest." Myrddin's breath came in gasps.

"In here." Arthur maneuvered him through the door to his receiving room and onto his own padded chair. He motioned to Nell to shut the door behind them. "Better to talk in private."

The room contained two more men: Bedwyr, as always, since he never left Arthur's side while he was at Garth Celyn except to sleep, and a much younger man standing with him, a youth, no more than sixteen or seventeen, albeit full grown—tall and well built—with shoulders used to wearing armor. Arthur straightened as Myrddin collapsed into the chair and Nell put a hand to his upper arm to keep him from falling out of it.

Not giving Myrddin a chance to catch his breath, Arthur held out a hand to the boy, who took a step closer. "Myrddin," Arthur said.

Myrddin looked up. Arthur's tone had been abrupt, but now an uncharacteristic smile—one Myrddin might even call gleeful—covered his face.

"Meet Huw ap Myrddin. Your son."

The boy looked straight at Myrddin, staring with an unrelieved intensity, and gave Myrddin a slight and very stiff bow. "Father."

"Wha—" Myrddin gaped at the boy, his head empty of any thought with which to work. "Who?"

"Huw ap Myrddin," the boy said. His spine matched his words, taut, like a bow string set to loose its arrow.

Myrddin's eyes ranged from the top of the boy's head to his boots, stunned speechless.

"My mother was Tegwan. From Brecon," Huw said, still quivering.

Tegwan. Dear God. He stared at the boy, this unexpected gift, and managed a nod. He remembered her—if the vague image of shape and form could be called a memory. Then Myrddin caught Huw's choice of words. "Was?" he said. "She *was* called Tegwan?"

"My mother died two months ago," Huw said. "I've been looking for you ever since."

"I do remember her," Myrddin said, not exactly lying.

Huw released a long breath and his shoulders sagged.

It was as if Myrddin had passed a test he hadn't known he was taking. If he'd had the strength to pace, he would have, but as it was, Myrddin shifted in his chair, hot and uncomfortable. "She never told me about you. I would have acknowledged you as my son had I known you existed. Surely Tegwan knew that?"

"My mother married someone else," Huw said. Then he paused, swallowed hard, and continued. "A Saxon. He knew I wasn't his son because she was already pregnant by the time they married, but he preferred to say I was his. I grew up thinking that he was my natural father. They had no other children and when my father died two years ago, my mother told me the truth."

Myrddin waited for more. He could hardly accuse Huw of neglecting to search for him sooner, given that Huw knew nothing of Myrddin or where he was. And he'd been raised half-Saxon. That wasn't easily put aside.

"My mother was ill herself by then, a wasting disease, and I couldn't leave her beyond my regular duties to my lord," Huw said. "I came north to Gwynedd as soon as he gave me leave to find you."

"And who is your lord?" Myrddin said.

Huw bit his lip and glanced at Arthur, who nodded. Huw hemmed and hawed for another few seconds, and then blurted it out. "Lord Cedric of Brecon."

"Ho!" Nell said from beside Myrddin. "Well, that's a tangle, isn't it?"

"Did you tell him my name?" Myrddin said. "And that I served King Arthur?"

"Of course," Huw said. "For what it was worth, as you go only by your first name. My lord Cedric had less need of me during these few weeks of the Archbishop's truce. He didn't want me to come with him to Anglesey so he gave me permission to search for you."

And to act as his spy in the Welsh camp? The though rose unbidden, but once admitted, couldn't be ignored. Myrddin looked at the King. "It was Cedric, with Nell and Ifan's assistance, who freed me from the Rhuddlan dungeon."

"Did he now?" Arthur scanned Myrddin's wounded body. It was impossible to hide the damage to his face or the awkward and uncomfortable way in which he was sitting. Every square inch of him, hurt, except perhaps his eyebrow, as Nell had noted.

Huw, too, perked up at the mention of his patron's name. "My lord freed you?" he said. "But who did this?" Uncertainty entered his eyes for the first time. "Surely not Modred!"

"Surely it was Modred," Myrddin said. "Or rather, Modred's guards on his behalf."

"Tell me that Lord Cedric wasn't present at the time!"

"He was not," Myrddin said. "I spoke with him at length earlier in the evening. We were dining together when the guards took me away."

"I have always found Lord Cedric to be fair and honorable," Huw said.

"We know." Myrddin flapped a hand in his direction and managing not to laugh at him openly. "Stand down."

Arthur turned to Nell. "Perhaps you could find our young man some food and drink."

"Yes, my lord." Nell straightened and released Myrddin's hand, which she'd been holding tightly. Myrddin nodded at Huw and hoped that Nell understood that it was not she who was being dismissed, but Huw.

The boy came forward. As he reached Myrddin's chair, Myrddin held out a hand to stop him. "Wait." With one hand on the table in front of him for support, he got to his feet so he could stand face to face with his son. They possessed similar coloring and were of a height, although Huw was perhaps a half inch taller. The boy had Myrddin's straight nose but his mother's blue eyes, where Myrddin's were hazel. Myrddin settled a hand on each of Huw's shoulders and gripped them. "I'm glad you came to find me," he said. "Any man would be proud to claim you as his son."

Huw held Myrddin's arms, his fingers tight around his biceps. "Thank you, sir." He still carried himself with a tenseness that kept his shoulders back and his jaw firm, but some of the anxiety seemed to have left him.

"Nell is a good friend," Myrddin said. "She'll take care of you."

"Yes, Father." With a last, direct look, Huw left the room with Nell.

Myrddin sank back into his seat, his head in his hands. King Arthur, having lost his usual chair to Myrddin, perched on the edge of the desk. Bedwyr found a seat on the bench under the window.

"I'd be delighted to know what's going on," Arthur said.

Myrddin looked up. "Damned if I know, my lord. Huw. . ." Myrddin made a helpless gesture towards the door. "I didn't know."

Bedwyr spoke from his corner. "Didn't your mother neglect to divulge the identity of *your* father before she died?"

"Yes," Myrddin said. "At least Tegwan gave the boy my name and encouraged him to find me, once her husband was dead."

"What was your mother's name again?" Bedwyr said.

Myrddin glanced at him, not sure why he wanted to know. "I don't know that I've ever told you," he said. "Her name was Seren ferch Gruffydd."

"An unusual name, Seren," Bedwyr said.

"Did you know her?" Myrddin checked Bedwyr's face again, which he was always careful to keep blank. Lord Cedric could take lessons from him.

"I never met her," Bedwyr said.

Myrddin nodded and clutched at his hair. Arthur had risen from the table while Bedwyr and Myrddin talked, and now moved to stand at the window, looking out at the flickering lights of the torches in the bailey, his hands clasped behind his back. "I did."

Myrddin's jaw dropped.

"Her father was an ally of mine until he defected to King Icel of Mercia the year before my uncle died. His action left his daughter alone, here at Garth Celyn, as one of my Aunt Juliana's ladies."

Towards the end of the 490's, King Icel of Mercia had appeared unstoppable. He'd wooed many a Welsh lord away from Ambrosius with promises of land and power, were he to conquer Wales once and for all. Instead, King Ambrosius and Arthur had defeated the allied Saxon forces in the summer of 500 AD at Mt. Badon. Unfortunately, Ambrosius had died in February of 501, followed six months later by Arthur's father, Uther. This left a gap in authority, filled instantly—if inadequately—by Arthur himself, then aged twenty-one.

Myrddin had been born into Madoc's household in September of 501—into a year of upheaval and strife. Each of the remaining Welsh lords, along with all of the Saxon barons, saw themselves as possible heirs to Ambrosius' throne. They'd fought among themselves for control of Wales. Though it was Arthur, of course, who triumphed. It was to avoid that horror again that many Welsh lords supported Modred now, preferring an orderly transition to possible war.

"I didn't know that," Myrddin said. "I thought my mother had grown up in Madoc's charge."

"No."

"But—"

"Speak to me of Cedric," Arthur said.

Myrddin blinked, not wanting to leave the subject of his mother, but unable to disobey. "I don't know if you're going to like what I have to say, my lord. I took some liberties . . ."

"And paid for them, by the looks." Bedwyr's lips curved into a smile.

Myrddin coughed and laughed at the same time. "You could say that. Although as I told you before, these wounds were courtesy of Modred." Myrddin took a deep breath, his abdomen aching at the effort. "After I gave Modred your letter, he directed me to bring Lord Cedric of Brecon to him. Thus, Cedric and I had a few moments of privacy in his room. I took the opportunity to suggest that you, my lord, would be open to a discussion of the disposition of various lands in Wales, if Cedric reconsidered his allegiance."

King Arthur swung around to stare at Myrddin.

"I apologize, my lord," Myrddin said. "It seemed like a good idea at the time, and the odds of him agreeing, or of anything coming of it at all, seemed worth the slight risk to my neck."

"It was obviously worth far more than that to Cedric," Bedwyr said. "And the fact that he had already heard your name from Huw sheds new light on the entire matter."

"It does," Myrddin said, although he was having a hard time figuring out what exactly it told him. He was feeling more and more wobbly and desperately wanted a drink, a bed, and Nell's gentle hand on his forehead, not necessarily in that order. "One more thing. Modred knows that you've sent Lord Gawain to Powys to marshal men against the Saxon lords there. Worse, Cedric told him of Edgar of Wigmore's letter to you. I don't know how he knew of it, except if Edgar himself told him."

The two men observed Myrddin, unspeaking, too well-practiced at absorbing bad news to show it openly, but clearly nonplussed. Bedwyr put down his cup of wine and leaned forward. "Go on."

"They are convinced, both of them, that Edgar is not sincere in his desire to ally with you and intends to lure you into an ambush, my lord King," Myrddin said, and then ventured to assert his own opinion. "I would think that likely."

"Thank you, Myrddin," Bedwyr said, implying he wasn't at all thankful for his advice, and then continued, half under his breath to the King—"The uncertainty in the air reminds me of the days after your uncle and father died, before you fully grasped the reins of Wales, my lord."

"Go to your son," Arthur said, his expression softening at Myrddin's evident distress. He nodded his head towards the door. "I don't want to see you in the hall tomorrow."

"And watch Huw closely," Bedwyr said.

Myrddin looked up, dismayed at the warning in Bedwyr's tone—and yet understanding it, for he'd had the same uncomfortable thought.

"He is Cedric's man," Bedwyr said. "He's already seen too much. I would be wary of allowing him to return to Brecon."

"Yes, sir," Myrddin said, not liking his observation but knowing he was right. He also didn't want the presence of his son to jeopardize Arthur's new found trust in Myrddin himself.

Still, Myrddin didn't move. His head felt like it weighed fifty pounds. Before he knew it, Arthur and Bedwyr were on either side of him. They pulled him up, just as the guards had done in the hall at Rhuddlan, but more gently, and half-dragged, half-carried him down the hall, out the door and across the courtyard to the sleeping quarters in the guest house. The small closet space in which Nell and Myrddin had slept before was vacant. The pallets lay on the floor, beckoning Myrddin with their softness and warmth. He reached an arm towards one. Bedwyr and Arthur laid him down.

"I'll find Nell," Bedwyr said.

It seemed Myrddin nodded agreement, but he couldn't be sure because a second later, he was asleep.

14

17 November 537 AD

"*Myrddin, damn it, get over here!*"

"*Coming, sir!*" *I hurried towards Gawain, my boots slipping in the snow, and we met in the center of the clearing by the church. In the growing darkness, the temperature had dropped and snowflakes had begun to drift down from the sky, filling in our footprints. I would have been happier to have had four more eyes in order to see in all directions. The Saxons were coming. I sure as hell wanted to be ready when they did.*

"*The King is inside, waiting, but I'm impatient with Edgar. I expected him here by now," Gawain said. "I think we need to leave this place.*"

"*Yes, sir," I said. "I'll tell King Arthur.*"

I strode towards the door to the church, glad that Gawain had decided to follow his instincts. I reached the

*bottom step and was just beginning to mount the stairs
when the world blew apart. An arrow whipped by my left
ear. I ducked and spun around, my sword in my hand.
"The King! The King!" . . .*

The first time Myrddin woke, Huw sat beside his pallet. A
low candle guttered in a dish on the floor, the light flickering and
reflecting off the walls of the room. Someone—Nell, perhaps—had
removed his boots and covered him with a wool blanket or three;
Myrddin was warm enough, even if his nose was cold since the
room was one of the few in the manor house without a fireplace.
He rolled onto his back, noting that someone had also taken his
cloak. He spared a thought for his armor, left behind at Rhuddlan,
and reconciled himself to the knowledge that it was gone forever.
He trusted that Arthur would see him properly protected when it
came to it again.

Pushing aside the changing dream and what it meant,
Myrddin turned his head to study his son. Huw sat upright
against the wall, his eyes closed. At Myrddin's movement, Huw
opened them.

"Hello, Father." He didn't appear to mind saying it;
Myrddin certainly wouldn't ever grow tired of hearing it. He still
couldn't believe that Huw could be his.

"What is the hour?" Myrddin said.

"The chapel rang Matins not long ago," Huw said. "Your
friend, Nell, said she'd relieve me at Lauds."

"You don't have to stay," Myrddin said.

Huw shrugged. "After the events of the day, I doubt I could sleep anyway." He smiled. "It's an honor to watch over you."

His obvious admiration—a sharp contrast to his earlier near-hostility—confused Myrddin, until he considered a possible source. "Someone's been talking."

"You have many friends," Huw said. "Ifan, certainly, but Lord Geraint joined us for the evening meal. They spoke of you at length."

"Do *not* believe everything they say."

Huw laughed. "Ifan said you'd say that."

"He was there when your mother and I met. Did he speak of it?" Myrddin said.

"Only that you were a squire in King Arthur's company. You came to Brecon in the fall of 520," Huw said. "But I knew that already from my mother."

"I was nineteen," Myrddin said. "Older than you, but in no way ready to be a father." He looked at Huw. "Your mother must have known it."

"I believe she did," he said. "Else, why keep you a secret? It's not as if you ever came looking for her again."

Christ. What do I say to that? "I did love her," Myrddin said. "I was careless with my heart and hers."

"And that's your excuse?" Huw's voice rose and the admiration of a moment ago was forgotten in favor of long-suppressed resentment.

"Is that why you came to find me?" Myrddin said. "To accuse me of abandoning your mother? Of abandoning you?"

Huw looked down at his hands, clenched in his lap so tight his knuckles whitened. Then he relaxed them, smoothing the palms on the fabric of his breeches. "Yes. My anger just now caught me unawares, but I've felt it ever since my mother told me the truth."

"I served my King," Myrddin said. "I was with your mother in the fall and winter but even with the upheaval in Brecon the following year, King Arthur never called me south of Buellt again. It's my fault that I never asked leave to go." He paused, hesitating. The real truth shamed him; yet, at this late date, it was a truth from which he should not hide and which his son deserved. "And I'd not asked to go because I was afraid to see your mother—I was afraid that she would ask for a commitment from me which I felt unable to give."

"Did you ever think of her?" Huw's voice didn't reveal anger now so much as pain.

"I was a coward, Huw," Myrddin said. "The longer I waited to see her, the worse the guilt. And after a year or two, I told myself that your mother would have forgotten me; that it was better for both of us if I didn't return." Huw didn't answer straight away and then Myrddin added, his voice as gentle as he could make it, "For all that our acquaintance was short, your mother and I enjoyed each other's company."

"My mother said as much to me," Huw said.

"But she still never wanted you to know about me."

Huw shifted, discomfited. Myrddin sensed he'd only added to his questions. "My father's family has served Lord Cedric for many years. My . . ." He licked his lips, " . . . father was a knight to his grandfather." He paused, and glanced at Myrddin, a rueful smile on his face.

"Go on," Myrddin said. "I know the history."

"After Badon, Lord Cedric's family lost Brecon to King Arthur, but not their interest in it. My step-father was often in the area," Huw said. "He'd had his eye on my mother for some time. She was with you, and then she was with him. She wouldn't tell me more than that."

Myrddin sighed, not even remembering the nineteen-year-old he'd been. It was so long ago, he had to wade through misty memory to catch a glimpse of those long ago battles. All Myrddin truly remembered of Tegwan was the hint of a laugh when he touched her, and his own eagerness.

"I was a fool to let her go," Myrddin said, noting the sturdy lankiness of his son and knowing how different all their lives would have been if he'd had as much courage in his personal life as on the battlefield.

"I loved my father—my mother's husband," Huw said. "But I've always been half-Welsh." He turned his head to look at Myrddin, his face intent. "I have resented you, it's true, but it is my hope that I will no longer have to be torn in two."

Myrddin had been a father to Huw for half a day and already he needed counseling. Myrddin didn't know that he was the right one to give it, but as he was the only one available, he had no choice. "Help me sit up."

Huw grasped Myrddin's hand and hauled him to a sitting position. Myrddin swung his legs over the edge of the pallet so he could rest next to Huw, their backs to the wall. Myrddin reached for the water cup and took a long drink.

"The world is not divided as simply as the lines between countries make us think," Myrddin said, setting down the cup. "You are full Welsh, by blood, but you were raised by an Saxon."

"Yes," Huw said.

"A man who loved you," Myrddin said.

"Yes." Huw paused and Myrddin let him say what he was feeling, not at all offended. "And I loved him."

"I'm glad," Myrddin said. "If I wasn't a father to you all these years, I would much rather you had a different father, than none at all."

"Was that how it was for you?" Huw asked. "You have no paternal name; you are just Myrddin."

"My mother took the name of my father to her grave," Myrddin said. "Apparently, she never told him either—or he was dead too, before my birth."

"That must have been hard," Huw said.

Myrddin was a bit surprised that Huw would speak to him of it. "It certainly made it difficult to dress me down as my betters would have liked." Myrddin smiled. "Nobody could say, *Myrddin ap Geraint ap Bedwyr, get over here!*" As Myrddin hoped, Huw smiled too. "I was not unique, certainly. Many of my companions growing up had lost their fathers early in life."

"But they knew who they were," Huw said.

"Yes," Myrddin said, "but as I had no choice, I didn't dwell on it." Myrddin paused. "Although, admittedly, I learned to fight almost before I could walk."

"And nobody seems to have any difficulty remembering who you are," Huw said.

Now Myrddin laughed. "Apparently not."

"When I began my search, I still called myself Huw ap Tomos, after my . . . father," Huw said. "But as I approached Gwynedd, I met more people who knew you, or had heard of you. They mentioned one battle in particular, many years ago in the south, along the border with Mercia. You saved King Arthur's life that day."

Myrddin nodded at his son. "The King knighted me after that. It's his way to choose one man after each battle upon whom to confer the honor, and that day it was mine."

"I would like that for myself," Huw said. "Or, at least, I always saw myself serving in my lord's retinue. But now, I don't know what I'm meant to do; whom I'm meant to be or which lord I should serve."

"If you live honorably within yourself, it doesn't matter so much whom you serve," Myrddin said. This was Huw's real concern, and what had hovered over their conversation from the first.

Huw turned his head to look at Myrddin. "You believe that?"

Myrddin's eyes crinkled and his mouth twitched with sudden laughter, because Huw had caught him out. "Except in this case. If King Arthur loses this war, our country will fall to the Saxons. Modred cares only for himself and his own power—despite the fact that he himself is half-Welsh. He desires to completely subjugate my people—your people too—and all evidence suggests that he will settle for nothing less. Your lord, Cedric, knows this."

"Which is why he might be willing to ally himself with King Arthur," Huw said.

"Possibly," Myrddin said. "Cedric fears that were Arthur to die, or lose this war, it will embolden Modred. Cedric himself does not possess such a high standing with Modred that he might not lose everything too."

"Even though he and Modred are cousins through their fathers."

"Yes."

"So you're saying that it matters this time," Huw said. "You're saying that it has reached a point where I have to decide the greater loyalty."

"Yes, if Cedric sticks with Modred. You can't both be Welsh, and serve him. When Cedric himself freed me from Modred's grasp, however, he took a step towards shifting allegiance. It is also possible that Modred wanted me free, but wanted me freed covertly."

"Lord Cedric ap Aelfric has always dealt forthrightly with his men," Huw said, back to being a staunch supporter. "He is a good leader."

"I'll grant you that," Myrddin said. "But I must warn you, my son, that not everyone in this castle trusts your motives." Myrddin had deliberated with himself as to whether he should mention it, but the time seemed right.

"They fear I would betray King Arthur?" Huw asked, eyes wide, a typical youth who still saw everything in black and white instead of realizing the world was mottled shades of grey.

"Think, Huw," Myrddin said. "This shouldn't surprise you. King Arthur has been betrayed by family, friends, and hidden foes more times than he can count. Is it any wonder some of his counselors would look askance at my newly claimed son who so conveniently rides to me from Brecon?"

"I see your point." Huw nodded, although Myrddin wasn't sure if he quite did.

"Just watch yourself," Myrddin said. "Better to keep silent and your eyes open."

"Yes, sir."

They were quiet a moment, and then Huw spoke again. "It was only chance, you know, that had me risk crossing the Conwy River and entering Eryri."

"Chance?" Myrddin said.

"In a tavern in Ruthin, I came upon a man who claimed to know you—or at least know the man whom the King knighted back in 525—but he told me you were dead. My heart fell. It seemed it was time to turn aside and return to Brecon."

"But you didn't," Myrddin said.

Huw shook his head. "Later in the evening, an argument developed between the man to whom I'd spoken and another. That man accused the first of being a liar and a traitor. The latter owed fealty to Arthur while the first had supported his brother, Cai, throughout his years of treachery." Huw glanced at Myrddin, his eyes thoughtful. "That was the tipping point. With my Lord Cedric on Anglesey, I was still free to search. I decided I wouldn't take the word of one man who did not hold with your allegiance."

"Praise God for that," Myrddin said.

"So what happens now?" Huw said.

"Cedric asked me to come to him at Brecon for the return of my horse. He's not ready to turn wholly away from Modred or turn to King Arthur. He intends, I think, to continue our discussion."

"Lord Cedric and his father once fought with Arthur." Huw tipped his chin upwards and stared at the rafters.

"They did," Myrddin said. "God willing, Cedric will again. I hope that once I've healed, you and I can journey together to convince him to honor that tradition."

* * * * *

Myrddin thought a single night at Garth Celyn should have been enough to heal him. Nell, on the other hand, was quite happy to have him more contained than usual. Bruised ribs could take weeks to mend. If they were right about what was coming for Wales and the King, Myrddin wasn't going to have the luxury of

196

that much time. At least he was mobile, even if he looked and felt terrible.

The second evening back from Rhuddlan, Nell helped Myrddin hobble into the hall to share a meal with Ifan and Huw. The joy of Huw's very existence filled Myrddin's heart each time he said, *my son*, as if no man before him had ever had one. She could see it. It brought her nearly to tears every time—for Myrddin's sake and because her own heart lifted at the thought of one of her long-dead sons walking through the door. Huw was only two years older than her Llelo would have been.

They were halfway through the meal when instead of a beloved son, Deiniol pushed open the great doors and walked into the hall, an enormous grin on his face. Immediately behind him were Lord Gruffydd and his son, Owain. Cai, who'd been sitting at his place at the high table on Arthur's right, rose to his feet. "By God, I prayed you'd come!"

He headed around the table and in several long strides he and Owain met in the center of the hall, careless of who watched or what they thought of this development. As Owain and Gruffydd had been co-conspirators with Cai eight years before when they'd plotted to assassinate Arthur, it was understandable that some of Arthur's men might give him a rather less-than-effusive greeting.

Arthur, a smile on his lips that didn't reach his eyes, canted his head in greeting to Gruffydd, who strolled down the aisle between the tables until he reached the point opposite Arthur's seat.

"My King." Gruffydd bowed his head, although not perhaps as far as he could have.

"Gruffydd." Arthur gave his guest a similar, slight nod. The King gestured with his hand to the space beside him on his left, which Geraint had hastily vacated two seconds before. Normally, Bedwyr, Arthur's closest confident, sat next to him on the other side, but he'd not appeared for the meal. Could be, he didn't want to sit next to Cai, who'd taken his customary chair.

Then, inexplicably, Deiniol detached himself from Cai's side and strolled directly towards the four of them.

"What's he doing?" Myrddin said.

Nell put a hand on his arm, just in case he acted first and thought later. She didn't want Deiniol to insult her again, but didn't want Myrddin to cause a scene either. In his weakened condition, Myrddin was more vulnerable than she. Deiniol, for his part, remained polite. He stopped two feet from their table, put his heels together, and bowed to Nell.

"Madam," he said.

"Deiniol," she replied, aiming for graciousness, although she couldn't stop the twitch of a smile that lurked in the corner of her mouth at having to be polite to him. Perhaps humor might conquer Myrddin's loathing.

"So you didn't have a death wish after all," Myrddin said.

Nell elbowed him under the table, hitting a painful spot that left him gasping, and then smiled at Deiniol. "It was a great thing you did, bringing Gruffydd and Owain here. It must have been a dangerous journey."

Deiniol smiled, his eyes scanning Myrddin's bruised face. "It looks as if you had it rougher than I."

"It's been an eventful week in your absence," Myrddin said.

"Was the road difficult?" Nell said, still speaking as sweetly as she could.

"It was no trouble to serve my lord and bring new allies into his circle," Deiniol said.

Nell wasn't so sure about that.

"Does Modred know that Gruffydd's here?" Myrddin asked Deiniol.

He shrugged. "I doubt it. Gruffydd has always followed his own road." He lifted his chin, pointing at Huw. "Who's this?"

"My son," Myrddin said.

"Sir," Huw said. He held a cup in his hand and motioned to Deiniol with it, the same amused expression she'd seen on his face at times when he talked to Myrddin, as if he couldn't quite believe he was actually in Garth Celyn, sitting beside his father.

Deiniol gave a laughing cough, saluted Myrddin with a slight motion of his hand, and moved on towards Cai, leaving the four companions staring after him.

Myrddin's eyes crinkled in the corners. Nell was glad to see his anger easing. Wearing a half smile, he sat back in his chair. "Three days ago, who would you have said were the three weakest links in Modred's control of Wales and the borderlands?"

"The lords Cedric, Edgar, and Gruffydd," Nell said.

"And now all three have come to call," Ifan said.

199

"Can he have all three, do you think?" Nell said. "Will they work with each other as well as with us?"

Myrddin made a 'maybe' movement with his head. "They've each fought Arthur in the past but they've also fought each other. It's Modred's response when he finds out that should give Gruffydd pause."

"If it's so dangerous, why is Gruffydd here?" Nell said.

"Because he's worried that Arthur will win," Ifan said. "He's afraid that if he waits too long to change sides, Arthur will no longer need him and when he wins, give his land to someone more deserving and loyal."

"Are we that close to victory?" Nell said.

"Gruffydd appears to think so," Myrddin said. "Perhaps the pressure from the Saxon barons Modred is trying to unite is greater than we thought."

15

19 November 537 AD

"Excuse me—uh—Father—what are you doing?"

"I'm up," Myrddin said. "I am alive. I refuse to lie in that bed one hour longer."

"Are you really planning to ride today?"

Myrddin had entered the stables, thinking to get out of the hall and put aside his endless dreaming. It seemed that every time he closed his eyes, some new manifestation of his dream of Arthur's death swam before his eyes, each one different from the last.

"No," Myrddin said. Snow had begun to fall and at his son's words, Myrddin swung around to look behind him at the flakes floating in gentle wisps from the white sky. It had the look of continuing all day. "Up until right now, I'd forgotten Cadfarch wasn't here. I was going to brush him."

"I'm sorry," Huw said. "My lord will take good care of him."

"No doubt," Myrddin said. Straw crunching underneath his feet, he walked to where Huw brushed his own horse. Myrddin picked up a brush to work alongside his son.

"I'm surprised Nell let you get up."

"She's seeing to a birth," Myrddin said. "She doesn't know."

"Is she your woman, like everyone says?" Huw carefully combed his horse's mane rather than looking at Myrddin.

"I don't know that she'd characterize herself that way," Myrddin said. "To her mind, she's nobody's woman but her own. At the same time, between you and me—and the rest of the garrison—no man should think otherwise."

Huw nodded. "I've spoken to Ifan of your injuries. When you said that they were at Modred's behest, I hadn't realized that he was actually *present* when his guards administered them."

"Yes," Myrddin said. He ran his hand down the horse's legs, feeling his sturdy hocks for damage. "Modred does as he pleases."

"My lord!"

The call shattered the peace and in four strides Myrddin and Huw arrived at the entrance to the stables to look out on a small company of men just coming through the gate. Gareth led them, the white plume on his helmet fading into the snowy landscape. The man beside him wore the garments of a member of the clergy, although he'd drawn up his hood to protect himself from the weather so Myrddin couldn't see his face. *Surely that's not one of Gareth's cousins?*

But then the priest turned to hand his horse's reins to Adda and Myrddin saw the face beneath the covering hood. The man was Anian, the Bishop of St. Asaph, who'd been party to the excommunication of King Arthur at Rhuddlan Castle.

"What's he doing here?" Myrddin said.

"Joining the fold, it seems," said Huw. He turned back to his horse. As he did so, he asked casually—although the question was anything but casual. "You distrust him?"

"I trust very few men," Myrddin said.

"Not Deiniol, certainly," Huw said. "Nell told me of your quarrels."

"It's more than a quarrel," Myrddin said, "for all that we've spoken no more than three sentences to each other in twenty years."

"And Cai?" Huw said. "You loathe him."

"That goes without saying," Myrddin said. "These men are known traitors to King Arthur. It's the ones who hide behind their loyalty while pocketing coins from Modred that concern me. Of them, there may be none or many, even here."

Huw picked up the brush for currying his horse and plucked at the hairs in it. Myrddin watched him, waiting for the question he knew was coming. "And me?" he said. "Do you trust me?"

If Myrddin could have told Huw without humiliating him that he was transparent, he would have. As it was, Myrddin clapped him on the shoulder. "I trust you. When I told you earlier that some here didn't, I did not mean me."

"What if my lord really did send me to find you in order to act as his spy among your people?" Huw said.

"Did he?"

"No," Huw said, indignant, despite the fact that he'd been the first to pose the question.

"Lord Cedric undoubtedly hoped that you would serve him in that capacity anyway," Myrddin said. Huw stuttered a protest and Myrddin held up a hand to stop him speaking. "Imagine you are a lord of Mercia and one of your men, one of the younger squires, tells you that his real father is someone other than the staunch companion of your youth. He's a Welshman you've never met. The boy asks to seek this new father out. You know that the boy's mother is Welsh. You understand how his two allegiances could pull him apart, regardless of how noble you believe him to be."

"So you send him north," Huw said, nodding. "And hope that he finds his father and that through that relationship, whether or not the boy wishes it, you discover something you didn't know about the King Arthur's plans."

"It is a sensible approach," Myrddin said. "Logical too. It's not even deceitful."

"If the boy comes home empty-handed," Huw said, "he has information about the disposition of Arthur's men and the interior of Wales you hadn't known before." Huw paused. "I would have been eager to tell Lord Cedric all I'd learned."

"It is the perfect plan," Myrddin said. "Cedric risks only you, who have requested this mission. At best, he gains knowledge; at worst, he loses a good squire."

"At worst." Huw studied his boots.

"When I met Cedric," Myrddin said, moving closer to Huw and taking the brush so Huw would look at him, "he was surprised at first. But he recognized my name, and because of that, he freed me from Modred's clutches."

"So I would find you," Huw said. "So I would spy for him."

Myrddin shook his head. "Cedric's position in Wales is unstable. You cannot blame him for using whatever weapons come to hand, especially if he can wield them at so little cost to himself."

This was too much for Huw. The knowledge that he'd been used by his lord stuck in his throat and he couldn't swallow it. He turned to Myrddin and stepped close, his face right in his father's. He wasn't angry as much as fierce. "Would you ever do that to me?"

"I would tell you," Myrddin said, "and make you a willing party to my plans. I promise you that."

Huw shot Myrddin an unreadable look from those pale eyes, nodded, and stepped away, back to his horse. Myrddin didn't know if Huw was truly reassured or if he no longer knew what to believe.

"But I am your father," Myrddin added. "In his present, precarious state, Cedric doesn't have time for niceties. Don't be too hard on him."

Huw didn't answer. Instead, he pawed through the saddle bags that rested on a hook in his horse's stall. He took out a wad of old cloth that looked like nothing more than a bandage yet to be used on an injured man. He unfolded it and held his hand out to Myrddin. A heavy gold cross on a thick chain lay in Huw's palm. At the sight of it, Myrddin stepped closer, his breath catching in his throat.

"Christ's bones, Huw, I've not seen that cross . . ." Myrddin's voice died as he realized where he'd last seen it.

"Since you gave it to my mother," Huw said. "I know."

Myrddin reached out a finger and touched it, feeling the smooth metal and remembering when he'd given it to her. The cross had weighed on his neck, dangling between them as Myrddin had made love to her. He'd placed it around her neck instead. In his mind's eye, Myrddin saw it settle between her breasts and warm there.

He'd spent the night in her bed; then left in the early hours of the morning at the command of his King. At the time, he'd meant for Tegwan to keep it. Myrddin had been nineteen years old, in love and a romantic. It seemed appropriate to give her the one thing of value that he possessed, barring his sword.

"It was my mother's," Myrddin said. "I've always assumed that her father gave it to her, although it has crossed my mind that she could have gotten it from mine." He looked into Huw's face. "It's yours, now."

"No." Huw shook his head. "You're still young enough to marry. Although my mother cherished it, I have many things from her, including sixteen years of memories. If you want to give it away again, give it to Nell." He pushed his hand towards Myrddin and Myrddin didn't resist him. He lifted the cross from Huw's palm by its chain, caressing the smooth links.

"Thank you." Myrddin forced the words past the thickening in his throat. "My nurse gave this to me when I was twelve, believing that I should have something of my mother. She had kept it hidden all those years, knowing that if Madoc found it, he could claim it for himself as payment for giving me house room until I became a man." Myrddin slipped the chain over his head and tucked the cross under his shirt. It was an unfamiliar weight against his breastbone, but a comforting one.

"May it protect you wherever you go," Huw said, "as it has me."

* * * * *

"I dreamed last night." Nell stood in the doorway of their room, gazing down on Myrddin who lay spread-eagled on his pallet. Huw remained in the hall where he would spend the night amongst the other squires and men-at-arms who were arriving in increasing numbers with their lords, in preparation for the meeting of the Welsh High Council.

Nell had asked Huw if he would prefer to share their room even though Myrddin no longer needed watching over. The appalled look on his face had prompted laughter from Nell. Myrddin and Nell had become more than friends, but what exactly they were to each other, Nell wasn't quite sure. The rest of the castle assumed they knew, however, and if that meant she could continue to stay with him, then that was fine by her. Like the breeches she'd worn to Rhuddlan, the idea was freeing.

"I dream every night," he said.

"Will you tell me about them?" Nell would have asked him about the dreams days ago, but he'd been ill . . . and she almost hadn't wanted to share them with him because once she did, they'd both be laid bare. While they'd admitted the truth to each other, what that truth entailed, and what they were going to do about it, wasn't at all clear.

"Do I have a choice?" Myrddin said, and then smiled, taking the sting out of his words. He gestured to Nell with one hand. She entered the room and closed the door behind her; then walked to the pallet on which Myrddin lay and knelt on the end of it. Myrddin pushed himself upright and braced his back against the wall. "All right." He scrubbed at his face with both hands. "Talk to me."

"My dreams have changed."

"Have they?" he said. "How?"

"Except for that first instance, I've always fought as you when I dream. But since before you went to Rhuddlan, it's been different. Sometimes you're not even there. Last night, more men filled the clearing than before, and there were no archers. In fact . . ." She paused, trying to think how to say this. "Although you were there, you didn't die."

"Really." Myrddin dropped his hands to his lap. "And that's different?"

"Yes, of course," she said.

"Certainly, I have no interest in dying just yet," Myrddin said. They sat silent for a moment, before Myrddin continued. "I don't just want to save King Arthur because I want to save Wales—I have this odd idea that if I save him, I save myself."

"There's nothing wrong with not wanting to die by a Saxon's sword," Nell said.

"In my dream last night, I didn't have Cadfarch," Myrddin said. "That might be the first time. And since just before I met you, I've not worn a mustache."

Nell's eyes widened. "And that's my fault! But I didn't know!"

"No," Myrddin said. "Only because I didn't tell you, and yet . . ."

"Does that mean that actions we take in the real world change our dreams, which in turn indicates a new course in the future?" Nell said. "That we're making progress?"

"What is progress?" Myrddin said. "We have no idea if everything we're doing right now is exactly what we need to do to ensure that King Arthur dies on December 11th. There's no reason to think otherwise."

"Except that if King Arthur's death is inevitable, why dream?"

Myrddin snorted under his breath. "You're assuming these dreams don't come from the devil."

"Oh, yes," Nell said. "I thought it at first, of course. I told my father of the vision the first time I had it. I ran home, screaming of the battle I'd witnessed and the dead men. Once past the clearing, the world reverted to what it had been. But when my father searched, he found nothing by the river. He was afraid for me, then."

"Did you ever tell a priest?"

"Did you?"

Myrddin gave a sharp laugh. "No."

"So what *did* you do?" Nell said. "Up until now, I mean."

"I came to serve the King as soon as I was able," Myrddin said. "But otherwise, I ignored the dreams. I drank."

"You drank." Nell strove to keep her voice even. "And what good was that supposed to do?"

"Goddamn it! I don't know!" Myrddin said. "Who am I to change the world? Who am I to have these visions?"

Nell bit her lip as she looked at him, realizing she'd pressed too hard. "You're Myrddin. Why not you?"

"What about you, then?" Myrddin said, still angry. "You were doing no more than I. Less, in fact. You were leaving Wales."

"Um . . ." Nell looked down at her hands folded in her lap, and then back up at Myrddin. "No, I wasn't."

"That's what you told me."

"I lied." Nell forced herself not to look away from Myrddin's face.

"You lied." He mimicked the flatness in her tone.

Nell nodded. "I was going to Rhuddlan, as I said, but my intent was to enter the castle."

"For what purpose?" Myrddin said. "As a spy?"

"Not exactly." Nell shrugged. She glanced away, unable to maintain eye contact. Now that it came to it, perhaps he'd find the truth far worse than his basest suspicions. She felt his gaze on her and still she wouldn't look at him. "I wasn't a nun anymore, you know."

"Christ!" Myrddin leaned forward to grab her chin. "You weren't going there as a spy! You were going as a . . . as a . . . as a whore!"

There it was, the truth at last. Nell pulled away, pummeled by Myrddin's horrified stare. She shrugged again. "It was an idea."

"My God! What were you thinking?"

"I'll tell you what I was thinking!" She looked up, her anger flaring. "The solution to our problems certainly wasn't to drink myself into a stupor every night. I was going to get close to Modred! And kill him if I could! It might even have been easy—just a knife in the back after I refilled his goblet. I might not even have had to sell myself to do it."

Myrddin's mouth was open as he stared her.

Nell gritted her teeth, determined to tell him everything. "My sisters had already suffered worse at the hands of Wulfere's soldiers. It was the least I could do! And it was the only thing I could think of that *I* could do to change the future."

Myrddin leaned forward and gripped her arms. "You must have realized that Modred's men would have killed you immediately afterwards."

"Of course."

"*Christ!*" Myrddin blasphemed again. "That was the stupidest idea I've ever heard!" He shook her. Once. While she glared at him, trying to hang on to her anger even though tears pricked at her eyes. She opened her mouth to speak but then he put one finger to her lips to stop her, his voice softening. "And the bravest."

With that, she couldn't constrain the tears. They spilled out the corners of her eyes and down her cheeks. Myrddin made a 'tsk' noise from between his teeth and pulled her to him. Nell wrapped her arms around his waist and sobbed into his chest.

"Sweet Mary, mother of God, that you would think that was your only choice," Myrddin said. "You would have died."

"That was, in part, the point," Nell said. "By then I would have done anything. Anything to stop the dreams. Anything to stop King Arthur from meeting Edgar by the Cam River."

"Thank God I found you. I wish I'd done so long ago."

"You didn't know of me," she said. "Better that I'd tried to find you. Silly of me not to think of it; I don't know why I didn't . . ."

"I'll be damned if I'll ever bow to a Saxon lord again!"

The fierce tones of Lord Gruffydd carried loudly through the wall. Nell froze in Myrddin's arms. As his words sank in, they eased back from each other. Nell wished she could see right through the wall to the other side.

"We've had little choice—" another voice said.

"He's talking to Cai," Nell said.

"You have had a choice!" Gruffydd hammered at him. "You would rather see Wales fall under the Saxon boot than lose an acre of what you possess? Even if Modred wins this war, you have no guarantee he will confirm you as Lord of Gwynedd. Look what has happened to Edgar of Wigmore!" Gruffydd sounded so much like Arthur, it was as if he'd become a different person.

"That's just one instance—"

Gruffydd cut off Cai again. "One instance that we are to take as an example for all of us! If he can do this to his loyal cousin, the man who stood by him through every war this century, he can do it to any of us."

"You've stood at Modred's side many times," Cai said, still defiant and forceful. "Why not now? Why not this time?"

"Because he betrayed me with my wife!"

The silence in both rooms was deafening. Gruffydd had married a much younger woman after the death of Owain's mother. His confession had Nell holding her breath, one hand clenching and unclenching around Myrddin's arm. Surely they must realize that the walls had ears?

Finally, Cai spoke again. "How do you know?"

"She told me that he'd asked for her. When I confronted him, he laughed," Gruffydd said. "He admitted he'd taken her." Now, Gruffydd lowered his voice, forcing Nell to lean in to hear the conversation better. She pressed her ear to the wall that separated the two rooms. "He thinks he controls me."

"Admittedly, Modred consorts with many women," Cai said. "It is well known."

"But never *my* woman," Gruffydd said.

"I can see that you are confirmed in your opinion." Cai returned to his normal speaking voice. "I will not try to change it."

"And you?" Gruffydd said. "You stand beside your brother for all to see, yet you mean to tell me that you spy for Modred?"

"I do not spy." There was a distinct *clunk* against the wall. Nell imagined Cai had pressed Gruffydd to it and she shrank back, as if Cai might be able to sense her through the wall. Ten heartbeats passed and then feet retreated across the floor. A door to the hall slammed.

"I see," Gruffydd said, presumably to himself.

"I don't see," Nell said. "Are we to understand that Cai's faithfulness is a front? A sham to gain power and land?" She turned to Myrddin, whose jaw was set in a more grim line than she'd ever seen it.

"Yes. That is precisely what we must understand. It is as it has always been. I just don't know what to do about it."

"You could tell King Arthur."

"Just like I can tell him about our dreams? He would not believe me, *could* not believe me without proof."

"Then Bedwyr or Geraint," she said.

Myrddin shook his head. "Not yet," he said. "We still have time."

"We hope."

16

21 November 537 AD

"**H**as it occurred to you that any one of these men could be your father?"

Myrddin turned his gaze on his son, amused to find the boy's eyes alight with mischief. "No." And then amended, "not for many years."

"Since my step-father's death, I wondered about you often," Huw said. "My mother told me that you served in Arthur's forces when she knew you, but that wasn't to say you still did. Or were even alive. I'm sure there are many Myrddins throughout Wales who wondered at the boy who questioned them about their activities when they were younger."

"I wish I'd been there, son." Myrddin rested a hand on his shoulder. "I can't say it often enough."

"You're here now," Huw said.

"So who looks most like Myrddin, Huw?" Nell sidled over to Huw and looked with him. "Huddled in the corner are those cousins named Rhys and there's three Gruffydd's over by the high table."

The other great men of Wales had come far for the meeting. Many had vacillated between Arthur and Modred over the years, depending upon who had the upper hand. Could it be that position now belonged to King Arthur?

"Stop it, Nell," Myrddin said. "My mother dabbled with a pig farmer. If he were noble, she would have named him."

Nell laughed, ignoring his protest. "I hate to say it, but I think you resemble Modred a bit." At Myrddin's glare, Nell laughed again. "I doubt, however, that he's your father, as he was just four years old when you were born and even for him, that would have been mighty precocious."

"Thank heaven for small mercies," Myrddin said. "How would I ever live that down?"

They surveyed the company for another minute and then Bedwyr and Geraint appeared. It was almost time to start the meeting. Men began filling the seats around the tables in expectation of King Arthur's arrival. "Modred would murder half the people in this room, given the chance," Nell said.

"And how many of them will turn to him anyway, seeing an opportunity," Myrddin said, "whether tomorrow, next week, or . . ." He glanced at Huw who had moved a few feet away in response to another man's query, "if Arthur falls?"

Nell met his eyes, showing sympathy for what could be, squeezed his hand, and headed for the rear of the hall and her herb hut. She'd made noises about dressing in her male garb so she would be allowed to stay in the room, perhaps to serve as a page, but Myrddin had dissuaded her of it. Whether she remembered it or not, these men knew her as a former nun and all hell would break loose if someone exposed her as a woman when she was thus disguised.

The commotion subsided. King Arthur had ordered the tables arranged in a large square and a sense of equivalence, if not equality, permeated the room. The King took his seat with Geraint and Bedwyr on either side of him as was his custom. Cai sat opposite Arthur, some twenty feet apart, more in the position of a rival than a brother. As a mere knight, Myrddin was lucky to be in the hall at all. With Huw, who was doing his best to make himself as unremarkable as possible, Myrddin found a place against the wall where they could see the faces of both brothers. Unfortunately, their spot turned out to be two spaces down from Deiniol. It was too late to move, so Myrddin stayed where he was and resolved to focus on the proceedings.

King Arthur had designated Anian, the Bishop of St. Asaph, as convener of the Assembly. Anian had spent as many years opposed to Arthur's rule as for it, but when he'd greeted the King upon his arrival at Garth Celyn, he'd said that he'd come to his own conclusions about who should rule in Wales and that the excommunication to which he'd been a party was not the Will of

God. In matters of faith, he would follow his conscience as he always had.

Anian began with an opening prayer, calling the assembly to silence. At its completion, he made a show of unrolling the letter from Modred to the Council that King Arthur had received back on November 8th and read it aloud. The letter was short and said, in a nutshell, that Modred wouldn't discuss what happened at Anglesey or the status of the four cantrefs of Wales, nor would he offer the council any promises in exchange for peace other than that he would deal with them mercifully as befitted an overlord. Anian then read the secret terms Modred had conveyed to Arthur and Cai, to which they had already responded.

By the time Anian's voice fell silent, the room was in an uproar. Many of the lords had heard rumors of what the letters contained. Cai had made no secret of his (false) new-found hatred of Modred, but Arthur hadn't shared the exact wording with any of his barons since that first day, wanting them all to hear it at the same time. Now, King Arthur himself had to rise to his feet to silence them.

"I've already responded to Modred's letter," Arthur said, "as has my brother." He nodded his head to Cai, who raised a hand, in acknowledgement of his action. "As the bishop has just explained, Modred demanded that we, in exchange for peace, give up all claim to our lands in Wales and our patrimony, and to leave our subjects in the hands of the Saxons. We have, of course, refused."

Again the uproar and King Arthur raised his hand to settle the room. Every man perched on the edge of his seat, even those who'd never wanted to listen to the King before.

"As a council, we must respond to Modred's letter with one voice," Arthur said, "but before we do, it is important that each man be allowed to air his opinions, grievances, and suggestions freely, in the company of his peers. From this hour, we all rise, or we all fall, together."

That calmed the assemblage somewhat. The Welsh were a more egalitarian people (at least among the elite) than many peoples, and everyone was used to this method of resolving problems. Thus, each of the lords stood in turn to state what he had won or lost in the war with Modred since the council had last met, and what he thought of Modred's letters. Nobody was happy; the list of grievances against the Saxons grew longer with every man who spoke. Once these preliminaries were over, Anian stood again.

"King Arthur has asked me to open discussion regarding the future of Wales," he said. "If she is to have a future, now is the time to speak of it."

Utter silence fell. Then, to no one's surprise, it was Cai who rose to his feet. "I have something to say."

"By all means." King Arthur gestured that he had the floor.

"What I want to know," Cai said, his voice level and conversational, "is why the Council has not disowned Modred long since?" He lifted his hand to show the scroll of paper he'd received from Modred. "Is this any kind of letter to send to a member of his own family?"

"No!"

Myrddin craned his head to see who'd spoken, whether a supporter of Cai, or just one of the many men who knew injustice when he saw it. A number of men shook their fists, presumably at Modred.

Huw leaned in to whisper. "That was Owain ap Gruffydd."

Myrddin glanced at him. "You don't like him."

"I don't like traitors, even when they're on my side."

Myrddin smiled, hearing the echo of Cedric in Huw's voice.

"I say we throw off that yoke, once and for all," Cai said. "It is well and good that we defeated the Saxons at the Straits, but Modred doesn't yet believe himself defeated. He thinks us beholden to him, a people in rebellion. He is already measuring his head for the crown. He has called my brother a usurper, when it is he who seeks to take the crown from us!"

"Excommunicate, by God!" That was Gareth, whom Myrddin had never pegged as one for spontaneous outbursts.

Cai nodded. "What gives Modred the right to stand between us and our God?"

"No right!"

Far more heads nodded and there were more clenched fists than before. Even Huw was moved, his hands gripping his knees and his back stiff as he hung on every one of Cai words.

"I say *no*!" Cai said. "I say we should be free of the constraints that Modred imposes upon us. No half-Saxon lord has a right to our throne!" He gestured to Arthur. "King Arthur has no heir of his body, but that is not to say that he doesn't have an heir of his heart!"

At those final words, the men around Myrddin swallowed hard, Cai paused, and Arthur gripped his goblet so tightly his knuckles whitened. Cai leaned heavily on the table, supporting his weight on both hands, and Arthur stood. When he spoke, his voice was gentle.

"What would you have us do, brother, that we have not already done? Did I not write to Modred that we spoke with one voice? Did not you? Did I not say that even were I willing to acknowledge Modred as my heir, the people of Wales would be unwilling to do homage to one such as he who has no respect for their laws and customs?"

A murmur of approval swept through the hall.

"I say we do not write it," Cai said. "I say we shout it! From the highest peak of Yr Wyddfa, we must cry aloud as one people and keep crying it until Modred heeds our words. I say we take what is ours for Wales, and only for Wales! I say we tell Modred what we think of his rights and his armies! I say we are a free and independent people and I, for one, am tired of living at Modred's sufferance!"

Cai's eyes were alive with triumph. He seemed to tower over the company with his power and eloquence.

Arthur, however, remained unmoved.

"To deny his claim to the throne will only spur Modred to greater heights of aggravation," he said. "He will take it as we mean it—as an open declaration that our people will never abide a half-Saxon overlord, even if he is also half-Welsh and my nephew. It treads hard on his divine right to rule."

Cai shot back. "We are already at odds with him. We thwart him and his church at every step. What more can he do to us that he has not already done? If you fear to place yourself at the head of such an endeavor, I do not!"

His shout rang throughout the hall. Then, silence settled and it was as if everyone was holding his breath—Myrddin and Huw among them—waiting for Arthur's answer.

"You are not afraid to renew the fight, brother?" Arthur said.

"I am not afraid, brother," Cai said. "For the good of her people, I would stand tall and never again bend to a Saxon lord or allow Modred to set his boot on the back our necks."

Another pause. The energy hummed among the men, just below the surface, threatening to come out.

Arthur released it.

"Then, so would I. I will take that chance." For the first time, Arthur's voice boomed out to every corner of the room. "Who will stand with me against Modred and his Saxon toadies, now and forever? Who would see the Kingdom of Wales renewed?"

Bedwyr shot his fist into the air. "Aye!"

A half second behind him came Cai, and almost in the same instant, Myrddin was one of dozens of others who matched him. Even Deiniol, who must have been taken up in the excitement and Myrddin feared would find himself with second thoughts by the time the doors to the hall opened, thrust his fist into the air.

Everyone shouted together. "Aye! God is with us!"

Arthur focused on his brother, who met his eyes. Cai's glowed with exhilaration and something else that Myrddin read as deceit. Then Arthur nodded, straightened, and turned from the table. Leaving Bedwyr to sort out the other lords, he strode from the hall.

* * * * *

"I hear that the barons have promised Arthur more money and men," Nell said, when Myrddin found her in her herb hut, boiling a concoction on the brazier. "Is it true? I didn't dare believe it until I heard it from you."

"That is what they've pledged. That's what King Arthur has sworn. He promises to have pushed Modred out of Powys by Christmas." He paused as their eyes met. "If we live that long."

"What does Huw think?" Nell said.

"He has discovered what it means to be Welsh," Myrddin said.

"We all feel it." Nell forcefully set down the jar she held and it almost tipped over. She righted it and then put it on the shelf above her head. "If the lords of Wales would stop fighting among themselves and unite, as they did at Mt. Badon, we would have the peace we need—not the peace that Modred wants."

"Modred has more men at his disposal than we do," Myrddin said. "This won't be easy."

"He is a vicious man, Myrddin," Nell said. "You do understand that if you ever cross paths with him again, you're dead." She held his eyes, like she once might have focused on one of the novice nuns, unsure if he was really listening. Myrddin went his own way, with a strong sense of *rightness* that Nell trusted, but she feared might cost him his life.

"I know it," Myrddin said.

"You say that so casually," she said, "but I don't want you to die."

Myrddin mouth twisted. "Nor do I." He glanced away.

Nell studied his profile and then turned away herself. Her back to him, she rummaged among her vials in the cupboard behind her. After the deaths of all her family, she'd carefully buried that part of her heart that cared too much—loved too much. But despite her best efforts to suppress it, she'd started caring for this man from the moment he'd stormed into the clearing to rescue her at St. Asaph, even before she knew him as the Myrddin from her dreams. That she'd loved that man since she was eight years old didn't help.

"Are you well?" Myrddin said.

Nell found herself smiling, her back still to him, studying the label of each of her jars in turn. "I am well, Myrddin. Thank you for asking."

17

24 November 537 AD

The feast showed all the signs of fading into drunkenness. It was growing late—or rather, early, as midnight had come and gone—and the hall remained full of drinkers and diners, many of whom would be returning to their homes tomorrow with a fine headache.

The lords of Wales had met one more time that afternoon, to give final approval for the wording of the letter to Modred. If the Welsh were anything, they were lawyers and the national pastime was suing each other over the smallest issue. A man moved a boundary stone, his opponent moved a fence, and they went to court to dispute their differences. They would settle them and then repeat the process the following year—sometimes over the same stones and fences. It was a wonder it had only taken three days with clerks and vellum to agree on the wording of the letter to Modred. There were years when it would have been too thorny an issue and tabled.

Bishop Anian had read it aloud, to the general approval of the hall:

> *The people of Wales, for their part, state that even if their King desired to give his nephew rule of them, they themselves would not do homage to any Saxon, of whose language, customs and laws they are utterly ignorant. For by doing so, they would be brought into perpetual captivity and barbarously treated . . .*

King Arthur had retired from the hall long since; Cai had been absent since before the last course. His behavior at the Council, once again, had been patriotically Welsh. How could Myrddin accuse him of betrayal when all eyes saw differently?

"I need you to help me with something." Nell plopped herself between Myrddin and Huw.

"Help you with what?" Myrddin said.

"I've felt something. Again."

"Felt, or *seen*?" Myrddin said.

"Not *seen*." Nell turned her body to shield them both from Huw's eyes, put her hand on Myrddin's, and gently squeezed. "I can't explain it. It's like when you went to Rhuddlan. Ever since we overheard Cai speaking to Gruffydd, I've been afraid. I can't articulate it, but something bad is going to happen tonight."

"All right," Myrddin said, intrigued.

"Tunnels lie underneath Garth Celyn. Will you poke around them with me? I thought you'd be angry if I followed one of the passages and didn't tell you, especially after what happened at Llanfaes."

"I surely would," Myrddin said, glad that at long last she was paying attention to what was good for her without him having to tell her.

Huw, whose mental image of himself definitely included tunnel exploring, perked up too. Huw and Myrddin followed Nell out of the great hall, past Arthur's receiving room, to one of the towers that buttressed the administrative building. This particular tower was the most northwestern; the garrison used it to watch the sea for enemy ships and to store equipment, beyond what was regularly kept in the barracks across the courtyard by the gatehouse.

When they entered, two men sprawled in chairs on either side of a table set against the far wall. They'd been drinking, but were sober enough to think of duty as Myrddin entered.

"Sir," said the first, a man named Tristan.

"We thought we'd see to the security of the sea tunnel," Myrddin said, working hard to keep a straight face.

"It's dusty down there," Tristan said. He walked to the trap door, set in the exact middle of the floor, knelt, and stuck his fingers through the recessed iron ring. He yanked on it. As the trap door came up, Myrddin grasped the edge to help him lift it. Below, a stairway led downwards.

Myrddin met Nell's eyes and she mouthed, *thank you.*

"It's been a long time since I've trod these steps," Myrddin said.

"There's another that leads to the mountains behind us," Tristan said. "It empties into a meadow below Aber Falls."

"We'll have to try that next," Nell said.

Myrddin swallowed a sarcastic reply about unbecoming behavior in an ex-nun, not wanting to squash her enthusiasm and because her concern was forcing him to reassess how seriously to take this.

Tristan handed Myrddin a lantern and in a file they walked down the surprisingly broad treads. Huw and Myrddin had to duck their heads so as to not hit the floorboards above them as they descended. Fifteen steps down, they arrived in a small room, much like the foyer in front of the cells at Rhuddlan, except there were no cells with prisoners, just a closed door.

Myrddin didn't recall a door there at all from his forays with Ifan or other boys as a youth, but admittedly, it was a long time ago. He raised the lantern high to inspect the stones around the door and the dust at its base.

"Look, Father." Huw pointed to fresh footprints in front of the door. Myrddin crouched to inspect them with him.

"Someone got here ahead of us," Nell said.

Huw lowered his voice. "Do you think something's really wrong? The hinges on the trap door were oiled and the stairs were swept clean. Everybody knows about the tunnels."

"I realize that," Myrddin said. "But whoever swept the stairs, pushed the dust right onto the floor here. Everything would have been cleaned in preparation for the Council meeting, up to and including the stairs. That means that these footprints are very recent."

Nell, her arms folded across her chest, stared down at the footprints. Myrddin glanced at her and then beyond her, up the stairs to Tristan who still stood at the top.

"What is it?" Tristan said.

Myrddin straightened. "Did someone come through here tonight before us?"

"Not on my watch," he said.

"Keep your eyes open." Myrddin lifted the latch on the door and a gust of air wafted through it. "And you might tell Lord Geraint where we've gone."

"Yes, sir," Tristan said.

"I can smell the sea," Nell said.

Huw loosened his sword in its sheath. Myrddin took Nell's hand and led the way into the tunnel. It was five feet wide. Every six feet along it, a stone archway supported the wooden roof, which itself was at least six and a half feet high. Both Huw and Myrddin could walk comfortably along it. Water seeped through cracks in the walls; eventually the wood in the roof would rot, given the wet climate, but it was still solidly holding up the tons of earth that pressed down from above.

Huw stared around them. "Who built this, Father?"

"I believe the Romans started it."

"You can see the footprints again." Nell pointed at the ground.

Huw had his sword in his hand now. "Do we go on?" He stepped past Myrddin and Nell and along the corridor.

"Yes," Myrddin said, his eyes straining to see beyond the rim of the circle of light thrown out by the lamp.

Huw gestured at the floor with the tip of his sword. "There are two sets of footprints. One man walked behind the other, and over there where the tunnel widens, the footprints go side by side."

He paced ahead of them, his left hand on the wall. Myrddin gripped Nell's hand more tightly and put his head close to hers. "How did you know, Nell?"

"I didn't." Nell shook her head. "It's like when you left for Rhuddlan. I can't believe . . ." She broke off.

"Well, *feeling* or not, you may have saved all of us."

The smell of the sea grew stronger. After twenty minutes, the tunnel curved to the left. As they came around the corner, a light flickered, reflecting off the moisture on the stone pillars. They retreated back around the curve and Huw doused the lamp. It wasn't entirely dark, as the light in front of them continued to flare. Myrddin peered around the corner, making sure he stayed low to the ground in case someone looked their way. The light came from a source a short distance outside the entrance to the tunnel. The sound of the surf was louder now, but with it, when he stayed still, voices echoed.

Myrddin listened, trying to understand what they were saying. Then Nell moaned. "Oh, no."

"What?" Huw and Myrddin spoke together.

"Listen," she said. "Those are Saxon voices."

Myrddin didn't need to hear them himself to believe her. He pushed her towards Huw. "Relight the lamp and run as fast as you can to Geraint. Tell him there are Saxons outside the sea tunnel, who are being aided by two men from Garth Celyn."

Huw hesitated, but Nell understood immediately.

"It's better if just one of us stays, Huw. Myrddin speaks Saxon just as well as we do, and better Latin, if it comes to it. Someone needs to warn the King so that he can plan our defenses. They must think to sneak into the castle with us all unawares. Come!"

That Huw understood. With a quick strike of flint, he relit the lantern and then took Nell's hand to run back the way they'd come, Nell holding her heavy skirts off the ground with one hand. Myrddin spared them a last glance before swinging back to face the sea. He swallowed hard. They would kill him if they caught him. Nevertheless, he hugged the wall and crept around the corner.

As Myrddin moved closer to the exit, the individual voices became clearer. Ten paces from the opening to the tunnel, he crouched low and listened. Several different conversations were going on at the same time, but the one occurring closest to the doorway was in Saxon.

"I will return to the castle overland to ensure that no alarm is raised and that the men I left guarding the exit remain true." The voice belonged to Owain, who'd evidently decided to continue his stand with Modred. Myrddin shook his head, choking down

bile at this betrayal and fearing for the safety of Nell and
Huw—and everyone in the castle.

A second man spoke, his voice ringing clearly down the
passage even through what had to be clenched teeth. "No! That is
not part of the agreement!"

"You dare threaten me?" Owain said. Feet scuffled and
Myrddin imagined them facing off against each other, swords
drawn. "Modred will hear of this!"

"He certainly shall," said the second man, "especially when
I tell him that our Welsh traitor lost his nerve at the last moment!"

A third man spoke, this time in Welsh. "Be reasonable,
Owain. They are looking out for their own interests, just as you
are. I, for one, will be glad when this night is over, but we said we
would lead them into Garth Celyn and that we must do."

The second voice spoke again, still in Saxon. "Enough! I
will leave five men with the boats. The rest of the company must
march now if we are to have the cover of darkness for our work.
Let's see this tunnel of yours, and then I alone will judge if you are
true to your word."

Myrddin backed away from the entrance. A second later,
he was around the corner and running, as fast and as urgently as
he'd ever run before. He worried briefly about the echo of his
pounding feet, but hoped he would be far enough away when the
Saxons entered the tunnel such that the sounds of their
movements would mask his own.

Myrddin ran the first quarter mile flat out, brushing his
fingers along the right hand wall to guide his steps in the dark. He

settled into a slower jog for the second half of the journey, which brought him into Garth Celyn within ten minutes of leaving the beach. Huw had left the door to the tunnel cracked open. Myrddin hit it with his shoulder and nearly impaled himself on half a dozen swords, their owners ready for a fight. He skidded to a halt and blinked—and the men-at-arms gave way.

"Pardon, my lord," Tristan called to Myrddin's back as he ran past him to take the stairs three at a time. Huw waited for Myrddin at the top.

"Lord Geraint was still awake," he said. "He sent me to Gareth, who is rousing the men in the hall and barracks. He's sent Nell to wake the King."

They crossed the courtyard between the administrative building and the sleeping quarters. Once inside, they jogged up a stairway and turned down the hallway to King Arthur's room. Nell had just knocked.

Arthur's deep voice boomed through the oak. "Enter!"

Nell pushed the door open and hovered on the threshold with Myrddin just behind her. The fire burned hot in the room and a wave of warmth met them. Arthur had been lying on top of his bedcovers, fully clothed. When he saw them, he sat up and swung his legs over the side of the bed. It seemed likely he hadn't slept at all.

"My lord." Myrddin bowed.

Arthur made an impatient gesture, as if to say, 'you woke me, now tell me what the trouble is'.

"A Saxon company is coming through the sea tunnel as we speak, led by Owain ap Gruffydd," Myrddin said.

Arthur had surged to his feet before Myrddin finished his sentence. A second later, Geraint brushed passed Myrddin, already booted, cloaked, and in full armor. Arthur's valet, an old fellow named Daffi, followed immediately behind. He hurried into the room, fixing the ties on his jacket. Geraint flung open the chest in which Arthur kept his armor.

"Keep talking," Arthur said, with a nod to Myrddin.

"The traitors spoke of allies in Garth Celyn who guarded the trap door entrance." Myrddin turned to Nell with a questioning look.

She shook her head, denying any knowledge of it. "When we returned to the stairs, Lord Geraint stood in the tower room, talking to Tristan with four other men."

"Tristan had come to find me," Geraint said, "but I needed more information before I raised an alarm."

While they spoke, Daffi helped the King with his armor and boots and then Geraint tightened the sword belt around Arthur's waist. Arthur nodded, ready to ride. "I'll see you in the courtyard when you've armed yourself. We must ride to the beach if we're going to catch them, once they discover we've barred the way into Garth Celyn." The Saxons could be back at their boats in half an hour. The King's company needed to intercept them before they could put to sea.

The King left the room. Although Huw and Myrddin wore boots, cloaks, and the swords they always carried, neither were

235

dressed in mail armor, which they'd need to fight the Saxons. "Help us arm, Nell?" Myrddin said, as they hustled after the King and Geraint.

"Of course," she said.

Together, they burst through the front door, ran down the stairs, and crossed the courtyard of the castle, heading for the barracks. Myrddin's new armor lay in a chest in the armory, alongside the equipment belonging to the rest of the men in the garrison. Once in the armory, Myrddin had to brush past Ifan to reach it.

"A wild night, eh?" Ifan shrugged into his surcoat which he'd pulled over his mail tunic. He stretched his arms to the sides, loosening his muscles. "It feels good!" He shot a smile at Nell, who patted his shoulder as she passed him.

Huw stripped to the waist and Myrddin tossed him his thin shirt, padding, and mail vest. All of them were rushing. In her haste, Nell fumbled with the fastenings to Myrddin's bracers.

"Damn you, Myrddin," Nell said as she finally managed to buckle them. "Another battle. More dead men. Haven't you done enough?"

"I love you too, Nell," Myrddin said.

She stopped, frozen, her hands at his belt and her head bent forward.

When she didn't give him the reply he expected and wanted, he gripped her arms. "I feel what I feel," Myrddin said. "I can live with it if you don't feel the same." He pulled her close, wrapping his arms around her. "This fight is not an end in itself.

It will be a small battle with a hundred men, perhaps fewer." He looked over at Huw. "Stay close to me when it comes to it. Get the horses and meet me in the courtyard."

"Yes, sir," Huw said, his eyes bright.

"Quickly now!" Myrddin said to his retreating back, and then under his breath, "There's nothing more exciting than a chance to get oneself killed."

Nell had her forehead in Myrddin's chest and was clenching and unclenching her fists around the edges of his cloak. She choked on sob that she turned into a laugh and lifted her head to look into his face. "I don't want you go."

"I'll be back."

She nodded and at last wrapped her arms around him for a hug, which he returned, thankful to have reached her at least that far. "Go with God, Myrddin."

Myrddin pushed past the few men still in the armory and out into the courtyard which seethed with men and horses. As he forced his way through the crowd to where Huw stood with Myrddin's new horse, christened Gwynfor because of her size and color, he searched for King Arthur. He eventually found him near the gatehouse, Cai already mounted beside him. Myrddin gritted his teeth at the sight of him, not wanting Cai within a sword's length of Arthur.

Owain's father, Gruffydd, had stopped Arthur as he was mounting his horse. Gruffydd's bellow carried over the uproar. "What is it you claim? You accuse my son of treason?"

"Where is your son?" Arthur said. "He would have us murdered in our beds and the castle fired. Produce him and we'll see if he has betrayed us. You have spent your life in service to Modred and his Saxons. Is it any wonder that I suspect treachery from your house?"

"Where is the proof?" Gruffydd said.

His challenge hung in the air; then other men shouted. A few spilled from the tower in which the trap door was located.

A man called. "They've reached the door!"

"We need more men!"

Arthur hissed. "There's your proof." He threw a leg over his horse's back. "Now is the time to make clear where your loyalties lie. I tell you there's no room in my country for the Saxons or their Welsh spies who betray us." Arthur gathered the reins and stood in the stirrups. He called to the men around him. "We ride to the sea! Let all who will, follow me! We will show no mercy for those who would have none for us!"

Men cheered, as men do when they are fired up, and two guards pulled open the gate. Ifan joined Huw and Myrddin and they followed Arthur and Cai through the gate and down the old Roman road, three abreast, moving faster than was reasonable in the dark, but trusting to their horses' sight. They followed that road for a short way before turning onto a smaller track that took them the last quarter mile to the sea.

At that point the three companions trotted their horses along the side of the column until they reached Gareth, who nodded at Myrddin as he approached, having been expecting him.

They'd worked well together when they'd fought at the Straits. Huw and Ifan fell in behind.

"We'll keep the men out of sight until the Saxons issue from the tunnel's exit," Gareth said. "Then we will fall upon them."

"That sounds nice and simple," Myrddin said, "provided they aren't expecting exactly that."

"Even if they are, they won't be able to do anything about it," Gareth said. "Bedwyr sent men ahead of us the instant Huw sounded the alarm. We'll know soon where we stand."

Myrddin glanced back at Huw, who gave him a sickly smile, just visible in the half-light of the waning moon.

Gareth noted Myrddin's attention and smirked. "This is a battle we can't lose. We have over a hundred men on horseback—far more than Garth Celyn's normal garrison. The Saxons intended a lightening raid, not a siege. As we saw at the Straits, when the enemy is on foot, a cavalry charge across open terrain is impossible to turn aside or survive."

"I don't understand why the Saxons are taking this risk," Huw said. It was the first time he'd referred to their enemy as *the Saxons*, as if he was no longer one of them. He didn't seem to notice what he'd said, and continued, "Even with a hundred men, they couldn't have hoped for more than a few minutes of surprise."

"Where's the risk?" Gareth said. "At worst they'll lose a company of men. At the Straits the commitment was much greater, and thus the loss. Any lives lost here are a small price indeed, compared with the opportunity to kill three dozen Welsh noblemen—and King Arthur. Their captain had no reason to think Owain couldn't have brought them successfully into the castle. It's only because of you that we hold a position of strength now."

Gareth paused, with a glance at Huw, and then turned to Myrddin. "Do not think the King is unaware of your role in this. You will be well rewarded."

Myrddin tipped his head in acknowledgement.

Ifan spoke for the first time. "Myrddin didn't do it for a reward." Myrddin turned to glower at him and Ifan shrugged. "It's the truth."

"All the more reason to acknowledge your loyalty." Then Gareth caught his breath at a shout from the head of the line. Arthur had raised his sword above his head. With Cai beside him, he charged forward.

The Saxons had abandoned their attempt to enter the castle through the trap door, admitted their defeat, and turned back the way they'd come. As Gareth had supposed, the cavalry caught them on the beach, just short of the water.

Huw and Myrddin raced towards the ranks of Saxons with a dozen of their companions, spread out across the length of the Saxon line. His eyes wide and face pale, Huw killed his first man with a slash across the neck, blood soaking him and his sword. Myrddin moved with him, his arm rising and falling with a deadly monotony, while Myrddin tried at the same time to keep his eyes on Arthur who fought just ahead of him. But Arthur and Cai were working together, fighting side by side, first one slicing through an opponent and then the other. All the while, Cai buttressed his brother with his own horse, body, and shield.

With Ifan emitting a steady stream of curses beside him, Myrddin, for his part, killed four Saxons in succession. When he had no more opponents, he turned to come at them again. But there was no need—so many men had already fallen.

Huw and Myrddin came to themselves simultaneously and sighted three Saxons heading up the beach, looking for safety in the woods that lined its edge. Myrddin spurred Gwynfor after them with Huw, who'd reacted a heartbeat sooner, just in front of him. Huw had his sword raised high, ready to thrust it into the neck of the first man he came upon. When he reached him, however, he hesitated—only for a heartbeat, but it was enough.

The man sensed Huw's approach and didn't waste his opportunity. As Huw aimed a blow at his head, the man stopped abruptly, spun on a heel, and swung his sword two-handed. He would have sliced right through Huw's arm if Myrddin hadn't reached him in time to grasp the man's wrist with his left hand, preventing him from completing the downward stroke. While Myrddin had arrested the man's movement, his own overbalanced him and he went down, falling off Gwynfor and pulling the man with him.

The Saxon fell at an awkward angle and Myrddin heard—and felt—an ominous crack when he landed on top of him. Unfortunately, Myrddin's momentum also brought him in contact with the Saxon's sword and it sliced through Myrddin's leather armor into his thigh above the knee. As Myrddin rolled off the dying Saxon, Ifan arrived, his eyes wide and staring at the blood soaking Myrddin's leg.

"It hurts," Myrddin said. *"Christ."*

"You might as well call on Him," Ifan said. "He'll be more forgiving than Nell. She's going to be very put out that you've given yourself another injury."

The sight of the wound brought spots to Myrddin's eyes. The fire that had rushed through him—through all of the warriors—died and he breathed heavily, curling inward on the pain. At the sight of Myrddin down, a Welsh man-at-arms ran over with a lighted torch. Huw threw himself from his horse to crouch beside his father. In the flickering light, Huw's face showed more white than its usual Celtic pale.

Myrddin caught his eyes. "Is that what is taught among the Saxons?"

Huw bit his lip, unable to avert his eyes from Myrddin's wound. "No, sir."

Ifan unbuckled Myrddin's armor to get at the wound and pulled the torn fabric of his pants aside. Gritting his teeth, Myrddin straightened. With Huw supporting his shoulders, they both looked at the damage. Ifan's hands shook as he tended the wound. Myrddin's eyes blackened but Huw's grip kept him conscious as he fought the buzzing in his head. Fortunately, the cut was not deep, just bloody.

"That man was as much our enemy as any other, Huw," Myrddin said, after all three had regained some measure of control. "Why did you hesitate?"

"I meant to kill him . . ."

Ifan ripped a strip from a scrap of cloth he kept in his scrip and began to bind the wound so Myrddin could no longer see it. That was all to the good. Myrddin had doctored many wounded men in his time, but he'd never been quite as sanguine about his own injuries.

Myrddin took a deep breath, still staring down at his leg. "I know you did, son. You fought well, up until the end."

"I'd already killed three men," Huw said. "As I chased this last one down, he was one too many. I didn't want to kill him, not from behind. If he'd been facing me, I wouldn't have cared, but from the back . . ."

"It's not wrong to regret the loss of a life or to show mercy," Myrddin said, "but this war we're fighting . . ." he trailed off too as Ifan wound the last cloth around his leg and pulled it tight. Myrddin felt like puking.

Ifan finished for him. "This war isn't about honor or justice or mercy. Only winning matters, by whatever means necessary. Neither side is going to have any honor left by the end of it."

"The one with honor is going to be the one that's lost?" Huw said. "That's what you mean?"

"We didn't make the rules," Myrddin said.

"You don't mean what you're saying." Huw gripped Myrddin's hand. "Not you."

"He doesn't." King Arthur had dismounted ten paces behind Huw, who now jerked around to face him.

Myrddin reached a hand out to Ifan. "Help me up."

"Father!" Huw turned back to Myrddin. "You can't! You're wounded!"

"I've had worst cuts than this," Myrddin said. It was no less than the truth. Besides, he wasn't going to get back to Nell any quicker by lying in the sand. Ifan grasped Myrddin's forearm and with the help of his sword, Myrddin levered himself to his feet. He was shivering badly now, most likely from shock as well as the cold November air. He grasped Ifan's shoulder with his left hand to stay upright.

Arthur studied Myrddin as he wove in front of him on his one good foot, nodded, and then gestured with his sword to Huw. "Kneel before me."

Huw hesitated, blinking, and then walked stiff-legged to within five feet of the King.

"Give me your sword." Arthur pointed the tip of his own sword at Huw.

Eyes wide, Huw turned his sword, bloody as it was, and presented it hilt out to the King. King Arthur, in turn, gave it to Cai, who grinned as he cleaned the blade with quick, efficient movements. He handed it back to his brother, who gestured to Myrddin. Finding that his pain had faded, and by using Ifan as a crutch, Myrddin took short hobbling steps to stand beside Arthur. Myrddin grasped the sword and drove it tip down into the sand in front of the kneeling Huw.

"I would have your oath," Arthur said. "Are you man enough to give it?"

Huw stared up at King Arthur and Myrddin, standing side by side before him. "Yes, my lord."

"Do you swear to fear God, to obey His laws, to serve your lord, to protect the weak, and to be honorable, chivalrous, generous, and truthful in all things?" Arthur said.

"I swear." Huw's voice cracked as it hadn't for months.

Myrddin tried to take a step towards Huw, but before he'd moved his foot three inches, his leg buckled underneath him. Ifan grabbed Myrddin's arm to keep him from falling and it was Arthur who stepped forward and backhanded Huw across the face. Huw rocked from the blow, and then straightened, letting no emotion show on his face, knowing that was expected of him as a man. Arthur pulled Huw's sword from the sand and held it out to him. Huw took the hilt, astonishment clear on his face.

"Stand as a knight, Sir Huw ap Myrddin," King Arthur said.

Huw popped to his feet as only a sixteen year old can, his initial nervousness transformed from disbelief, to astonishment, to joy. He crossed the sand to Myrddin in two strides, a smile a mile wide on his face. Myrddin put a hand to the side of Huw's head and pulled him closer. He grinned, no longer feeling the pain in his leg. Suddenly, they found themselves in the center of a ring of men, cheering and pummeling them, jubilant in their victory.

Ifan wrapped his arm around Huw's shoulders. "You're a good man."

Huw laughed, and everyone laughed with him.

Into the midst of the joviality, rode Gruffydd. "Where is my son? I don't see him among the dead."

245

Cai and Arthur had stepped out of the ring of men, once it became raucous, and now it was Cai who strode forward to stand at Gruffydd's stirrup. The rest sobered, recalling the seriousness of the morning's events.

"He is not among the Saxons," Cai said. "My brother sent men through the tunnel, as well as overland to Garth Celyn, to inform those who guard the trap door that it should be safe to open. We should have news soon of those who never left the tunnel."

Gruffydd didn't look satisfied, but within ten minutes, Cai's word proved true. One of Arthur's personal guards jogged from the entrance. "If it pleases you, my lords, Lord Bedwyr asks that you return to the castle. Owain ap Gruffydd lies at the foot of the stairs."

Myrddin stared up at Gwynfor's back, sure he was never going to be able to mount her. Still, between Huw and Ifan, they got him astride and heading home. They entered Garth Celyn through the main gate and Myrddin dismounted awkwardly. Along with many other men, he limped to the top of the stairs that led to the tunnel.

King Arthur was just ahead. "This way, sire," Bedwyr said, his expression grave.

He and Arthur walked down the stairs and through the door at the bottom. Nobody stopped Myrddin from following, although the bandage around his thigh received more than one look. The activity had him bleeding through the cloths. Nell was *not* going to be happy.

Owain lay just inside the doorway to the tunnel, propped against the wall and alive—barely. A body sprawled on the other side of him, a knife thrust through his midsection. Myrddin didn't recognize him, but Cai did. He stood at the man's feet with his hands on his hips, staring down at the body, his eyes narrowed in recognition and disgust.

Owain was speaking to Nell as Myrddin arrived. "Don't try to save me. If I survive until dawn, I'm for the gallows."

Nell had been pressing hard on his wound to stop the flow of blood, but now he pushed at her hands and she removed them. Owain rested one hand on the spot just above his left hip. The blood began to flow freely through the cloth. Choking on a sob, Nell got to her feet. Just as she moved away, Gruffydd rumbled up and fell to his knees in the place Nell had vacated.

He took Owain's hand. "What is this, my son?" His voice was gruff. "What are you doing here?"

Owain's face twisted into a grimace. His voice came harshly. "I followed your example, Father. All my life we've fought against Arthur. You meant me to believe you sided with him this time? I'm afraid that I could not."

Gruffydd bowed his head and his shoulders sagged.

Owain's next words were for Cai. "I understand you've been looking for this man." He tipped his head towards the fallen traitor.

Geraint spoke softly in Myrddin's ear. "He belongs to Cai's own guard, from the former garrison at Denbigh. Do not forget that we cannot trust this man."

As if I could.

Cai said nothing, merely toed the dead man's heel and shot a glance at Arthur, who didn't notice it, as he still watched Owain.

"What do you want from me?" Owain said.

"From you, nothing," Arthur said. "For Wales, peace. That is all I have ever wanted for her. We'll leave you to say goodbye to your father."

Arthur moved towards the door and Myrddin reached for Nell's hand. He led her away, his vision etched with a picture of Gruffydd, his head in his hands, kneeling beside the failing body of his son.

18

27 November 537 AD

"**Y**ou're the last person I'd have expected to see here, Myrddin," Gareth said. "When was the last time you darkened the door of a church?"

Myrddin half-turned to look at Gareth, who continued smirking. Myrddin opted not to mention to Gareth that he set foot in a church every night in his dreams, on the way to dying.

They were standing at the rear of the packed Church of St. Deiniol to honor the date of the church's dedication. They might be in the middle of a war and all of Wales might be under interdict, but Arthur ap Uther lived a pious life. It was a holy day, and all of Garth Celyn had turned out to celebrate it.

It had been an amusing scene, in fact, when the King had arrived at the church. Neither Brother Rhys, who ran the church, nor Brother Llywelyn, who led the adjacent monastery, had been prepared for the crowd that had ridden the three miles from Garth

Celyn and descended on Bangor at four o'clock on a Friday afternoon in order to celebrate the service before sunset.

"What is this? What is this?" Rhys had said, running around the sanctuary in a panic, having been unable to waylay either the King or Anian, who'd accompanied him. Because Rhys then refused to hold the service, Anian himself had ordered the candles on the altar lit.

Now, they were two hours into the service and Myrddin was tired of standing. But as was increasingly the case, he wasn't going anywhere without Nell. He lifted his chin, indicating to Gareth where she stood with bowed head, Huw beside her. A few feet beyond stood Cai. He'd found religion, apparently, and no longer left King Arthur's side. If that wasn't irritating enough, Arthur had reminded the company a dozen times these last three days how brilliantly Cai had fought. To Myrddin's mind, it was as if he was spitting into the wind, daring the fates to disagree with him.

"I see," Gareth said. "Do you trust your son to see her safely back to Garth Celyn?"

"Of course." Myrddin looked at Gareth more closely. "Why?"

"All may not be as it seems."

Myrddin snorted under his breath. He could only agree with that assessment. He despised standing in the same room with so many traitors. While Rhys had disappeared, refusing to countenance the use of the church under these circumstances, Brother Llywelyn had stayed, hovering on the margins of the crowd as if to prevent someone from stealing the candlesticks. It was insulting.

"Tell your son you'll be staying behind," Gareth said.

Myrddin nodded. Twenty minutes later, as the service ended, he caught Huw's eye. "I've a task to do," Myrddin said, when they reached him, Nell's arm in Huw's. "I'll see you at the castle."

"That will be fine," Nell said. "One of the villagers from Bangor tells me her niece is laboring with some difficulty. Huw can see me there, and then home when it's over."

Huw nodded, obliging as always, although his eyes on his father were intent. Myrddin clapped him on the shoulder to indicate all was well and watched them leave, heading towards the horses with the rest of the crowd, the bulk of which was easily visible from the dozen torches that lit up the clearing in front of the church steps. King Arthur was among them, bareheaded, half a head taller than most of the men. He mounted his horse and rode away, flanked on one side by Gruffydd and on the other by Bedwyr.

By Bedwyr?

"You note it too?" Gareth said, looking past Myrddin to the King's entourage. "His mistake was to be *too* attentive. The King may think nothing of his absence—in truth may even be relieved to ride without him—but it's glaring to me who has tailed our traitorous prince these last three days."

"What is it you suspect?" Myrddin said.

"Cai wanted to be here alone—he said as much to King
Arthur when he broached the subject of the holy day. Cai
discouraged King Arthur from coming—but Arthur refused to take
the hint."

"So all of Garth Celyn came. No wonder Rhys and
Llywelyn were taken aback," Myrddin said. "Does King Arthur
know you're spying on his brother?"

Gareth snorted a laugh. "No. He would not countenance
it. But I do what is best for Wales. Come."

They re-entered the church, slipping back into the nave to
wait for the last of the parishioners to leave. Anian hadn't
extinguished the candles he'd lit and they flickered on the altar,
minutes from going out. Eventually, all was dark and quiet.

"There's no one here," Myrddin said.

"Isn't there?" Gareth said. "Cai hasn't left the church."

"Could he have used a different exit?"

"There's only the one," Gareth said. "I suspect he's in the
belfry, if only because I saw Llywelyn's skirts disappearing up the
stairs earlier."

With a tip of his head, Gareth indicated a curtain on the
northern wall. Myrddin realized he'd never looked behind it,
never thought to. Together with Gareth, he poked his head past it,
observed the shadowed stairs, and hastily retreated at the sound of
voices above them.

"Hide," Gareth said.

Myrddin slipped behind one of the limestone statues that
lined the walls of the nave, an older one, but with a large base.

Gareth spun on his heel and at first Myrddin thought he was looking for a similar spot for himself. But he wasn't. Instead he waited, planted in the center of the floor with his hands on his hips.

Three men came through the curtain, Llywelyn in the lead. He lit the way with a lantern which threw shadows on the wall that separated the nave from the foyer. Because they spoke among themselves, distracted by their own issues, the three men were almost upon Gareth before Llywelyn halted abruptly.

"You!"

"Cousin," Gareth said. "I thought I'd find you here among your betters." He nodded his head at Cai, who stepped out from behind Llywelyn.

"What do you want?" Llywelyn said.

"I knew you had to be up to something," Gareth said. "And now I know what it is."

"Just kill him," the third man said. Myrddin didn't recognize either his voice or his shape. Nor did he dare stir from behind his statue to get a better look.

"Ahh," Gareth said. "My dear Agravaine." And Myrddin understood that Gareth said the man's name for his benefit. "*You're* the secret they've been keeping. King Arthur might rationalize a meeting with my slippery cousin, but you—you he wouldn't forgive."

"Which is why we need to kill him," Agravaine said.

Gareth spread his arms wide. "Go ahead. I suspect the consequences might be greater than you know." Myrddin's hand went to his sword, his stomach churning and his head spinning with the shock of this situation. If he'd expected anything, it wasn't this.

Agravaine made to step forward, but Cai put out an arm to stop him. "He's Modred's. You can't touch him."

"You tell me false!" Agravaine's tone dripped with disdain and outrage. "He can't be."

"He was spying for Modred as early as 532," Cai said. "I know because I was at Modred's court then."

"Why didn't I know of this?"

"Perhaps because you don't know everything!" Cai said. "Be quiet and let me think." A pause, and then Cai spoke again, directing his words at Gareth, who was the only man he appeared to view as more-or-less an equal. "What do you want?"

"Assurances," Gareth said.

"Don't listen to h—" Llywelyn said.

Cai cut him off. "Shut up, Monk." And then to Gareth. "You have them. What is your concern? That Modred won't like what we do?"

"More that you'll muck it up, just like the attack on Garth Celyn," Gareth said.

"That was Owain's plan," Cai said. "He's always been long on ideas and short on follow through."

"It would have worked but for this . . . Myrddin," Llywelyn said. "I told you we should've removed him sooner."

"He'll be taken care of before too long," Cai said. "Agravaine has it in hand."

"Good to know as Myrddin's a nosy bastard," Gareth said.

"Are we done here?" Agravaine said. "I have a boat to catch." Dismissing his fellows with a wave, he strode towards the exit and flung open the door. The cold night air blew over Myrddin, accompanied by the staccato of rain.

Llywelyn and Cai followed, though Cai paused on the doorstep. "We'll speak later," he said to Gareth before disappearing.

"Yes, my lord."

The door swung home, leaving the foyer completely silent but for the drip of water from the roof. Myrddin was loathe to rise from his hiding place lest they return—and even more reluctant to face Gareth.

"You heard some things I would have preferred you hadn't," Gareth said, into the quiet.

"Does King Arthur know your role in this?" Myrddin finally stood and stepped from behind the statue.

"He knows Modred thinks I spy for him," Gareth said. "He doesn't know that I once truly did."

"Am I to believe you remain loyal to King Arthur now? After what I heard?"

"It's the truth."

Myrddin contemplated Gareth's face. He seemed sincere, but Myrddin felt manipulated. "Admittedly, you could have come alone and confronted them without me. It would have been safer for you."

"But not safer for the King," Gareth said. "Knowing that Cai and Agravaine are allies, I cannot now believe that he should go south. They may well be using Edgar for their own ends. You should know, in addition, that Modred confirmed Edgar in his inheritance a few days ago."

"*Cnych!*" Myrddin said.

"I share your sentiments," Gareth said. "I brought you as witness because I found what I was looking for, but I'm not in a position to speak to the King of the dangers that face him in the coming weeks."

Myrddin stared at him. "What? Why ever not?"

"I play a dangerous game, Myrddin," he said. "Modred trusts me; Cai trusts me. So does my King. Few could have played this role so well for so long. But if I speak to King Arthur of Cai's betrayal, I throw all to the fates."

"You're afraid," Myrddin said.

"Cautious," Gareth said. "What if Cai discovers I've deceived him? I will have lost all ability to serve Arthur effectively."

"So you leave it to me?"

Gareth waved a hand dismissively. "You're one of his household knights. Your loyalty is without question. He will listen to you."

"I pray you're right."

19

28 November 537 AD

He threw me out of his office, Nell." Myrddin paced around the work table in the center of her herb hut. He and Gareth had ridden home and Myrddin had gone straight to Arthur, leaving Gareth drinking in the hall as if nothing untoward had happened. Myrddin's subsequent conversation with King Arthur had been short, lasting five minutes at most. In that time, Myrddin had explained what he'd seen. Arthur had shouted Myrddin down before the words were half out of his mouth. Even Geraint, who was witness, was taken aback by Arthur's rare display of temper.

"Sit, Myrddin," Nell said, "before you upset all my tinctures and salves. Besides, it's very late. You'd do better to sleep than think."

Myrddin sat but was on his feet again an instant later, too restless to stay still. "He and I have always maintained a good relationship, and now he thinks I'm a traitor."

"Tell me what happened again."

"I told him that Cai, Llywelyn, and Agravaine had met in the belfry at Bangor. I told him that I believed the letter from Edgar a trap and asked if I could go in his stead, or, as an alternative, travel south to Brecon as Lord Cedric suggested. Arthur ignored my request, instead asking if I knew what the meeting had been about. I told him I didn't know. He asked if I'd actually seen Agravaine's face. I hadn't, and since I couldn't reveal Gareth's role in all this, the King instantly disbelieved my whole story. He didn't want to believe it.

"And then Cai came into the office, that incessant sneer on his face, before he wiped it clean and denied everything."

Nell moved to stand beside him, her hand on his shoulder. "The King loves his brother, all reason aside. And without Gareth, you have no proof. This isn't your fault."

Myrddin grunted his disagreement and disgust, moving towards the brazier to raise the fire. When he'd left the hut earlier, he'd banked the coals so they'd continue to burn low, but he'd been gone so long they were almost out. Soon, Myrddin had the coals glowing again. The hut was small enough that the heat from it would make some headway against the cold. The activity calmed him and he found his shoulders sagging with his acceptance of his failure. "I must return to the hall and speak to Geraint. I cannot leave it there."

Now it was Nell's turn to pace and she circled her table. The light glinted off the blonde highlights in the wisps of hair that escaped her coif. Myrddin had never noticed them before; he knew he'd never seen anyone as beautiful as she. He'd lost track of his sensible decision to keep her at arm's length. It sucked the air from his lungs to realize how much she still kept inside her own head; he could only hope that she, too, loved despite herself.

At last she stopped in front of him. "Tell Geraint everything."

He studied her face. "Everything?"

"Yes," she said. "I'll come with you if you think it will help."

"Not yet," he said. "Let me try again alone first." He moved away, ready to leave and glad to have the decision made. But Nell caught his arm before he'd gone two steps.

"What you did was very brave."

"It had to be done." He turned back to her. "Time is too short to waste." He started to pull away but she didn't let him go, tugging him closer and forcing him to focus on her again.

"You be careful," she said. "I told you the only way to prevent myself from weeping was to laugh, but I can't face the coming weeks with laughter."

He looked down at her, seeing the concern in her eyes. "I lived thirty-six years with nobody to worry about me. I can take care of myself."

"I know." She stepped closer, placing her hands flat against his chest. "And is that what you want?"

Myrddin didn't look away. His hands found her waist and rested there, one on each hip. He looked into her eyes. "I've never had a choice before." He leaned forward and kissed Nell's forehead, his lips lingering in her hair.

"I shouldn't have let you go into battle without an answer," she said.

Their faces were inches apart, hers upturned looking into his. Time and silence stretched out as Myrddin stared down at her. Then without a conscious decision on his part, he brought his lips down on hers. She wrapped her arms around his neck and he pulled her tight against him.

"God, Nell." He forced himself to take a breath. "I don't want to lose you."

"You won't," she said. "No matter what happens, you won't."

His arms encircled her. He didn't want to let her go, but knew he had to. He groaned, his forehead to hers and his desire for her a deep ache within him. "I must see Geraint." He eased away.

"I know that too." She allowed him to lift her hands from his chest. He squeezed them once, and then left the hut, heading down the garden walkway to the kitchen, his mind full of Nell.

Halfway there, Geraint stepped out of the darkness. "What is it that you cannot leave?"

Myrddin pulled up short.

"The King leaves for Powys in three days. I must know what it is you aren't telling me," Geraint said. His tone was forceful, but not menacing. Urgent, rather.

"Over here." Myrddin glanced around to make sure that nobody had followed him and that Nell had shut the door to the herb hut. It wasn't so much that he didn't want her to overhear their conversation, but rather he didn't want her to suffer for his failings if this went as awry as in Arthur's office.

"Speak," Geraint said, once they'd retreated to the far corner of the kitchen garden where the side of the keep met the garden wall.

"If you're worried that Modred turned me to his side in his dungeon at Rhuddlan," Myrddin said, "that is not the case."

"I have no such concern," Geraint said. "If you'd been bought, there'd be signs."

The compulsion to tell the truth had Myrddin pressing his lips together to keep the words back. And then, for better or worse, he gave up the fight. "I fear for the King's life because I already know the future. I know what will happen by the Cam River if he goes to meet Edgar of Wigmore."

Geraint stared at him. "What in Christ's holy name is that supposed to mean?"

"I've seen it," Myrddin said. "I've seen him fall, stood over his body to protect him, and fallen myself. I've seen all Wales weep."

In the darkness, Myrddin couldn't read Geraint's expression, but he stood so still that if not for the light coming through the open kitchen door he would have been indistinguishable from the wall at his back. The scar that slashed across his forehead stood out white against his darker skin.

"No." Geraint shook his head. "You can't know what you're saying."

Myrddin stepped away, rethinking his approach. "Come, my lord. A cup of wine wouldn't go amiss."

Geraint hesitated, and then nodded. They returned to the hall, Geraint walking several paces behind Myrddin. By the time Geraint lowered himself onto a bench near the fire, a cup and carafe in front of him and Myrddin settled across the table, Geraint's intensity had lessened. He took a swig and wiped his mouth with the back of his hand.

"Let's try this again," Geraint said. A twinkle appeared in his eye that told Myrddin he didn't believe a word he'd said, and for that, Myrddin was almost grateful. Geraint might treat him like a lunatic from now on, but not so much that he'd hang him as a traitor. "I'd like to hear the rest."

Geraint's expression was such as a man might wear when he was settling in to hear a bard's tale of how Gwydion, son of Dôn, brought pigs to Math ap Mathonwy when he ruled Gwynedd as its king, or how Gwydion and Math conspired to make a wife for Gwydion's nephew out of flowers. They were stories that he didn't believe but at the same time, thought might provide good entertainment for an evening.

Myrddin folded his hands around his cup, took a sip, and set it on the table in front of him. "On the 11th of December, King

Arthur will go to St. Cannen's church at the request of Edgar. It is a trap, as I told you before, and he and the eighteen men of his personal guard will die. The Saxons will remove King Arthur's head and send it to Modred."

"And you know this . . . how?"

"Since I was a boy, I've dreamt it. I have fought and died for our King more times than I can count—always at the church by the Cam River; always straddling the fallen body of the King. Lately, I've had the visions even while awake."

"So you're what? A saint? A seer? A wizard?" Geraint said, his amusement of before gone.

Myrddin leaned forward across the table, determined to defuse Geraint's anger if he could. "This is me, Geraint. Myrddin. I've ridden with the King for twenty years and I tell you I've *seen* it. I've lived it. This is what is coming and it has haunted me my whole life!"

"And you've kept these visions hidden all this time?" Geraint said, mocking. "I'm the first to know?"

"If this is your response, is it any wonder I've told no one?" Myrddin said. "Look what happened when I tried to tell the King about something I saw with my own eyes! I only tell you now because we are so close to the end."

Geraint rubbed his chin with one hand. "All right. Say I believe you. What do you propose?"

"It's as if I've had a path laid before my feet—like footsteps in the snow—that I've followed time and again to my death. I refuse to follow that path any longer. We must forge a new one."

Geraint leaned back in his chair, ran his fingers through his hair, and then scrubbed his face with both hands. "Christ, Myrddin." He dropped his hands to rest them helplessly in his lap. "I don't want to know this. I don't want to hear this."

"I know," Myrddin said. "As long as you protect the King, I don't care if you believe me, but you mustn't stop me from doing what I can to help him and Wales."

"I will protect the King," Geraint said. "But perhaps it would be best if you do as you suggested and ride south to Brecon and Buellt."

"So I don't embarrass you with my delusions?" Myrddin said.

Geraint looked straight at Myrddin, meeting his eyes, his jaw set. "No. That's not it at all. You must ride to south so that what you describe never comes to pass."

* * * * *

"I need you to get up, Huw," Nell said.

Huw rolled over and his eyes met hers. Instantly, he was awake and attentive. "What's wrong? Father—"

"Myrddin's fine. He's getting the horses. I'll tell you on the way."

"Where are we going?"

"Brecon. And Buellt after that if we have time."

Nell was already moving away. Huw, fortunately, had slept close to the door and had been easy to find. The other men were used to her by now and nobody else, even if awake, had stirred to stop her.

Huw caught up with her by the time she reached the door, shrugging into his coat and cloak. "I'll need my armor." He slept with his sword, as befitting a newly dubbed knight.

"Your father has it," she said. They left the barracks and trotted across the courtyard towards the stables.

"And you're coming with us?" Huw said.

Nell glanced up at Huw. "Yes. Don't you dare take Myrddin's side in this!"

"He's trying to stop you," Huw said, not as a question.

"Of course he is, but he's wrong to. I can help. I've cobbled together a nun's habit. If I wear it as we travel, it will provide an adequate ruse for our journey."

Huw pursed his lips in thought. "That's a good idea, actually." They turned into the stables and came to a halt in front of the horses. Myrddin was adjusting the stirrups on the last.

"No it isn't." Myrddin straightened and glowered in Nell's direction.

Nell whirled on him, finger pointing. "You don't get to decide this! I already cleared it with Geraint."

They glared at each other for a count of five, and then Myrddin gave way. "I don't like it."

"I know you don't," Nell said. "But you won't regret it."

Regardless of his doubts, Myrddin had saddled three horses, not two, one for each of them. As she grabbed the bridle of her horse and prepared to mount, Nell smiled inwardly, not so much at his capitulation or that she'd 'won,' but because he respected her enough to bring her even when every fiber in him protested.

"*Jesus Christ!*"

Nell had half-pulled herself into the saddle when the curse came from behind her. She swung around to see Myrddin, his hands up and helpless, with Deiniol behind him pressing a knife to Myrddin's throat.

"Well, well. You're leaving Garth Celyn in the wee hours, *mochyn*? Have I caught myself a traitor?"

"You would know far more about that than we would!" Nell said. She took a step towards the pair but arrested her movement as Deiniol tightened his grip on Myrddin's hair. The knife pressed far enough into Myrddin's skin to draw blood.

"Stay back, love," Myrddin said. He'd placed his hand on the hilt of his sword, but could do nothing more than that. Huw had moved beside her but was helpless as she, staring at Deiniol and Myrddin.

"What do you want?" Nell said.

Deiniol gazed at her through narrowed eyes and then spit out the truth—maybe for the first time ever. "I've caught him now. He can't get away with his treachery this time. He's always had it easy—the one touched by God, the one everyone always trusted and believed, and for whom everything came easy. He's a nobody! He took from me what was mine!"

That was such a different perspective from the one that Myrddin had expressed, Nell couldn't reconcile the two. She met

Myrddin's eyes, trying to speak without speaking and discover a way out of this predicament in which Myrddin's throat didn't end up cut.

"Let him go, Deiniol," Huw said.

Huw was drawing his sword, despite the danger to Myrddin, when Gareth appeared out of the darkness of the stalls. A finger to his lips, he approached silently from behind Deiniol, his sword out. He pressed the tip into Deiniol's back. "That's enough," he said.

Deiniol started.

"Your grievances have no place here," Gareth said. "Let Myrddin go."

Deiniol clenched and unclenched his hand in Myrddin's hair, and then eased up on the knife. He straightened and slipped it into the sheath at his waist. "My lord." He bowed stiffly in Gareth's direction.

Myrddin swung around to face him. "The next time you touch me, I will run you through," he said, his face in Deiniol's, "even if it would anger my lord and yours!"

"Why are you here, Deiniol?" Gareth placed a hand on Myrddin's chest and stepped between the two men.

"Lord Cai believes we have a traitor among us," Deiniol said. "He charged me with discovering his identity." He gestured towards Myrddin. "Who but a traitor would leave Garth Celyn in the middle of the night."

"You know what Modred did to me," Myrddin said, "and what it took for me to escape."

Deiniol smirked. "I admit, to suffer those wounds simply to put on a show would imply an unprecedented devotion to duty, even for you, Myrddin."

"There are men among the King's company who are more deserving of your knife than I. Including your own lord."

Gareth shot Myrddin a quelling look. "How long have you been following Myrddin?"

"Long enough," Deiniol said.

"Be off." Gareth threw out a hand and stepped back. "Your duties lie elsewhere."

Deiniol gave Myrddin an evil look but turned away, disappearing through the far doorway of the stables.

Gareth turned back to Myrddin. "I heard what happened with King Arthur. I'm sorry."

"You set me up," Myrddin said.

"Myrddin—" Nell took his arm. She'd never seen him this angry. Gareth's appearance, instead of easing his temper, appeared to have increased it. He was vibrating with the effort it took to contain it.

"I did not foresee this outcome," Gareth said. "But I do not believe all is lost. Cedric could be a valuable ally. Even Edgar might turn out to be sincere—I find it more likely now than before I knew of the alliance between Cai and Agravaine, since Edgar despises them both. I take comfort in the fact that you, of all people, are going south to determine the truth."

Myrddin's jaw remained set. "I, at least, will do my duty. We will see you along the Cam at the King's camp—or I will see you in hell." With that, he threw himself onto his horse and urged her out of the stables.

Gareth moved to help Nell mount and she opted not to shake him off. Still, she couldn't quite be civil. "I don't trust you. You are far too concerned about your own neck."

"And your man is too noble for his own good," Gareth said. He paused. "I'm glad of it."

Nell looked at him for another heartbeat; then pulled at the reins, turning her horse's head to follow Huw and Myrddin. Geraint waited for them by the wicket gate, having apparently missed the exchange in the stables entirely; it was by his power that they were leaving and he'd sworn to assuage Arthur's anger when the King discovered their absence.

"May God go with you," Geraint said, as they passed through.

20

6 December 537 AD

"**Y**ou were right not to leave her behind." Huw leaned across the space between him and Myrddin to murmur the words. "It's always better to do as Nell suggests."

"I heard that." Nell glanced at Huw and gave him her sweetest smile. "But you are correct."

The three of them were jogging along well down the old Roman road to Brecon. The weather had eased, turning warmer and bringing overcast skies and threatening rain instead of the snow of the past days. Huw and Myrddin flanked Nell, as her escort and protectors. Even masterless men would find the prospect of attacking two armed men and a nun daunting.

The eastern slopes of the Cambrian Mountains were as rugged and barren as their northern counterparts, but as they followed the road eastward, towards the farmlands along the Welsh border, the air warmed further. The snow was reduced to pockets, mostly tucked into the northern slopes of the hills. Nell was looking forward to reaching Brecon not long after nightfall, which always came too early this time of year. They'd slept safe but not overly warm in a series of castles and hunting lodges that linked Eryri with Powys and whose castellans were loyal to Arthur. She was cold, tired, and smelled of horse—and they hadn't even gotten to the hard part yet.

They'd skirted the hill of Yr Allt to the north of the Usk river valley and were continuing east, expecting nothing untoward, when up ahead a horse whinnied, the desperate pitch carrying through the still air. The sounds of men shouting and swords clashing followed. Huw slowed to listen. "That can't be good."

"Definitely not," Myrddin said.

The two men shared a glance and then spurred their horses forward. Nell hung back, knowing that she would only hinder the men in a fight. Twenty yards ahead, Huw outpaced Myrddin, his sword held high. In that formation, they rode around a corner, heading towards the ford of the fast-running Cilieni River, swollen from the autumn rains. Another eighty yards further on a dozen men battled—or what remained of them. One group had caught another in an ambush at the ford.

Dead men and horses lay in the water. A cry rose in Nell's throat at the sight of a lone man in Cedric's colors standing astride another who sprawled on the ground, unmoving. The knight held off four others in red and white surcoats from a good position, even if a desperate one. In order to reach him, his enemy had to climb the bank leading up from the river.

In the excitement of the fight, only one of the men noted them coming and half-turned in his seat. He had a single heartbeat to register Huw's approach, without even time to raise his shield to defend himself, before the boy swung his sword in a mighty sweep of his arm and severed the man's head from his body.

"Huw!" Nell found her voice, afraid Huw would barrel right into the other men and fall under their combined assault. The taste of fear was sour in her mouth.

But Huw was a good soldier and while his horse carried him another few steps down the bank, he was able to recover. Before he went into the water, Myrddin caught up with him. In parallel formation, the two men charged towards the three remaining soldiers, two of whom were struggling to turn their horses in the river. The third was still intent on running the lone defender through.

One of the attackers danced around Myrddin. Their swords connected. To Nell's eyes, it was the same as she imagined any other fight: hack, slash, twist, each trying to gain advantage over the other. Then Myrddin's horse found a hole and her leg twisted. Going down, Myrddin threw himself from her back, barreling into the man he was fighting to bring him off his horse and into the water.

They landed with a terrifying clunk, instantly soaked, their boots filling with water and their soaked clothing adding to the weight of their mail. The man's head hit the stones under the water and he lay stunned, with the wind knocked out of him.

Myrddin pushed up on one knee—and having lost his sword and shield in the fall—drove his fist into the man's jaw. His head fell back into the water.

The man coughed and sputtered, trying to rise, but Myrddin held his head under the water for a count of ten to subdue him and then grasped his arm and began to haul him to the far bank of the river. Huw, meanwhile, had dispatched his opponent. The man lay on the southern end of the ford, bleeding from a mortal wound, before floating off of it, heading downstream. Turning away, Huw urged his horse out of the water and up the bank towards the final enemy soldier.

That man noted Huw's approach. Rather than continue to fight a battle he might not win, and having dispatched Cedric's last knight, he spurred his horse eastward, down the road that led to Brecon. Huw visibly warred with himself as to whether or not he should follow, and then didn't. Instead, he dismounted and fell to his knees beside the body of the man who'd had such a staunch defender.

"It's Lord Cedric himself!" Huw looked back at Nell, still on the other side of the river.

Myrddin dragged his combatant up the slope and dumped him half-in and half-out of the water. Mentally pushing aside the violence she'd just witnessed, even if the memory of it would haunt her forever, Nell trotted her horse into the river and across the ford. Once up the other side, she dismounted and crouched opposite Huw.

"Let me." She felt for a pulse, which was hard to discern as her own heart still beat in her ears, her outward calm a false front for the choking horror inside her. "He's alive. His heart is strong."

Soaked, Myrddin limped up the bank. After a brief inspection, he rolled the body of Cedric's defender off his shins where he'd fallen. "The wound is here." Myrddin gestured to a slash across his right thigh, not dissimilar to Myrddin's own healing injury. The stroke had slid just under his mail armor, cutting the thick muscle but not the bone or tendon.

Long ago, Nell's husband had explained to her why so many soldiers were wounded in the same way when fighting well-armored opponents. A man must direct his attack toward legs or faces, or deliver crushing blows, because it was nearly impossible to pierce an opponent's mail in hand-to-hand fighting. In this case, Cedric's opponent would have gotten his weapon underneath Cedric's shield while Cedric was astride his horse. The man then hoped to deliver the killing blow once he'd put Cedric on the ground, but Cedric's man-at-arms had protected him from that.

"He's out of his senses," Nell said. "Perhaps he hit his head." With gentle hands, she removed his helmet, set it to one side, and then felt at the back of Cedric's head. She glanced at Myrddin who'd slumped beside her on the ground and looked a bit green around the edges too. "Give me a moment to get my supplies."

Myrddin sat with his legs splayed in front of him, spent. His horse had righted herself on the far bank and now stood, one leg lifted, on a grassy verge. If her injury was a sprain, they might be able to save her. Otherwise, it would be more humane to slit her throat right now.

"I'll see to her." Huw met Nell's eyes and acknowledging their joint concern for Myrddin's well-being.

"Thank you," Nell said. She removed her healer's pouch and flask from her saddlebags and returned to Cedric.

Myrddin, meanwhile, had gotten himself more under control. While she crouched again beside the wounded lord, Myrddin grabbed one of the linen scraps from her bundle and ripped a strip with his teeth. Nell held the flask of alcohol above the wound, hesitating, knowing that if Cedric was at all conscious when she poured it on him, he would leap from the ground, shrieking in pain. As it was, when she tipped the liquid over the wound, Cedric's body stiffened, his back arching. And then he bucked.

"Help me hold him!" Nell said.

Myrddin dropped the bandages on top of her leather pouch and pressed down on Cedric's shoulders while Nell mopped up the remaining liquid and smeared calendula salve along the length of the wound.

"You sew him up," Myrddin said. "You've the finer hand."

She nodded, while adding, "Riverside medicine. Not my favorite." With a hand that didn't tremble, she threaded her needle. Myrddin leaned in to hold together the edges of Cedric's skin above his right knee while she sewed. Then, he lashed bandages around Cedric's thigh and with his stronger hands, tied them. About the time Myrddin finished, Cedric opened his eyes.

275

"I know you." Cedric looked into Nell's face. "Am I in heaven?"

"I'm a nun, not an angel," she said, "although, I'm not even that anymore." With a swipe of her hand she removed her headdress. Her thick braid swung loose, the end tied with a leather thong.

Cedric turned his head as he sensed Myrddin on the other side of him. "It's you." He blinked.

"Myrddin, again, my lord. I've come with Huw, my son."

"Ah," Cedric said. "He found you, then."

"He did."

"Help me up."

Nell opened her mouth to protest and then closed it. 'Riverside medicine' was not subject to the conventional rules of healing. The man needed to stay prone, but the sun had set and the light was fading. None of them wanted to be caught by the windy ford once it got dark, fair game for marauders, both animal and human.

With Nell's help, Myrddin levered him to his feet. Upright, Cedric surveyed his dead companions. "Did any of my men survive?"

"None that I know," Myrddin said. "One of the enemy fled and we chose to care for you rather than to follow him."

"Under the circumstances, I can hardly protest," Cedric said.

Nell was glad to see that his dry humor was still in evidence, despite his pain. "Are we going to talk about whose men they were?" She studied the man by the river, who'd begun to moan. He put a hand to the back of his head.

"Their colors tell me they belong to Arthur," Cedric said, matter-of-factly, "but your presence here makes me question it."

"Thank you for that," Myrddin said. He walked down the bank, his boots sliding in the mud, to the injured man-at-arms. At his approach, the man opened his eyes.

"Just because a man wears certain colors, doesn't mean they belong to him," Nell said. "Remember Modred at Shrewsbury." At the battle where Cedric's father died, Modred had deceived them by raising a friendly standard. The opposing forces had allowed Modred's men to get too close and ultimately trap them.

"Such was my thought," Myrddin said, his voice as flat as Cedric's. He squatted beside the injured man and spoke in Welsh. "What's your name?"

The man didn't answer and his eyes remained unfocused. Myrddin repeated the question in Saxon.

"Carl," the man said. His face had been flushed when Myrddin first crouched beside him, but now it paled and he twisted towards his left side, his pain evident.

"Was it truly your mission to kill Cedric ap Aelfric?"

The man didn't answer; all of a sudden he just ceased to be. Myrddin checked his pulse. "He's dead." Myrddin stood. "I didn't think I'd done enough damage to kill him."

Nell refused to chastise herself for the fact that she didn't seem to care that another man had died and turned to Cedric, all business. "You shouldn't be able to stand, but given that you're doing it anyway, can you ride?"

"Of course," he said, and then amended, "with help."

Just then, Huw returned, leading a single horse, his own. His face said, *I'm sorry.*

Myrddin sighed. "It is what it is."

Cedric's own horse had strayed along the river bank, cropping the short grass along its fringe. Huw and Myrddin retrieved it, along with another for Myrddin whose owner no longer needed it. Between the three of them, they managed to get Cedric astride with Nell behind him, to hold him should he weaken.

"You all right?" Myrddin asked her, once she was seated.

She gazed down at him, warring between disbelief and humor. "I held you like this," she said. "I've been around you long enough to get used to wounded men."

Myrddin grinned back at her and then mounted himself.

Despite their efforts, it was immediately clear that Cedric couldn't ride one mile, much less the eight that would bring them into his castle at Brecon. His head lolled back onto Nell's shoulder. "Is there anywhere else we can go?" Nell said. Myrddin had brought his horse closer so he could brace Cedric with his right hand.

"There's a small manor house not far ahead, perhaps a quarter of a mile," Huw said. "I've ridden by it a time or two."

"Its owner was one of my men," Cedric said, his voice a rasp. *Was*, meaning *dead.*

They plodded forward, Nell clutching Cedric around the waist, Myrddin with one hand out, holding Cedric's shoulder, and Huw leading the way. The horses picked their way along the road and then within a dozen yards, they reached a trail and turned onto it, following it north. Fifteen minutes later, they found the house of which Huw and Cedric had spoken, squatting in a clearing amidst the trees.

It wasn't quite what Nell expected for a 'manor house', although it was a cut above the huts that dotted the countryside, in which lived families like the ones who'd worked her father's land. Still in good condition, despite being abandoned, the house was roughly built, one story and a half high, with a wooden door and one shuttered window. Beside it sat an empty paddock, fenced with wood poles, and a barn. The house might even have a wooden floor instead of dirt.

Anxious to get Cedric to safety, they approached the house, ghostly in the moonlight that filtered through the shrouding trees. They arrived at the deserted front door and Myrddin dismounted to allow Cedric to slide off the horse into his arms. Despite the possible indignity of it, Myrddin bent forward and threw Cedric over his shoulder. Huw lashed the reins of their horses to the stockade fence to prevent them from escaping, while Nell reached around Myrddin and lifted the latch to allow them to enter the house.

Nell and Myrddin pushed at the door simultaneously, with Myrddin nudging the bottom of the door with the toe of his boot.

When it didn't immediately give way, he shoved it hard. It opened halfway, but then stuck on something behind it.

They froze on the doorstep. *"Mary, Mother of God,"* Nell said.

The smell of blood and death, oppressive in such a small and enclosed space, wafted over them. Huw, who'd had a hand on Cedric's back to keep him in place—and perhaps because he didn't quite believe he was still alive—stepped to the corner of the house and retched. Myrddin backed away from the door, swallowing hard.

"Let's get him into the barn," Nell said. "We can deal with this later."

She led the way across the paddock and through the barn door, which was open. The barn was bare in a way the house was not. Hay had drifted across the floor to pile near a broken shovel a past resident had left on the floor near the door. Myrddin followed Nell and after a minute, Huw came as well, holding his belly, but recovering. Once inside the barn, Huw kicked at a bed of straw to make sure it wasn't moldy and Myrddin laid Cedric on it. Nell knelt beside him to check his leg wound and feel again at his head.

"He's not fevered," she said.

"Maybe he'll get lucky," Myrddin said.

She shot him a look, a cross between hopeful and skeptical, and then turned back to her patient. "He needs warmth or he'll go into shock."

"If we could get into the house, we could make a fire," Myrddin said.

Nell and Huw looked at him in disbelief.

Myrddin held out his hands. "All I'm saying is that it would be preferable."

"But not possible," Nell said. "Even if we moved the bodies, we couldn't stay in there with the stink. We need to build a fire here."

"I'll get the flint and start it," Huw said. "If I build it at the entrance, we won't choke on the smoke."

Nell nodded, glad that Huw was capable. Then Myrddin put a hand on Nell's shoulder. "Can you manage if I find us firewood?"

"I'm as fine as I can be." She grasped his hand, squeezed once, and let go.

As Myrddin turned away, Cedric opened his eyes. "Thank you," he said. "You could have let me die."

"No," Nell said, leaning in to better assess his wounded leg. "We couldn't."

* * * * *

With a last check of Nell's face, and Cedric's pale one beyond her, Myrddin stepped out of the barn and set off towards the house. Huw was already gathering handfuls of straw. Myrddin worried that the light might alert an enemy to their presence—whether Saxon or Welsh, the choices were near

281

limitless—but a night out here without a fire might well mean Cedric's death.

Holding his nose and without entering the house, Myrddin latched the door to the manor, not wanting to draw wild animals to the smell of blood. Shutters blocked the window in the lower level, meaning that an animal couldn't have strayed inside and died. The remains were human. Myrddin was tempted to return with a torch and discover who was dead, but the pressing needs of the moment had him skirting the corner of the house and heading for the woods beyond it.

Once among the trees, Myrddin slowed, allowing the darkness to envelope him. The luminescence of the snow in the mountains had given way to dark earth and fallen leaves of the more balmy lowlands. Still, the moon was playing cat and mouse with the clouds, which were not as thick as before, so Myrddin wasn't blind. As he moved from tree to tree, picking up every likely piece of wood—wet or dry—he listened hard to the forest. Once he'd circled around to the far corner of the barn, he stilled and let his senses expand. The smell of smoke from Huw's fire filtered towards him, mixing with the scent of pine, but otherwise he was alone in the world.

It had been a long time since he'd stood this way; he could be anywhere in Wales, at anytime in his life. He felt as young as the twelve year old who'd had that first vision, and as old as the man in his dreams, whose only thought was the cold certainty of death as the Saxons closed in around him. He'd always thought it strange that his *seeing* showed him the end of his life, but never what it might take to avert it. He'd never *seen* this location before, had no prior knowledge of rescuing Cedric. Myrddin didn't know what was going to happen tomorrow. He tipped his head back to look up at the familiar stars and breathed in the cool, moist air.

Amidst his fear for Arthur's life, there was a excitement, and a joy, in that fact.

21

7 December 537 AD

Throughout the night, Myrddin, Huw, and Nell took turns with Cedric, staying near him and checking his breathing and pulse every hour to make sure his concussion wouldn't settle him into too deep a sleep. As dawn approached, when Myrddin sat by him and Huw and Nell slept, Cedric woke fully for the first time. Myrddin had just tended to the fire, so it burned hot and gave off enough light to see the outline of the ceiling of the barn, the rusting farming implements and equipment that hung on the walls or were stacked along them, and the shapes of his companions.

"It's been a long time since I've slept in a barn," Cedric said, his voice strong enough for Myrddin to note the amusement in it. "I must have been no older than nine."

"How do you feel, my lord?" Myrddin rested the back of his hand on Cedric's forehead, trying to sense whether he had developed a fever. He was cool enough.

"You've fought for Arthur your whole life," Cedric said, shifting and then wincing as pain shot through his leg. "I'm sure you know how I feel."

"True," Myrddin said. "In fact, I have a new scar on my leg that mirrors yours. I received it a few weeks ago when a Saxon company tried to take Garth Celyn."

At that, Cedric, who'd been gazing up at the ceiling, turned his head to look at Myrddin. "You say, 'tried'. I'd heard your enemies burned the castle to the ground."

Myrddin stared at him. "Why would you say that?"

Cedric pursed his lips. "Because that's what the messenger told me."

Myrddin had a sudden fear that the Saxons had attacked Garth Celyn since they'd left—that the first attempt had been a ruse to make them think they were secure. Warily, Myrddin said, "On the 24th of November, a fortnight ago, Owain ap Gruffydd and a company of Saxon soldiers attempted to enter Garth Celyn through a tunnel that runs from the beach, north of the castle, into Garth Celyn. We stopped them."

Cedric pushed up on his elbows, trying to straighten enough to sit up. Myrddin grasped him under his arm to help him. "You tell me truly?" Cedric said. "The date is correct, but the outcome is not what I was told."

"Did the rider say who'd been killed?"

"He said that Arthur's daughter was captured and taken to Mercia and a host of the King's personal guard killed, although

King Arthur himself escaped." Cedric paused. "I can see from your face that this is not true."

"None of it," Myrddin said. "Not even a morsel. Whom did the messenger serve?"

Cedric pressed into his forehead with two fingers, his eyes closed. "Agravaine."

"I don't understand it," Myrddin said. "Why lie?"

"To counter your victory at the Straits, of course," Cedric said. "To convince all of us who've wavered at times to stay true to Modred."

"But eventually you'd find out . . ." Myrddin's voice trailed off at the subversive logic. With helpless understanding, he nodded. "By then, Agravaine assumed he'd have killed King Arthur or severely weakened his cause. Agravaine isn't worried about you learning of his deception next year or even next week. He wants you steadfast now."

"News of a Welsh defeat could stiffen the spines of the lords in Modred's cause long enough for Agravaine to achieve his aims," Cedric said. He settled back into the straw, a look of satisfaction on his face at learning the truth. Then he changed the subject. "So Huw's been blooded?"

"He has," Myrddin said. "More than once. He's had some adventures since you sent him to me."

"He and I must have a long speech together."

When Myrddin didn't answer him, just allowed his eyes to meet Cedric's, Cedric nodded. "Ah. His allegiance isn't what it was."

"He was the first to wade into the fight at the ford," Myrddin said. "It was four against one and yet he didn't hesitate. He thinks of you as a father."

"But you are his true father and have claimed him," Cedric said, nodding again. "It was a risk I thought worth taking."

"You saved my life at Rhuddlan," Myrddin said. "I owe you that."

"Then we are now even." Cedric gestured to indicate his wounded leg.

Perhaps we are, at that. "Do you remember the events of the day before we arrived?" Myrddin said. "Why were you at the ford?"

"Simple scouting mission," Cedric said. "I try to ride with my men when I can. I'm not an old man just yet—younger than you I warrant—and we were about to cross the river when men I thought were Arthur's set upon us. I admit to entertaining dark thoughts about your lord . . . and yet, you came in on my side."

"They couldn't have been King Arthur's men," Myrddin said. "But whose they were—Cai's? Agravaine's?—I couldn't tell you. This move makes even less sense to my mind."

"Does it?" Cedric said. "You know as well as I that we border lords wage war against each other when we aren't allied with one another to fight the Welsh or perhaps our own Saxon allies."

"But why would anyone want to kill you?" Myrddin said, and then added with a smile, "beyond the obvious that is."

"Who knows of your journey? Could someone want to prevent you and me from speaking?"

That got Myrddin thinking grim thoughts. "Definitely. But it's more than that. Many would gain by your death. Your son is only six. You would die without a strong heir."

"My God, man," Cedric said as Myrddin's assessment sunk in. "I'm of the royal house of Mercia! This is unconscionable!" In his agitation, he struggled to return to a sitting position, even to go so far as to bend his good knee to get to his feet. His voice woke Huw, who hurried to his side.

"My lord," he said. "You'll start the leg bleeding again."

"I can't sit here," Cedric said. "I have to return to my castle!"

Myrddin put out a hand to stop him from rising. "We have a slight problem to deal with first."

Cedric spied an overturned wooden bucket and snapped his fingers at Huw to get it for him. Huw brought it and Cedric lifted himself onto it, his wounded leg outstretched. "I'm not going to like this either, am I?"

By now, Nell had also risen and come to sit on the upturned water trough to re-braid her hair. "Not much, my lord."

A hint of a smile flickered at the corner of Cedric's mouth as he took in her clothing, still the nun's habit, and loose hair. Then he turned back to Myrddin. "What is it?"

"Something lies dead in the manor house, just there." Myrddin pointed at the house with his chin. "The stench is oppressive."

Cedric sighed. "You say 'something'. You don't know who or what?"

"We've not yet found out," Huw said. "Whoever it is wasn't going anywhere and we couldn't sleep in the house even if we knew. Better to wait until the sun rose."

Myrddin checked the sky. It was still dim in the barn, but the sun shot rays that glittered on the puddles in the paddock. The temperature had dropped over the last hours and their breath hung in the air in front of them.

"None of my men came through here in the night?" Cedric said.

"No," Myrddin said.

"I pray Brecon isn't under siege," Cedric said.

"Surely not," Huw said.

"I wouldn't have thought the ford would prove dangerous either," Cedric said. He turned back to Myrddin. "Let's see this, then."

With Huw on one side and Myrddin on the other, Cedric hobbled across the snowy paddock to the front door. Myrddin lifted the latch and pushed the door open. The smell was the same. Cedric pulled a handkerchief from his scrip and put it to his nose. In a row, they stepped into the main room, angling so they'd all fit through the door, and surveyed the chaos inside.

Two men lay on the lower floor, the first behind the door. It was his body that had kept it from opening all the way. Black boots, smaller than the ones Myrddin himself wore, stuck out, but the rest of the man remained hidden by the door. The second dead man lay in plain sight, leaning against the wall underneath the loft, his legs sprawled in front of him. Someone had skewered him through the gut.

"Check the loft," Myrddin said to Huw, who obeyed, heading towards a ladder on the right side of the room.

Nell remained in the doorway, hovering on the threshold without entering. "They're all dead?"

Myrddin turned to her. "Yes. There's nothing you can do."

She nodded and stepped outside again, moving out of sight and smell of the men in the house.

Huw called down to them. "There's another one up here."

"What are the man's colors?" Cedric said.

"Gold lions on blue," Huw said. "Same as the others."

"Christ's bones," Cedric blasphemed. "Mine."

"But who killed them, and why?" Myrddin said.

He left Cedric propped against the door frame and went down on one knee near the dead man behind the door to roll him onto his back. He too wore Cedric's crest. In his left hand, however, he grasped piece of torn cloth. Myrddin pulled it from his grip and held up the prize. The emblem on the cloth was the same as that worn by the men at the ford: a crimson dragon on white.

"Gwynedd colors again," Myrddin said.

"Enemies are friends and friends are enemies," Huw said, now coming down the ladder. "This becomes more and more strange."

"And less and less to my liking," Cedric said, his face very pale, although Myrddin thought that was less from the dead men than from the effort of staying upright. "We must return to Brecon Castle immediately."

Nodding his agreement, Myrddin threw Cedric's arm over his shoulder as before and hobbled with him towards the barn and the horses.

Myrddin boosted Cedric onto his horse, with Nell behind him once again. They left the manor, riding south along the trail to the main road, and then east as they'd intended the day before. Cedric didn't speak until they were within sight of his castle. Myrddin had left him to himself, not wanting to disrupt his focus on staying upright. But Cedric had been considering his situation.

"When I invited you to retrieve your horse, I could not have predicted the events of yesterday," he said.

"No, my lord," Myrddin said.

"I am reconsidering your King's proposal," Cedric said.

"He will be pleased to hear it," Myrddin said.

Cedric shot Myrddin a quick glance. "I cannot meet with him myself at this time, but perhaps a small gesture on my part wouldn't go amiss."

"A gesture that doesn't commit you fully, but indicates to the King your goodwill?" Nell said.

The smile flashed again. "Exactly, my dear."

"Give a company of your men leave to ride north with us when we depart from Brecon," Myrddin said. "As you told Modred last month, Edgar of Wigmore—and Agravaine with him—intend to lure King Arthur into a trap near the Cam River. I fear the King will meet them with too few men."

"That I can do," Cedric said, satisfaction in his voice.

Myrddin congratulated himself for latching upon the perfect solution. It was a way for Cedric to show support, without showing too much. At worst, if Agravaine accused him of switching sides, Cedric could claim his men had been in the wrong place at the right time and waded in on Arthur's behalf. Cedric was justified in not wanting to see Arthur, a noble kinsman, struck down, even if he was ostensibly an enemy. Agravaine might not believe Cedric. Nor might Modred. But they could prove nothing. If Arthur did die in four days, God forbid, Myrddin wouldn't have Cedric lose everything just because he'd had honor enough to listen to him.

22

8 December 537 AD

Snow spit arrhythmically against the pane. Nell gazed through the chapel's unusually large glass window at the accumulation—more than enough for this early in December. It sifted and swirled in the bailey of Brecon Castle. The small chapel possessed intricate carvings, stained glass windows with Cedric's crest, and family tapestries on the walls. All trace of King Arthur, who'd held it for decades, had been erased, not just here but everywhere.

Myrddin walked to stand behind her. He hesitated—she could sense his tentativeness—and then placed a hand on each of her shoulders. She trembled beneath them. "What are we doing here, Myrddin?"

"We've come a long way from St. Asaph haven't we?" His hands rubbed gently on her arms to warm her.

"Do we trust him?"

"Can we trust anyone at this point?" Myrddin said. "But yes, I do. I've no reason not to and we're so close to the end now that the price of failure is no worse than that which already faces us."

"Your dreams consumed the whole of last night," Nell said.

Myrddin shrugged. "And yours didn't?"

She canted her head in acknowledgement of his point, though in truth she'd hardly slept. "And what do you see? Is it still the same dream?"

"It's odd; you've told me I'm no longer present in yours, which is something in which I find great comfort, but I'm watching from above in my own dreams now too. It's disconcerting, frankly, and I find myself trying to force the dream into the long-remembered patterns."

"But it won't go," Nell said.

"No," Myrddin admitted.

"Shouldn't that mean we're doing something right?" Nell said.

"The King still dies, Nell," Myrddin said. "I can no longer see his face, but the Gwynedd crest is bloody on the ground every time, just like at the ford."

Nell turned to him, wrapped her arms around his waist, and put her face into his chest. "We're doing everything we can. If King Arthur goes to meet Edgar, it's out of our hands."

"We are *so* close—not only to saving the King but to *winning* this war," Myrddin said. "I refuse to back down now."

Nell breathed deeply and squeezed Myrddin once more. "It's time we started for Buellt. How soon can we leave?"

"I would have liked to have left this morning," Myrddin said. "The last thing I want is to be too late to the castle or the church."

"I share your concern, but you can't ride today," Cedric said from behind them.

Myrddin swung around, pulling Nell with him. Cedric stood framed in the doorway to the chapel.

"You shouldn't be up—" Nell cut herself off. Telling Cedric he shouldn't be up and around two days after a sword sliced through his leg was just as effective as saying it to Myrddin.

"And why is that?" Myrddin said.

"Because it would do you no good to arrive at Buellt Castle when Edgar is not there. You don't want to spend two days waiting for him under the eyes of Agravaine."

"How do you know this?" Myrddin said.

"Edgar has just sent me word that he intends to leave Wigmore tomorrow, at the head of a host of men, break his journey at Buellt, where he will see to the status of the garrison and confer with Agravaine, and then journey on to Brecon after hearing mass on Sunday."

"And his men?" Nell said. "What of them?" The combined forces of Agravaine and Edgar would be considerable, more than enough to counter the men that King Arthur might be able to collect once he reached Powys.

"Likely, he will leave the majority of them with Agravaine, to bolster his numbers and prevent King Arthur from besieging Buellt Castle," Cedric said. "Both sides are wary of each other now. They see the end game and are maneuvering their forces to strike at the most opportune time."

"As are you," Nell said.

Cedric canted his head at her, an amused glint in his eye, but didn't answer. Instead he turned to Myrddin. "I trust your horse is undamaged from his stint in my stables?"

"Yes, my lord," Myrddin said. Nell had been there when he'd located Cadfarch and Myrddin had been very pleased. "He's an old friend."

"Always the best kind to have at your back," Cedric said.

Nell didn't know how to interpret that, since even if Cedric was their friend (not yet determined), he certainly wasn't an 'old' one. Meanwhile, Cedric turned on his heel and departed.

As he disappeared down the corridor, heading for the stairs, Nell shook her head. "I can't read him."

"Neither can I," Myrddin said. "I wouldn't want to cross him."

"Do we know what we're doing?"

"No," he said. "We don't."

* * * * *

Myrddin found Huw in an open space between the stables and the smithy. The wall and buildings sheltered it from the worst of the wind, and the ground, although frozen, was clear of snow. Huw had grown to manhood in this castle after King Arthur's defeats earlier in the decade. In the last day, he'd fallen into old patterns, willing to take up where he'd left off to the point of holding a dull sword to face down a boy of similar age to him. Unlike Huw, the boy was not yet a knight. By the look in his eye and the determined set of his jaw, he was ready to put Huw back into the place he thought Huw belonged.

But Huw, for all that he was young, had earned his title and was equally determined to show it. As they fought, Myrddin recalled another castle and a different fight, this one overseen by the captain of Arthur's guard, a man long dead, but much revered. Those first months Myrddin had lived among Arthur's court, the captain had taken Myrddin under his wing. Even now, he could hear the man's words:

'A man is divided into four quarters,' he'd said, gesturing to Myrddin with the point of his sword. 'Every attack you make should draw your opponent's defenses to a new quarter, degrading his ability to counter you. At the same time, your opponent will be trying to attack you in the same way and you must parry his blows. Remember that, and that we slash, not thrust, unless it is for the final blow when you force the point of your sword through a man's mail.'

It had been a lesson Myrddin had heeded; despite Huw's hesitation at the battle at Garth Celyn, it was one he'd learned well too.

"I will miss the boy," Cedric said, silently coming up behind Myrddin as was his custom. Myrddin found it disconcerting. Then again, it seemed to be his way, and extension of his desire to hide what he was thinking and feeling at all times. As a Saxon lord, this ability had undoubtedly stood him in good stead.

"Thank you for giving him leave to find me," Myrddin said. "It isn't every lord who would have done so."

"It was either that or find him gone one day, the imperative of his birth overcoming his allegiance to me," Cedric said. "It would have cost him more than needful to have refused him."

Huw parried another blow. Then in a quick movement, he upended his opponent to pin him to the ground. Watching with Myrddin, Cedric gave a snort of satisfaction. "As I said, I'll miss him."

"I'll do my best to ensure that you never find yourselves on opposite sides of a fight," Myrddin said. "If I can protect him from that, I will."

"When I was sixteen, I saw my father cut down in front of me. There will be worse things for him in this life than having to fight in a battle not of his choosing."

Huw left the ring of boys and men, stripping off his tunic as he walked away. Steam rose from his torso. Even in the cold and snow, his young blood ran hot from the fight. Cedric glanced at him once more and then turned to Myrddin. "Come. I have something to show you."

Myrddin followed Cedric into the great hall, both walking with identical stiff right legs, though Myrddin told himself his was the more limber, and then up the stairs to Cedric's office. Like the chapel, it had one window with glass in it which in this case looked northwest. Snow had built up along the window ledge and a sheen of ice coated the inside edges of the glass. Black clouds lay ominously low on the horizon, threatening more snow. Cedric's steward sat at a desk near the fire. Upon Cedric's entrance, he stood, bowed to Cedric, and left.

Myrddin faced Cedric across his desk, expectant but not expecting anything. Cedric reached up to a shelf above his head and brought down a box. Setting it on his desk, he opened it. Several cloth bundles nestled inside. Cedric chose one and unwrapped it, revealing a gold cross. Myrddin stared at it, speechless, for it was a match to the one he wore.

Wordlessly, Myrddin lifted his own cross over his head and laid it on the table beside the box.

"Your cross fell on your chest during the fight beside the river and I noted it," Cedric said. "Where did you get it?"

"From my mother," Myrddin said. "She died at my birth, under the protection of one Madoc, a household knight of Lord Cai, King Arthur's half-brother."

"But Madoc was not your father."

"No." Myrddin's stomach lurched at the thought. "At least, he never claimed me, for all that he allowed me house room until I became a man." Myrddin paused. "And yours?" He almost didn't want to know.

"My mother died when I was two. She left this cross for me, her eldest son," Cedric said.

Myrddin absorbed his news, wondering and uncertain. There was no doubt the crosses were brothers, made by the same goldsmith and likely purchased together.

"There's more you should know." Cedric watched Myrddin carefully as he spoke, while Myrddin endeavored to copy him—to give nothing away of what he was thinking. "This cross was a gift to my mother from her sister, Juliana, when Juliana was near death."

"Juliana had it made?" Myrddin kept his eyes fixed on the matching crosses, recalling what King Arthur had said: that Myrddin's mother had been a lady-in-waiting to Juliana for a time before Myrddin's birth.

Cedric shook his head. "Juliana's husband had it made for her; he gave it to her the Christmas before he died."

Myrddin's head came up at that. Together, yet unspeaking, he and Cedric contemplated the import of his words. Juliana's husband had been Ambrosius, uncle to King Arthur and ruler of Wales after the death of Vortigern. Myrddin ran his finger along the intricate carvings on the cross. Celtic in appearance, the crosspieces flared at the tips. "How is it that you came to me?"

The cross lay on the table, not answering. Shaking his head at all he didn't know, about his father and everything else, Myrddin picked it up and hung it around his neck, tucking it under his shirt as usual.

Cedric studied Myrddin's face and then scanned his clothes, his worn scabbard with its fine sword, and tattered cloak. "Who was your father, Myrddin?"

Myrddin shook his head.

"You really don't know?" Cedric said.

"No," Myrddin said. "Once I was grown, it no longer seemed to matter."

"Has your King ever seen that cross?" Cedric said.

"No," Myrddin said again. "Not that I'm aware."

Cedric picked up his own cross. "You might show it to him. Sooner, rather than later."

23

10 December 537 AD

Myrddin had Nell tucked against him under their blanket—fully clothed—with Huw sleeping not far away. They'd found shelter at a small castle half-way to Buellt whose owner swore allegiance to Cedric. The place was primitive in the extreme, but it was warmer than outside. The threatened snow had turned into a whiteout in the higher elevations that rose between Brecon and Buellt; it was the difference of a few hundred feet, but it was enough to turn a snowstorm into a blizzard. Thus, they'd come all of five miles from Brecon in an entire day. They had only eight more miles to go, but it could have been eighty for all the difference it would have made. Nothing could have been more pathetic—or impossible.

Nell had lain quiet against Myrddin a long while, neither of them sleeping, just absorbing each other's company and their growing closeness. She knew now that if nothing else in the entire world made sense, she was sure of him. She was no longer nervous or afraid that she was risking her heart. Better to risk it than not live the life she'd been given, even if it only lasted one more day.

"We're going to have to ride on in the morning, no matter what," she said. "Even if we lash ourselves together with rope."

"I know," Myrddin said. "And we'll be losing Cedric's men at Penrhiw."

"I suppose, at the very least, they're loud and good at plowing snow." Nell laughed, and then sobered, turning in Myrddin's arms so she could see his expression. The small amount of light given off by the candle they'd not yet blown out made his face just visible. "If something goes awry in Buellt, you save yourself."

Myrddin took her face in his hands and studied it. "Meaning what?"

"There's so much here we don't know or understand," she said. "I'm afraid of what may happen. If you need to flee, you do it, even if it means leaving me behind."

Myrddin shook his head. "I will not desert you. I'm no longer the unthinking warrior I once was." Then his voice gentled and he rested his forehead against hers. "I'm not afraid of dying, Nell. I've died in my dreams more times than I can count."

"And I've died with you," she said. "As you. I don't want to live in a world without you in it." She reached up and stroked a stray hair off Myrddin's forehead. "We need a place to meet if the worst happens and we get separated; I need to know where I can find you."

"Some place safe," Myrddin said. "Some place that one of us can stay until the other one gets there."

"A tavern?"

"In what village?" he asked. "If this goes bad, the Saxons will control the coasts, the border, and be pushing inward."

"Then an Abbey," she said. "Cwmhir, where Arthur himself might be sleeping tonight."

Myrddin nodded. "That's a wise choice. The monks are loyal to Arthur and always will be. Wait there, no matter how long it takes for me to arrive."

"And if you don't find me?" A tear leaked from the corner of her eye. Myrddin wiped it away with his thumb.

"I will find you." Myrddin brushed his lips across hers.

Unable to resist, she tightened her arms around his neck. "I want to see this through with you. I love you."

"You do?" Myrddin pulled back.

She smiled through her tears. "For a man as old as the hills, you certainly are thick."

Myrddin stroked a second, stray tear from her cheek. "It's going to be all right," he said. "When next we see the King, all will be forgiven; he'll give me land on which I can settle with my new wife and I can retire from fighting forever."

"Wife, is it?" she said. "A second ago you didn't know how I felt about you!"

"Ah, Nell," Myrddin said. "You are my world. Marry me. Say you will."

"We may have no future—"

"All the more reason. Say you love me," he said. "I need to hear it again."

Nell buried her face in Myrddin's shirt, her hands entwined in the cloth. "I love you, Myrddin."

"Marry me." Myrddin threw off the blanket and got to his feet. He kicked at Huw who grunted and rolled over. "Right now."

"Now?" she said. "How are we going to do that?"

"There's a castle chaplain. We'll wake him up."

"I'm supposed to be a nun!"

Myrddin flapped a hand at her. "It's a disguise. Everyone here knows that."

She stared at him, her mouth agape, and then she laughed. "You're crazed."

"The King could die tomorrow; I could die tomorrow." Myrddin reached down and shook Huw.

Huw opened one eye. "Wha—?"

"Get up," Myrddin said. "Nell and I want to get married and we need you as a witness."

Huw was instantly alert. "Excellent." He popped up from his pallet and onto his feet, pulling on his boots a second later. "But wait." He paused. "As King Arthur's men, we are under interdict. The priest can't bless you."

"The chaplain's is sympathetic," Nell said. "If we ask him, he'll do it anyway."

"I know we've no contract . . ." Myrddin swung around to look at Nell, the first sign of hesitation in his eyes.

Nell laughed. "We've no money, Myrddin. No possessions other than what we stand up in. No family other than Huw. The priest will make it right."

After rousing one of Huw's squire-friends as witness, they filed into the chapel on the top floor of the keep.

"What's this about a wedding?" The priest came into the room, buckling the belt to cinch his tunic at the waist and shrugging into his cloak of office.

"Nell and I would like you to bless our marriage," Myrddin said.

The priest took in Nell's loose hair and green dress which she'd worn under her habit. "Have you asked her father?"

Momentarily at a loss for words, Nell looked at Myrddin and then back to the priest. "My father is dead," she said. "No one is alive to gainsay us."

The priest's face turned very serious. "What about your lord?" he said to Myrddin.

"King Arthur told me to find a wife and he would give me land to support her in the new year," Myrddin said. *I pray that's still true!*

The priest nodded. "That's very good. I will bless you, even if some will say that I can't see to my parishioners in this fashion."

"Those men are not Welsh," Myrddin said. "Even the Bishop of St. Asaph refused to put out his candles. If it matters to you, we can ask again for a blessing when the interdict is lifted."

"If the interdict is lifted." The priest grumbled under his breath; then said something about, "upstart half-Saxon telling me how to do my job."

Nell and Myrddin exchanged a look, and both smiled. The priest placed a cross about his neck, turned back to them, and lifted his hands to the heavens to begin his prayer. Myrddin moved his hands to Nell's waist to pull her closer, bending to touch his forehead to hers.

After the priest finished speaking, Myrddin lifted the chain that held his mother's cross and settled it around Nell's neck. Surprised, she looked down at it, and then up into his eyes. "Myrddin—"

"Sshh," he said, a finger to her lips. And then recited, "*For as long as there's wind in the mountains; for as long as there's salt in the sea; for as long as rain falls on these green hills; I will stand with thee.*" It was the native ritual with which they'd both grown up. "Nell ferch Morgan, I claim thee as my wife."

Nell brought her hands up, one in each of his, and Myrddin clasped them to his chest. They stood close, breathing each other in, as the priest called down the blessing they wanted but didn't need.

24

11 December 537 AD

The storm hadn't lessened by dawn. Myrddin lay on his back, listening to the wind howling around the castle, not wanting to face the morning. The King couldn't see the chasm opening at his feet which threatened to suck him in. It had already pulled in Myrddin and with only ten hours between now and the rendezvous, there was no way he and Nell were going to get everything done that needed doing.

"Five minutes," Nell said from the doorway to their room. As they'd agreed, she wore her habit. That was going to be a surprise to the priest if he saw her before they left. "Huw's got the horses ready."

"I'm coming," Myrddin said. Now that he was awake, he noted the stamping of the two dozen horses in the castle bailey, just on the other side of the wall. "How'd you sleep?"

"Did I sleep?" she said, and then smiled. "When this is over, they'll be plenty of time for sleeping."

Myrddin got himself upright, kissed Nell on his way out the door, and walked with her into the bailey. He had some hope that the snow wouldn't be falling quite as hard as yesterday, but once they left the shelter of the castle walls and were again on the road to Buellt, the wind picked up. It shrieked down the canyon through which the road ran and into their faces. They bent forward into the storm, cloaks clutched and shoulders hunched. Myrddin pulled his cap more securely over his ears and his scarf tighter around his neck. He'd tied his helmet to his saddlebags. He would only put it on in great need, since metal and cold were synonymous in a snowstorm.

As Cedric and Myrddin had agreed, they said goodbye to Cedric's men at a crossroads. The company turned northwest to St. Cannen's church where they would wait for Arthur—or for Myrddin once he'd finished his business with Edgar. Nell, Huw, and Myrddin carried on the last miles alone.

Myrddin had hoped to have easily reached this point the day before. He'd wanted plenty of time to determine the lay of the land, even if it meant sleeping in a ditch or an abandoned barn last night. But they'd run out of time for maneuvering. The eight miles to Buellt took them long hours of hard slogging, pushing on past the point they wanted to stop and refusing to give up. Thus, noon had come and gone by the time they reached the castle.

"We have to find way to talk to Edgar," Nell said as they approached the gates, which rose up black before them. Agravaine had a small army outside the walls, but the encampment showed no signs of imminent movement, which was a great relief.

"We're walking in like blind men," Myrddin said. "I don't like it."

"Aww. This is what makes it fun," Huw said, parodying Ifan and trying to cheer up his dour elders.

"No question of that, son," Myrddin said. "Go on, then. Your face and Cedric's colors can get us inside."

Myrddin hoped the garrison and its leaders were so busy with the threat of Arthur's approaching army that they'd not question Myrddin's presence. In contrast to Huw, he wore a deep green surcoat that claimed allegiance to no lord. Nell said his tunic brought out the green in his hazel eyes and it occurred to Myrddin that if it pleased her so much, he would only wear this color from now on, even if it clashed with Arthur's crimson and white—if he still had leave to wear those colors.

As they hoped, at such a busy hour of the day and with all the coming and going through the gatehouse, few marked their presence and those who did were appropriately dismissive. The man-at-arms who allowed them through the gate looked them over and then waved a hand to let them pass. Given that the snow still fell unrelentingly, a man would have had to be pretty hardened to turn away a nun and her escorts—one of whom wore Cedric's crest—under those conditions. They found housing for their horses in the sprawling stable complex and then made their way to the great hall.

"This needs to be quick if we are to reach the church in time," Myrddin said. "We are already too late to warn the King before he reaches it."

"That's what Cedric's men are for," Nell said.

"I spoke with a stable boy," Huw said. "He told me that no one has seen Edgar since he arrived. Could he have returned to Wigmore Castle or left already for Brecon?"

"No," Nell said. "If he'd gone to Brecon, we would have passed him on the road. Edgar is here." Nell tipped her head to indicate a man-at-arms walking from the barracks to the stables. "Those are his colors."

"I would have to agree," Myrddin said. "Modred finally approved Edgar's inheritance. He'll want to be in the thick of things to emphasize that Modred chose right in restoring to him his lands."

"Which is why we don't think Edgar ever intended to betray Modred in the first place," Nell said. "Or if he did for a fleeting moment, he certainly doesn't now. There's too much at stake for him to risk Modred's disapproval."

"But then why isn't he in evidence?" Huw asked. "We have to find him—for Lord Cedric's sake, if not for King Arthur's."

The rescue of Cedric had done nothing to dampen Huw's admiration of his former lord and Myrddin couldn't blame him. What most concerned Cedric was his own power, but you had to admire the man for making it this far, given what had happened to his father at Modred's hands.

Like the bailey, the great hall was full of soldiers. Huw led the way to a spot on the end of one table, but before they could sit, a jovial shout split the air. "Huw!" A young man rose from his position on the other side of the hall and walked toward his friend.

Huw smiled, somewhat sickly Myrddin thought, and held out his hand. The two grasped forearms and then Huw introduced him. "Father, this is Peter, one of my companions growing up. Lord Cedric sent him to Agravaine as a squire several years ago." Huw turned to Peter. "I'm glad to see you are well; you've found a place here."

"That I have." Peter slapped Huw on the back. "Come. Eat!" Then, Nell's habit registered and he turned fully to her, his face flushed with embarrassment at his lapse. "Madam," he said, with a slight bow. "Might I be of some service to you?"

Nell stuck her nose in the air and sniffed. "I wish to speak with Edgar of Wigmore. On a private matter."

At the mention of Edgar's name, Peter reacted swiftly, moving closer and waving his hand at her in a shushing movement. "You cannot see him! Don't say his name."

Huw studied his friend. "Why? What's happened?"

"Lord Agravaine believes him a traitor to Lord Modred!" Peter said, relishing his role in imparting the news. "Supposedly, Edgar is unwell and confined to his bed at the top of the keep, but in truth, my lord leaves men to guard his door."

Nell opened her mouth to speak but Myrddin put a hand on her shoulder to stop her. "Thank you, Peter. We appreciate the news."

Myrddin caught Huw's eye and he tipped his head at his son. Catching on, Huw said, "I'm starving. I'll sit with you and we can catch up."

"For a few minutes only," Peter said. "I'll be riding out shortly." He winked. "We have a mission."

Huw shot Myrddin a look of pure dismay and Myrddin caught his arm before Peter could lead him away. "Watch your back, son."

"I can do this, Father," he said. "Trust me."

Myrddin nodded, reluctance sickening his gut, but he let him go. As soon as Peter and Huw had turned away, Myrddin steered Nell towards the back of the hall, to the stairwell that led down to the kitchens or up to the apartments above.

"That boy is one of the men Agravaine is sending to the church," she said.

"I know," Myrddin said. "We can't stop them now. Given that we've made it here at this hour, Cedric's men should have reached the clearing too. The King will have allies and it won't be the uneven fight for which Agravaine is hoping."

"But what are we going to do?"

"We're going to speak to Edgar," Myrddin said. "Agravaine distrusts him and that's good for King Arthur. Then we're going to get out of here as quickly as possible. If Modred's dungeon was bad, the one here would be catastrophic."

Nobody stopped them from climbing the stairs to the rooms above, although when they reached the landing on the second floor, intending to continue to the third, a guard confronted them. He dropped a pike to block the way, looking apologetic once he took in Nell's apparel. Myrddin had to give Nell credit. Bringing her along on this journey dressed as a nun had been one of her better ideas.

"I've orders to let nobody pass."

Nell opted for her cloak of meekness, rather than authority; all Myrddin could do was admire it. "Please, sir. I've word that Edgar requested someone with whom to pray. Since it is uncomfortable for me in the hall, the priest sent me here. My former husband served the old lord before both of their deaths. I believe Lord Edgar would want to see me."

The man gaped at her. "I've no orders—" He stumbled over the words.

Myrddin looked at him, then, with his best *how foolish do you want to be?* stare.

"Yes, Madam." The guard recovered enough to shrug his shoulders. "Tell the two men on the door that Walter sent you."

"Thank you," Nell said, befuddling him further with an uncharacteristic giggle, and moved past the guard, Myrddin hard on her heels.

"You simpered at him," Myrddin said as they circled the stairs to the uppermost rooms.

"It worked, didn't it?"

Myrddin couldn't argue with her, although surely it was unbecoming conduct in a nun, not to mention his wife. He shook his head and remembered Ifan's laughter. *Myrddin with a wife.* He prayed they'd have more than just this one day together.

In short order, they arrived at the landing of the third floor. Two guards occupied the space. A ladder to the battlements rose from the middle of the floor; a locked door, barred from the outside, lay behind it.

"She's here to speak with Lord Edgar," Myrddin said. "I was to tell you that Walter sent us."

One of the men sneered but didn't argue. He peered through the narrow window in the locked door. "Got a nun to see you." Myrddin couldn't hear the reply, but the man nodded. "Go on in."

Nell smiled and tipped her head. "Thank you."

The guard unbarred the door and she slipped past him. Myrddin made to follow, but the guard stopped him with a hand to his chest before he could pass through the doorway.

"You stay here." He closed the door.

Myrddin had expected as much. He stepped to the side and leaned against the wall, ready for when Nell and Edgar came through the door—if that was indeed what was going to happen. He would find out soon enough. He'd caught a glimpse of Edgar before the guard had blocked the way. He'd been facing away from them, staring out the lone window, which was located high up in the northwestern wall.

Although it couldn't have been far into the afternoon, the sky was dark, less because the sun was setting than because of the storm clouds that had been their constant companion for the last four days. Blessedly, the rate of falling snow had lessened over the last hour since they'd arrived.

The minutes stretched out in silence. The guards returned to their table and their dicing, and Myrddin waited. He couldn't make out the conversation beyond the door, just low murmurs between Nell and Edgar. Then the voices stopped, booted feet paced the floor, and a strong hand banged on the door.

"We're done here," Edgar said.

Earlier, Myrddin and Nell had agreed that if Edgar said those words, then she believed he was on King Arthur's side and Myrddin was to do what he could to facilitate his release.

The guards looked up, surprised they were needed again so quickly. One stood and came to the door. The other turned to Myrddin. "Our lord is cleansed of sin, is he?"

"It seems so." Myrddin returned his smirk.

Myrddin stayed where he was beside the door frame, seemingly unconcerned but inwardly bracing himself for action. The guard unbarred the door and pulled on it. As it began to open, Myrddin moved. Shoving his left shoulder into the gap between the door and the frame, he put the full force of his weight behind it to slam the top edge of the door into the guard's forehead.

The man stumbled backwards. Before he could recover, Myrddin came around the door, hit him with the heel of his right hand, and with a swipe of his right foot, had the guard's legs out from under him. The man fell hard on his back and cracked his head on the wooden floor.

Meanwhile, Edgar had bounded out of the room. The second guard had tried to pull out his sword but was still fumbling with it when Edgar drove Nell's knife into his chest to the hilt.

With two downed men between them, Edgar and Myrddin faced each other. Myrddin gave the former prisoner a long look, taking in his short-cropped dark hair, narrow face and black eyes, which like Cedric's, gave nothing away.

Edgar raised his eyebrows. "I think we're done here."

Walter called to them from the stairs below. "Is everything all right up there?"

"Prisoner's giving us a bit of trouble," Myrddin said, in as gruff a voice as he could manage and speaking in Saxon, the language of the guards.

"I'll come up." Walter's feet sounded on the steps. They had ten seconds to prepare.

Without Myrddin having to say anything, Edgar leapt to a position on one side of the archway that led to the stairs while Myrddin occupied the other. Nell stood some ten feet away in the middle of the room just in front of the ladder that led upwards. For a count of three, she waited, her hands twisting in her skirt. Walter spied her with five steps to go to the top and then bounded up the rest.

"Madam!" he said.

That was all he managed to say before Myrddin wrapped his arm around Walter's neck. Edgar pressed the knife to his breastbone, but in the end, didn't have to use it. Walter lost consciousness, slumped in Myrddin's arm, and Myrddin lowered him to the ground.

"You sent a letter to Arthur ap Uther," Myrddin said, turning to Edgar.

"I did." Edgar had started to ease away from Nell and Myrddin, as if unsure of his safety, but then arrested his movement.

"Was it sincere?"

Edgar coughed and laughed at the same time. "Was it? Do I even know? It doesn't matter now. Agravaine sends men to intercept the King. He's emptying the castle of his knights and men-at-arms in pursuit of this endeavor."

"It isn't too late to warn him," Myrddin said to Nell. "If we leave now, I can ride hard to the church."

"It is too late," Edgar said. "Agravaine has been communicating with King Arthur in my name for three days. The meeting will occur in less than an hour. He told me of it last night. As Nell entered my room, I saw that Agravaine's second in command had gathered his men in the bailey of the castle. They left in the few minutes we occupied in talking."

Myrddin spun on his heel. He strode through the open doorway to Edgar's cell and then to the window. "The devil take him. We *are* too late." He swung around to Edgar. "Has Agravaine gone too? Does he lead them?"

"Does the man fight himself? Ever?" Edgar gave a laugh that came out an ironic snort. "Of course not. He's too important to tarnish his sword with Welsh blood."

Myrddin had heard enough. "Do you want to get out of here?"

"And damn the consequences?" Edgar said. "Yes. I never intended, as Agravaine does, to murder my uncle. I do not want his death on my conscience."

"Then let's go." Myrddin covered the distance to the stairwell in a few steps, glad he didn't have to kill the Saxon lord.

They hurried down the stairs to the second floor, and then to the first. Before they continued to the kitchens, Myrddin held out a hand to stop his companions. Huw had been dining in the great hall but if Peter had left with the rest of the garrison, there was no telling where Huw'd got to. Myrddin peered around the doorway that led to the hall, looking for his son. The tables were deserted as Edgar had warned they would be. Only two men remained: Huw—his back to the fire—and another man. The man's voice had risen, berating Huw while Huw shifted from one foot to another, pained and uncomfortable. Myrddin recognized the tone. *Damn it! Agravaine.*

Huw didn't acknowledge Myrddin but flicked a finger in his direction. Understanding, Myrddin waved him off and retreated around the corner, furious at the cock-up this mission had become, and running through potential ways to rescue Huw.

"What is it?" Nell said.

"Huw needs help," Myrddin said.

"Let me see." Nell peered around the corner before he could stop her. Almost immediately, she popped her head back, her face drained of all color.

"What is it?" Edgar said.

"That man." Her breath choked her.

319

"You recognize him?" Myrddin said. "Have you *seen* him?"

"No." Nell switched to Welsh. "I didn't have too. But I know him. He's one of the men at St. Asaph. He was one of the knights who escaped."

Christ.

Meanwhile Edgar, not understanding their words, even if their tension was evident, had taken a quick glance through the doorway. "It's Agravaine," he said. "It would be better if he didn't see me."

They needed to get out now. "Go through the kitchens," Myrddin said. "Bring the horses into the bailey. I'll send Huw to join you and then I'll meet you as soon as I can."

Nell grabbed his arm. "No, Myrddin! We can't leave you here!"

"I'll be fine," Myrddin said, speaking in Welsh as she had, for her ears, not Edgar's. "I don't wish to die. I have a life with you to look forward to. I'll meet you. I promise."

Nell clasped his hand tightly. "I'm not ready for this. We've had so little time!"

"What are you going to do?" Edgar said.

"Rescue Huw." Myrddin looked at Edgar over Nell's shoulder. "And maybe kill Agravaine."

Edgar appeared amused at that, but not Nell, who'd gotten herself under control again. "Don't be an idiot. King Arthur is more important now."

She was right, of course. Myrddin pulled her to him in a brief hug and then let her go. Edgar grasped her arm. "I'll take care of her."

They turned from Myrddin, hurrying down the stairs to the kitchens. Once they moved, Myrddin strode from the stairwell. Agravaine was focused on Huw but Myrddin hadn't walked five paces before he drew Agravaine's attention. Agravaine paled at the sight of him and stopped speaking in mid-sentence. He stood with his mouth open, staring at Myrddin. "You!"

Myrddin checked his stride. Agravaine stepped backwards towards the fireplace, distancing himself from both Huw and Myrddin. He yanked his sword from its sheath and held it out, keeping them both at bay. Meanwhile, Huw sidled sideways towards Myrddin.

"What are you doing here?" Agravaine said. "You shouldn't be here."

"Have we met?" Myrddin came to a halt ten paces from Agravaine.

"You should be at the church!" Agravaine said. "I've *seen* you there!"

Agravaine's words hung in the air, the echo of them twisting between them—and in a single heartbeat upended Myrddin's world. He'd thought himself unique all these years until he found Nell. And yet, even with their union, it had never occurred to either of them that they were not alone in their *seeing*. That there could be others like them. The implications were staggering.

"Get the horses, Huw. Get out of here." Myrddin drew his sword to match Agravaine and pointed it at him.

"But—"

"Now!" Myrddin said. "Nell will explain."

"Yes, sir," he said, and Myrddin was grateful that he didn't say 'father' and reveal to Agravaine their connection. Huw walked quickly towards the stairs and disappeared down them.

"You've *seen* me there?" Myrddin said to Agravaine, once they were alone.

Agravaine brought up his chin, his eyes blazing. "You've died every night in my dreams since I was a boy." And then amended, "until recently."

Dear God, to borrow Nell's favorite phrase. Myrddin's stomach curdled with a strange sort of sympathy for Agravaine which he immediately gagged down. Agravaine didn't share it.

"You're nothing but a trouble-maker," Agravaine said, sneering. "I should have known as my dreams became more confused these last weeks, and then ceased to come at all, that something was wrong."

"If you knew what was to come, why harm the woman at St. Asaph?" Myrddin said. "What did that gain you?"

"Why not take her?" he said. "I knew the future."

Myrddin took a step back, involuntarily distancing himself from Agravaine's amorality. Agravaine had been haunted all his life, just as he and Nell had been. But in Agravaine's case, the result had been a life without consequences.

"You're a child," Agravaine said, the sneer permanently affixed on his lips. "There is so much you don't know."

At that, Myrddin refocused on Agravaine and stepped towards him again. "If that's true, then we can help each other," he said. "We can pool our knowle—"

Agravaine cut Myrddin off, shouting his disbelief. "I need nothing from you!" He brandished his sword at Myrddin, ready to fight even if Myrddin wasn't.

Realizing that Agravaine was in earnest and that he couldn't consider him an ally of any kind, Myrddin met Agravaine's blade with his own. The swords rang out as they clashed and then the men backed off from one another. "So how did you discover who I was?" Myrddin said. "Did Cai tell you?"

Agravaine's eyes glinted with amusement now instead of anger. "I've always known your name and your allegiance, of course," he said. "I *just* missed you at Rhuddlan; I shouldn't have talked Cai out of running you through at the first opportunity."

Myrddin had heard enough. The dreams might have overtaken Agravaine's reason, but he was still powerful; he still stood between Myrddin and the exit. "The King isn't going to that church alone, you know," Myrddin said, advancing on Agravaine.

Agravaine laughed. "You think you can prevent his death?" His query echoed off the walls of the empty hall. "You can't. I imagine he's dead already!"

At these final words, he attacked, driving at Myrddin with all his strength. Myrddin fell back, stepping away from him and allowing him to expend his energy unnecessarily. Every defense a

323

swordsman made should have an attack associated with it, and as Myrddin parried his blow, he positioned himself more strongly. When Myrddin caught Agravaine's cross guard with the tip of his own weapon, the movement pulled the sword down and away from Myrddin and he took the opportunity to close the distance between them. He wanted Agravaine on the ground and his sword in his throat.

But Agravaine was too quick and spun away. The two men clashed swords again—four, five, six times—and with every movement, Myrddin allowed Agravaine to push him closer to the door of the hall. This couldn't go on much longer before a member of the garrison—one of the few left in the castle—would hear, and then Myrddin would be outnumbered. Anxious to put an end to it, desiring Agravaine's death, but not willing to die himself to achieve it, Myrddin contemplated making a run for it.

At that moment, one of Agravaine's boots slid on a piece of abandoned food that a diner had dropped on the floor. The rush mats provided a poor footing, almost as bad as muddy grass. It was ignoble of Myrddin and he knew it, but as Agravaine went down on one knee, Myrddin moved in, batting Agravaine's sword to one side with his gauntleted left hand, and drove his own sword through the man's midsection.

Agravaine fell backwards, his breath guttering as he lost air. Myrddin ripped his sword from Agravaine's body and then kicked Agravaine's fallen sword away. It went skidding underneath a nearby table. Without a second look, Myrddin turned to the door, wiping his sword on the edge of his cloak as he did so, and then sheathed it on the run. He didn't want to reveal to all who might see him that he was fleeing from the aftermath of a fight and that a Saxon lord lay dying in the muck of the hall.

When Myrddin burst through the great doors and into the bailey, Edgar, Huw, and Nell were passing between the main gates out of the castle. Each sat astride their own horse, while Huw led Cadfarch.

Myrddin called in Saxon, on the off-chance that avoiding Welsh might give him a few more seconds before the guards caught on that he was an enemy. "Wait!"

Myrddin raced down the steps towards the gatehouse. Nell had turned her head at Myrddin's call but the others didn't notice him until he threw himself onto Cadfarch's back, delighted to have had such a close shave and survived again—and also knowing that the delight was a mirage, a false emotion that would fade as soon as the fire inside left him.

As he'd hoped, the guards had seen him coming but hadn't known if they should block his path. Usually their charge was to prevent people from entering the castle, not leaving it. Besides, no hue and cry rose from the hall and Lord Edgar, whom the guards would expect to be able to come and go as he pleased, rode at Myrddin's side.

At a steady canter, they left the castle, moving into a gallop once they came down from the gatehouse. They traveled the mile between the gatehouse and the bridge across the Irfon River in five minutes. It was distressingly dark by the time they crossed it, at which point Edgar pulled up.

"I cannot ride further with you," he said. "Tell King Arthur, if he lives, that I would talk with him, but not here; not now. I must first speak to Lord Modred."

"What was that?" Myrddin said. His heart still beat hard since he hadn't recovered fully from the fight or his flight from it. He forced himself to take a deep breath and encompass what Edgar was saying. "Do you think Modred doesn't know of the letter you sent? I assure you he does! Agravaine suspected you of treason. You cannot doubt that Modred does too!"

"Modred confirmed me in my lordship," Edgar said. "He deserves to hear my concerns from me. He needs to know that Agravaine seeks only his own power."

"Not anymore," Myrddin said. "To bring the news of Agravaine's death will not make you welcome in Modred's court."

"And yet I must go," Edgar said, "and accept the consequences of doing what is right. I am my father's son."

The man was too noble for his own good. Turning from Edgar, Myrddin and Nell faced off in the growing darkness. "What would you have me do?" Myrddin said.

She shook her head, looking from him to Edgar and back again without an answer.

"Lord Edgar cannot ride through Powys alone and without a guard," Huw said, sure. "As an ally, King Arthur would not allow it."

"Someone has to ride with him at least as far as Montgomery," Nell said. "Huw and I are the natural choice. We'll be safe on the road—especially given my habit—while you, a Welsh knight, will not. Find King Arthur. He is alive; I know it. And then we'll find you. Huw and I will come to the Abbey, as we agreed."

"I can't leave you," Myrddin said. "Agravaine's men—"

"Were met by ours, Myrddin," she said, and then switched to Welsh. "The King is alive. Even if he went to the church, even if Agravaine has tricked him into going, Cedric's men would have arrived in time to save him."

Myrddin nodded. "All right," he said, wanting her to be right, wanting to believe that the future they'd envisioned together would really come to pass.

"Did you say Cedric?" Edgar said, catching the reference. "What has he to do with this?"

"We're not sure yet," Myrddin said. He turned back to Nell. "Don't do anything stupid."

"I wouldn't," she said.

He reached for her, pulling Cadfarch close to her horse so he could kiss her.

Edgar muttered under his breath. "Some nun."

"They're married," Huw said.

"Of course they are," Edgar said, deadpan.

Myrddin released Nell who shot Edgar an amused look. Then Myrddin held out a hand to Huw, who grasped his forearm as one knight to another. "Take care of each other," Myrddin said. He wasn't used to caring so much about the immediate prospects of survival for people other than Arthur, but fear for Huw and Nell roiled his gut.

"I will, Father," Huw said.

Edgar threw up his hands in mock exasperation.

"I love you, Myrddin," Nell said.

Myrddin nodded, unable to speak through the knot in his throat. All three turned away. Myrddin watched them until they disappeared around a bend in the road. The ache in his chest flamed higher until it burned him. And then it went out as cold certainty set in. Nell might hold hope in her heart, still, but with her absence, Myrddin couldn't share it.

Turning Cadfarch's head, he acknowledged that it was better that Huw and Nell were out of it. To the east was Mercia and for all intents and purposes, peace. The danger was to the west. Alone, he could make better time and approach the church more circumspectly. If Agravaine's men had attacked King Arthur's, there was nothing Myrddin, as one man, could do to help them. At this point, he'd just be happy to find the King had stayed in bed, even if all his other plans had come to nothing.

Then Myrddin cursed himself for the questions he had forgotten to ask Agravaine, not that he would have answered: first and foremost, how many of the dangers that faced the King were his doing? The attack on Garth Celyn? On Cedric? *Ah well. Too late now. The man is dead.*

It was less than two miles from the Irfon Bridge to St. Cannen's Church. The road kept close to the Cam River and Myrddin followed it. The river rushed by, not quite in flood, and the wind howled in the trees, blowing the snow directly into Myrddin's face. The weather raged around him, but as he approached the churchyard, the strife of men drowned out all else. Up ahead, shouts came in Saxon and Welsh. As Myrddin got closer, a great column of smoke rose into the air. It flew above his head, a dark smudge blowing east. The smell of death and mortified flesh enveloped him.

Retreating to the safety of the trees that lined the river, Myrddin bowed his head and closed his eyes, a sickening horror in his stomach. Sure enough, after a short wait, a troop of men—thirty at least—marched around the corner, coming from the church. They bore torches that lit up the night, the light reflecting off the snow on the ground, in the air, and the white clouds above their heads.

The trees and the darkness beyond the torchlight hid Myrddin. Even without the protective trees, the troop made so much noise they wouldn't have noticed Myrddin if he'd shouted. Several of the men in the lead whooped and called their triumph. One call rose above every other, this one in Saxon: "He is dead at last!"

Not all the men were so exuberant. Towards the tail end of the company, five or six men rode straight and solemn. Every so often, one of them glanced upwards and Myrddin gagged at what rose above their heads: A severed head bobbed on a pike, blood matting the dark hair, a grisly testament to their accomplished task.

They passed Myrddin without a glance. He stayed in the trees, doing nothing, too late to save his King. When they'd gone, vanishing into the whirling snow, Myrddin directed Cadfarch towards the ruin of all his hopes. Men and horses had packed the snow in the clearing in front of the church so the blood stains showed clearly where they'd pooled on the icy ground. Here and there, grass poked through the snow where a heel had dug into the earth, evidence that men had dragged other men across it.

It was the first time he'd ever seen the place awake. Myrddin noted the differences and similarities to his dream—and knew they mattered not at all. He followed the signs to a spot to the northwest of the church. The Saxons had built a bonfire, their only tinder the bodies of the men they'd killed.

Upwards of two dozen men burned in the pyre—maybe fewer or more it was hard to tell—most marred beyond recognition. The fire hadn't yet consumed their gear but the torn clothes and disarrayed armor told Myrddin all he needed to know about how they died. His friends lay as they'd been thrown, haphazard and in every direction. Every one wore the dragon crest on their surcoats.

Myrddin walked around the pile in a daze, the smoke stinging his eyes, although he would have been blind from tears regardless. At the far end, he spied the headless and mutilated body of his King, fallen off the edge of the pile and stripped of its fine armor. Choking on the horror of it, he dragged the remains to one side, unable to look more closely at the other bodies for fear he'd find the faces of his friends staring up at him, lifeless and empty.

A lament rose unbidden in his ears. Its relentless rhythm drove Myrddin's movements as he labored to put out the fire, to throw dirt on bodies, and to provide some semblance of a decent burial for his King, although all that was decent had disappeared from the earth:

> *Can you not sense the turmoil amongst the oaks?*
> *Do you not see the path of wind and rain?*
> *And that the world is ending?*
> *Cold my heart in a fearful breast*
> *For the lion of Wales, that oaken door*
> *our warlord, our dragon-king*
> *Our Arthur . . . is dead.*

Exhausted and spent, knowing he'd done his best and it hadn't been enough, Myrddin wept over the fallen body of Arthur ap Uther, his lord, and the last hope of his people.

25

12 December 537 AD

High in the mountains to the northwest of Buellt, with the snow up to Cadfarch's knees, Myrddin stumbled towards the Welsh camp, drawn by the smoke and firelight. He'd buried King Arthur's headless body as best he could—but with the dark and no tools, only his ragged and bleeding nails, and the clouds blotting out the stars and moon, the body was more under rock and brush than earth. It had taken far longer than Myrddin had wanted. Once he'd finished, he'd given Cadfarch his head, merely directing him west towards what he hoped were the remains of Arthur's camp. Arthur's men might face a battle tomorrow that they could easily lose, now that they had no King to lead them.

And after that, if Myrddin survived the battle, he had to find Nell and Huw. They needed to decide what they were going to do next; if they were going to stay in Wales and live as best they could, or walk away. Or maybe die where they lay. The part of him that refused to surrender, that held onto hope amidst the desolation, died a little inside with every step that led him further away from them. With so many dead, his family was the only thing that mattered anymore.

Myrddin had just reached the first of the outer sentries, posted some two hundred yards from the camp, when a voice from behind hailed him. "My lord!"

Wearily, Myrddin swung around, every muscle protesting even that slight movement. Cedric's men, torches lighting up the forest, rode towards him. In response, the sentry beside Myrddin raised his pike. It was a brave stance, though what he thought two men could do against a company of soldiers Myrddin couldn't guess.

Myrddin raised a hand to Godric, the young captain, while reassuring the sentry. "They are friends."

Godric began speaking before he'd come to a halt. "We've just come from the church. I'm sorry. We were too late; we were lost for hours and ended up miles out of our way. The snow . . ." he broke off at Myrddin's look, knowing as Myrddin did that excuses were merely that, when the price of failure was the loss of a King and a country. If the blizzard had not delayed them, these twenty men could have been enough to change the course of history.

"Come," Myrddin said. "I was too late as well."

Myrddin turned from Godric, gave the sentry a nod, and led the company the short distance through the woods to the camp. If he'd had the energy to think on it, the scene when they reached it was far calmer than he would have expected: men walked around the fires; they ate and drank, but their movements held no urgency. If anything, the emotion Myrddin felt from them was positive—even cheerful—without the expected drunken despair.

And then it hit him . . . *Could they not know?*

If it was possible for him to feel more despairing, the emotion would have overtaken him then. He faced the truth: the Saxons had killed everyone else who could have reported back and it was he who would bring the news. Only he had survived and that by chance.

Myrddin dismounted in front of the pickets. "My lord Myrddin," the guard protecting the entrance said, "we've missed you."

It took a moment for Myrddin to recognize the man as one of Cai's—and then his already cold heart collapsed in on itself. *Of course.* Cai had come. It would be just like him. Perhaps it was he who'd convinced Arthur to meet Edgar, setting up his brother to die as he'd plotted with Agravaine back in the belfry at Bangor, and now he would get to act the grieving brother and take up the mantle of Wales in his stead. Myrddin's stomach churned in a foul pit and he felt like puking. Instead, he looked for Deiniol among the men at the fire pits for he was sure to be here too, but didn't see him.

Myrddin and Cedric's soldiers left their horses with the boys whose job it was to tend them and trudged through the camp to what had been Arthur's tent. When they reached it, voices inside rose and fell. Myrddin hesitated at the entrance, gripping the hilt of his sword. He speculated if it would be better to run the traitor through now, or see Nell and Huw safe first and then return to finish him. While he was deliberating, a man spoke from behind him:

"You're late, but I forgive you since you've brought so many friends."

Myrddin spun around at the familiar voice. Gawain smiled his greeting, leaving Myrddin unable to speak. *He should be dead! Why isn't he dead like in my dreams?* Oblivious to Myrddin's shock, Gawain leaned across Myrddin and held out a hand to Godric, who took it. He remained mute, but Myrddin managed to stutter, "You . . . but I saw . . . how can you . . . the King . . .?"

"What's wrong with you?" Gawain asked. "You look as if you've seen a ghost."

"The church—"

"The King didn't go to the church." Gawain looked from Myrddin to Godric whose mouth was opening and closing like a landed fish.

"Didn't go?" Myrddin was unable to think coherently. "Then who . . .?"

Gawain shook his head at Myrddin's evident stupidity and gave up on him. He gestured towards the entrance to the tent. "Go on. The King is waiting."

"He's dead!"

The shout came from the entrance to the camp and Myrddin turned to see Deiniol riding towards them, threading his

335

horse between fire pits. He was bent over his horse's neck, haggard of face and worn to exhaustion. He pulled up and dismounted. Once on the ground, he staggered towards Myrddin, wrapped his arms around his neck, and to Myrddin's combined horror and astonishment, wept into his cloak.

"Who's dead, Deiniol?" Myrddin grasped him by the arms and pushed him away so he could see his face. "Who's dead?"

"Lord Cai," Deiniol said. "At the church by the Cam River."

"Cai is dead?" Gawain's voice held disbelief.

Deiniol nodded. "When Lord Cai learned that his brother had passed up the chance to ally himself with his nephew, Edgar, he went in his stead. It was his right."

Gawain stared at Deiniol. *"Sweet Mary, mother of Christ!"*

Deiniol continued, caught in his own misery yet still defending his lost lord. "Lord Cai had arranged to meet with Edgar in the nave of St. Cannen's church, or so we thought. But shortly after we arrived, Saxon soldiers set upon us. Everyone is dead! Everyone but me."

Myrddin gazed into Deiniol's smoke-blackened face. "You mean . . . " Ordinarily he would have found some illicit pleasure—even triumph—at seeing Deiniol so unmanned by grief. But now . . . Myrddin stopped to take in a breath and refocus on the part of Deiniol's story that mattered most to him. "Then King Arthur—"

"What's this I hear about my brother?" The door to the tent swept open and a dark head ducked through the doorway.

The sight of his King walking toward him, with Gareth and Geraint behind him, had Myrddin weaving on his feet, his hollowed limbs barely holding him upright. "I thought you'd gone to the church."

"Of course I didn't go," Arthur said.

"Of course . . ." Lost, Myrddin swallowed the rest of his sentence.

Arthur shook his head at him. "How could I go to that meeting when you made it so clear I shouldn't? You who have served me unswervingly for twenty years; you who had the courage to speak the truth."

"But . . . you didn't listen to me. I failed . . ."

Geraint, coming to stand beside the King, smirked. "Only if failure means saving King Arthur's life—and Wales."

"What do you mean?" said Myrddin. "What has any of this to do with me?"

"My dear boy," Arthur said. "It has everything to do with you. Cai's increasingly desperate attempts to unseat me resulted from *your* continual interference in his plans. Who escaped from Rhuddlan to warn me that Edgar's letter might not be what it seemed? Who thwarted the attack on Garth Celyn? Who told me of Cai's treachery when no one else dared speak of it? Who related to Geraint your fears of my death? Who is possessed of the *sight*?"

This struck Myrddin speechless but Geraint nodded. Arthur glanced from one to the other before continuing. "Yes. You have a friend in Geraint. If more of my men had your courage, Modred would not have been able to constrain us as he

337

has." He narrowed his eyes at Myrddin. "I have underestimated—and you have downplayed—your abilities until now. We will not allow that error to continue another day."

"I thought you didn't believe me!" Myrddin recalled his desperation and the hours he and Nell had agonized over their choices, or lack thereof. "I feared for twenty years that I couldn't avert your death. Until ten minutes ago, I believed I *had* failed."

"And that is my fault," Arthur said. "That is my lapse for not seeing that one of my staunchest defenders and counselors had gone unacknowledged all these years."

"What changed your mind?" Myrddin said.

"The evening after you left for Brecon, I dined with my brother. It was as if I saw him for the first time. Noting my attention, he turned to me with a smile that never reached his eyes. I recalled your parting words, when you spoke to me of his treachery."

"Thou practice deceit through confidence; Alas! my brother, must that be?" Myrddin said. "From a poem by St. Llywelyn."

"I'd refused to listen to you. But you were right. Cai opposed me at every turn, even as he professed his support. My brother was the same man he'd always been, just as you were the same as you'd always been. In that moment I knew it, knew that I should be listening to you and not to my brother."

Arthur sighed. "I informed Cai that I would not be going to meet Edgar—though not why."

Gareth moved into the circle of men. "Cai was angry but he acquiesced, less he reveal his duplicity. With that, I came forward to confess my part in all this—that I also knew of Cai's treachery—that he had been working with the Saxons, specifically with Agravaine, for many months."

"But how did Cai end up at the church when he *knew* it was a trap?" Myrddin said.

"It is as I told you," Deiniol said in a loud voice, speaking for the first time since Arthur had appeared. "He sought Edgar's support for our cause."

"More like he thought to concoct a new plan to overthrow King Arthur," Geraint said, "and wanted Agravaine's help with it."

"You have the truth of it," Gawain said, with a half-laugh.

Myrddin was filled with a sudden compassion for the wayward lord. "Except that neither Edgar nor Agravaine went to the church to meet Cai and instead Agravaine sent men to kill him," Myrddin said. "Cai went to the church thinking he was among friends, only to find he'd outlived his usefulness. It was an opportunity to get rid of a rival and Agravaine took it."

Myrddin had dreamt his own death at that church, lived again and again the moment when he realized he was going to die. Cai must have known that feeling, there at the end. Myrddin hoped that as he died, he'd repented; that he'd understood he couldn't trust these Saxons and should have remained loyal to his brother.

"Edgar betrayed him," Geraint said.

"Mmmm," Myrddin said. "Not Edgar, in truth."

"What did you say?" Arthur peered into Myrddin's face.

"Edgar's initial letter to you *was* genuine, my lord," Myrddin said. "Agravaine imprisoned him in Buellt Castle because of it. We released him. Nell and Huw are accompanying him north even now. Agravaine, however, is dead."

Myrddin's companions openly gaped at him at that.

Myrddin shrugged. "It needed doing."

Arthur met the gazes of each of the men in his circle in turn: Geraint, Gawain, Gareth, and Myrddin, Godric, with his men crowded up close to hear the conversation better, and Deiniol, who stood a little behind Myrddin, listening but not one of them. "In one day, Modred has lost four allies: Cai, Cedric, Agravaine, and Edgar. In the morning, we will seal his loss by taking Buellt Castle from him too." He stepped back and gestured towards his tent, indicating that the men should enter. "We have much to do before dawn."

Myrddin, for his part, hung back to the last, coming to a halt in front of King Arthur after everyone else had entered the tent. The two men studied each other for a long moment, and then Arthur stuck out his hand to Myrddin. For the first time in his life, Myrddin clasped forearms with his King, one man to another, before they turned together into the tent.

For once, despair was in abeyance. A potent mix of joy, awe, and relief flooded Myrddin. Arthur ap Uther . . . lived.

The End

Historical Background

Historians are not in agreement as to whether or not the 'real' Arthur—the living, breathing, fighting human being—ever existed. The original sources for the legend of King Arthur come from a few Welsh texts. These are:

1) *Y Goddodin*—a Welsh poem by the 7th century poet, Aneirin, with it's passing mention of Arthur. The author refers to the battle of Catraeth, fought around AD 600 and describes a warrior who "fed black ravens on the ramparts of a fortress, though he was no Arthur".
http://www.missgien.net/celtic/gododdin/poem.html

2) Gildas, a 6th century British cleric who wrote *De Excidio et Conquestu Britanniae* (*On the Ruin and Conquest of Britain*). He never mentions Arthur, although he states that his own birth was in the year of the siege of Mount Badon. The fact that he does not mention Arthur, and yet is our only historian of the 6th century, is an example of why many historians suspect that King Arthur never existed.
http://www.fordham.edu/halsall/source/gildas.html

3) Taliesin, a 6th century poet, who wrote several poems about Arthur. Including the lines: " . . . before the door of the

gate of hell the lamp was burning. And when we went with Arthur, a splendid labour, Except seven, none returned from Caer Vedwyd."
http://www.maryjones.us/ctexts/t30.html

4) Nennius – "History of the Britons" (Historia Brittonum, c. 829-30)

"Then it was, that the magnanimous Arthur, with all the kings and military force of Britain, fought against the Saxons. And though there were many more noble than himself, yet he was twelve times chosen their commander, and was as often conqueror."
http://www.fordham.edu/halsall/basis/nennius-full.html

5) *Native Welsh Tales*: These connected works of Welsh mythology were named *the Mabinogion* in the 19th century by their first translator, Lady Charlotte Guest. These include the story of *Culhwch and Olwen*, in which Arthur and his men track down the thirteen treasures of Britain, and *The Dream of Rhonabwy*, a tale of Arthur that takes place after the Battle of Camlann (thus indicating that he survived it) and includes directions to 'Mount Badon' or Caer Faddon, as the Welsh call it. These stories are found in the *Red Book of Hergest* and/or the *White Book of Rhydderch,* both copied in the mid-14th century.
http://www.maryjones.us/ctexts/index_welsh.html

6) *The Annales Cambriae.* This book is a Welsh chronicle compiled no later than the 10th century AD. It consists of a series of dates, two of which mention Arthur: "Year 72, The

Battle of Badon, in which Arthur carried the cross of our
Lord Jesus Christ on his shoulders for three days and three
nights and the Britons were victors. Year 93, The Strife of
Camlann in which Arthur and Medraut fell."   The early
dates of the above works indicate little or no relation to the
later English/French embellishments of Arthur, which
Geoffrey of Monmouth
popularized. http://www.fordham.edu/halsall/source/an
nalescambriae.html

Later texts that are built on the above works, in chronological
   order, are:
1) William, Chaplain to Bishop Eudo of Leon – "Legend of St.
   Goeznovius, preface" (c. 1019)
2) *William of Malmesbury* - "The Deeds of the Kings of England
   (De Gestis Regum Anglorum)" (c. 1125)
3) *Henry of Huntingdon* – "History of the English" (Historia
   Anglorum, c. 1130)
4) *The History of the Kings of Britain*, by Geoffrey of Monmouth,
   dating to the middle 12th century. This is the beginning of
   the King Arthur legend as we know it. Geoffrey was born in
   Wales, but worked for his patron, Robert of Gloucester,
   who was particularly interested in legitimizing the claim of
   his sister (Matilda) to the English crown. Thus, the
   confusion of landmarks which moved Arthur from Wales
   to England proper, and the romanticizing of the tale,
   including the notion that Britain was originally conquered

by Brutus, the son of the Trojan hero Aeneas, and thus
Britain was 'classical' in origin.

5) *Roman y Brut* (**The Romance of Brutus**) is the translation of
Geoffrey's work into Anglo-Norman verse. It takes much of
Geoffrey's story and adds the round table, courtly love, and
chivalry, thus transforming Arthur from a Welsh warrior to
a medieval, Anglo-French knight. From this point, the
Welsh Arthur is all but lost, and the
Anglo/Norman/French 'King Arthur' is paramount.

By 1191, the monks of Glastonbury were claiming
knowledge of his grave, and soon after, the link between Arthur
and the Holy Grail, which Joseph of Arimathea supposedly
brought there. By 1225, monks in France had written The Vulgate
Cycle, telling of the holy grail from the death of Jesus Christ to the
death of Arthur, and included the romance of Lancelot and
Guinevere. This story became the standard version used
throughout Europe.

Whether or not King Arthur was a real person is an
either/or query. He either was or he wasn't. Many scholars,
researchers, and Arthurophile's have strong opinions on this topic,
both for and against. Because of the paucity of written records
(most notably, Gildas fails to mention him), much of the academic
work has come down on the side of 'wasn't'—or at least if Arthur
was a real person, his name was not 'Arthur' and he possible
wasn't even a king.

As a side note, the Welsh sources, particularly the dream of *Dream of Rhonabwy*, make Modred Arthur's nephew and foster-son, not his illegitimate son as many readers might know him. This version of events is carried through to Geoffrey of Monmouth's version of the Arthurian story. Arthur's illicit/incestuous relationship with his sister, Morgause or Morgan, is a later (French) addition.

For the purposes of my book *Cold My Heart*, I choose to believe that Arthur was real, that he was backed into a corner by his duplicitous nephew, Modred, and—as in the *Dream of Rhonabwy*—he did not die at Camlann as the Norman/French/Anglo version says, but lived to see his country securely in the hands of a worthy heir. At the same time, the world of *Cold My Heart* rests in the balance between the historical Wales of 537 AD, and the quasi-medieval Arthurian world that readers have grown to love throughout the ages.

Some points in particular where *Cold My Heart* is less than historically accurate:

1. The Christian Church was not as full blown and organized as portrayed in *Cold My Heart*. Although St. Dafydd was appointed Archbishop around this time, he did not have ecclesiastical control over Christianity throughout Wales and organized Christianity tended to center on small groups of monks/nuns or hermitages. Many people remained pagan.

2. Saxons had only just begun to fight on horseback. They rode horses, of course, but cavalry weren't necessarily part of their repertoire. Nor the use of bows.

3. A 'knight' is a medieval notion, but it is impossible to portray Geraint, Bedwyr, Gareth, and Gawain without using the word. Forgive me.

Thank you for purchasing *Cold my Heart*. Look for the sequel by December 2012 ...

Acknowledgments

I have many people to thank, not only for their assistance with *Cold my Heart*, but who have helped make my books better and my life sane for the last five years.

First and foremost, thank you to my family: my husband Dan, who told me to give it five years and see if I still loved writing. I still do. Thank you for your infinite patience with having a writer as a wife. To my four children, Brynne, Carew, Gareth, and Taran, who have been nothing but encouraging, despite the fact that their mother spends half her life in medieval Wales. Thank you to my parents, for passing along their love of history.

Thanks to my beautiful writing partner, Anna Elliott, who has made this journey with me from nearly the beginning. Thank you to the many support groups to which I belong, including the Indie Chicks, Indie Writers Unite, and the Writer's Café at the Kindle Boards. And thank you to my readers, who make it all worthwhile.

About the Author

With two historian parents, Sarah couldn't help but develop an interest in the past. She went on to get more than enough education herself (in anthropology) and began writing fiction when the stories in her head overflowed and demanded she let them out. Her interest in Wales stems from her own ancestry and the year she lived in England when she fell in love with the country, language, and people. She even convinced her husband to give all four of their children Welsh names.

She makes her home in Oregon.

Made in the USA
Lexington, KY
06 March 2012